RESONANCE

Ajay is currently with the Indian Revenue Service (IRS). His background as an engineer and his two decades of work with the Indian Revenue Service, his close association with different intelligence agencies around the globe, the World Bank and the International Monetary Fund in Washington DC, attachment with the Indian Embassy in USA and his training at Duke University, North Carolina, USA have given him a deep understanding of world geopolitics and the intricacies of how intelligence agencies and governments at different levels operate worldwide. All of this has fed into his first novel, Resonance.

Ajay is married to Sumita and they have one son, Pranjal.

RESONANCE

AJAY

Westland Ltd

westland ltd

61 Silverline Building, 2nd Floor, Alapakkam Main Road, Maduravoyal, Chennai 600095
No. 38/10 (New No.5), Raghava Nagar, New Timber Yard Layout, Bengaluru 560026
93, 1st Floor, Sham Lal Road, Daryaganj, New Delhi 110002

First published in India by westland ltd 2014
Copyright © by Ajay 2014

All rights reserved
10 9 8 7 6 5 4 3 2 1

ISBN: 978-93-84030-20-9

Typeset by Ram Das Lal

Prologue

"*Jihad* will never cease in Kashmir. To liberate Kashmir and to secure *azaadi*, Jihad is the only way! The Hindustānis have deprived our Muslim brethren of their just demand and treated our brothers like second-rate citizens. It is *Jihad*, which has forced Hindustān to sit up and take notice of the Kashmir issue. *Jihad* will gather strength because the Republican Party of George W. Bush will soon lose the coming election. American-led allied countries, France and Denmark, have run out of steam and have left Afghanistan. Very soon Italy, Germany and Canada will also abandon the US. Then, the ground will be ready for us, the Mujahideen. We will see how Hindustān will save herself from the wrath of Allah. We, His servants, will take the first steps to bomb the Baglihar Dam in Hindustān. Our destiny is not to sit back and watch our fertile land become barren. Let us release the floodgates and allow the deluge to cleanse us of the dirty marks of the *Kafirs*. Let the lands be inundated so that our green crops stand tall and bountiful, feeding each and every one of our Muslim brothers. Insha Allah, we will eliminate Hindustān soon."

An early morning speech by Hafiz Muhammad Saeed, Chief of the terrorist organization Lashkar-e-Taiba.

Post his speech, a thousand voices chorused together, *"Jihad, jihad!"*

*   *   *

A few thousand miles away in Amman, the capital of Jordan, Sundaram Iyer, the Joint Director of the Central Bureau of Investigation, checked into the Royal Suite, on the 24th Floor of Le Royal Hotel at 3rd Circle. After relaxing in the steam room, Sundaram Iyer let his body float on the bubbling jacuzzi. After a while, he stepped out and instructed the butler to prepare a large scotch for him while he got dressed.

Hafiz Muhammad Saeed's message still hung in the air, like an ominous cloud, when in the wee hours of the morning, two agents of the Inter Service Intelligence (ISI) of Pakistan visited the Royal Suite and turned up the 'Do not disturb' door-hanger. Sundaram welcomed the agents and offered them drinks. The officers politely refused. The agents waited while Sundaram savoured some more of his smooth thirst-quenchers and lay down on the silk sheets. A few minutes later, one of the agents took out freezing cold water from the refrigerator, while the other hauled Sundaram off the bed in one swift movement. With half shut eyes, Sundaram dragged himself behind them. The agents hurried Sundaram through the dimly lit corridor and then bundled him into the Mercedes-Benz, waiting at the back of the hotel.

The car sped off to the Royal Jordanian Airbase. A Pakistani private chartered plane took the flight path to CJL, the Chitral airport situated in Pakistan's troubled province of Khyber Paktunkhwa. Five hours later, the plane started to descend when it neared Panjsher. It maneuvered through the beautiful valley of the Hindukush Mountain Range and floated over the runway before touching down. A SUV was waiting for its passengers. From the airport, the SUV crossed a bridge on the Kunar River, steered across a dusty road, heavily guarded by the Elite Armed Force and reached its destination -- the three massive caves that lay nestled against the thick pine forest.

An all-important meeting was soon underway.

Somashekhar Rao, an engineer from India, spread the drawing sheet on a stone dyke as Imran Shah Malik, the retired Chief of the ISI and Saeed al-Masri, the Financial Chief of al Qaeda, pored over it. When the engineer ran a simulation on a powerful MacBook Pro, Saeed al-Masri patted his back. Imran Shah Malik had a pen drive in the inner pocket of his overcoat. However, he chose not to disclose its contents and thus unveil his plan, a plan aimed at altering the history of mankind. The other Jihadists gave the engineer a bored look. The technical and engineering aspects of the plan held no interest for them. What interested them was the annihilation of millions and the destruction of thousands of square miles of verdant land beyond the flowing Indus River and turning it into a swampy wasteland forever.

Part-I

More than a year later

NOVEMBER 2008, LAHORE

Imran Shah Malik, the retired Chief of the ISI, was proud of his new six-bedroom bungalow, in the heart of Mall Road, Lahore. A beautiful sprawling garden flanked the brilliant sapphire swimming pool that glittered under the canopy of an azure sky. A high fence with concertina wire secured the perimeter of the bungalow while elite forces from the Pakistan Army stood guard.

Right from the days of Zia-ul-Haq, Operation Tupac was aimed at disintegrating India by utilizing the ISI spy network to act as an instrument of sabotage, exploiting the porous Indo-Nepalese and Indo-Bangladesh border to set up bases and thus carry out anti-India operations.

Operation Tupac was Imran Shah Malik's driving passion. A fourth objective was added to the plan when Sundaram Iyer and his team agreed to execute the Joint Action Plan. He pompously renamed it Tupac-II. All the other members except Imran

Shah Malik wanted to go ahead with a trial run of Operation Tupac-II. This preface was called Project Karachi, a Jihadist attack on Mumbai. The main purpose of the Jihadi attack on Mumbai was to tactically shift the interest of the world from Afghanistan, as well as to instill a new spirit amongst the Jihadist cadre. The cadre was getting impatient because of their failure to carry out any worthwhile work that would invite world media attention. American drone attacks had demoralized the rank and file. Post their exploit, they wanted to gauge global reaction. If all went as planned, India would bleed and the Government of Pakistan would have a lot of explaining to do. Best of all, it would open up new avenues for the Jihadists.

However, Imran Shah Malik's interest lay beyond Project Karachi. He wanted nothing less than the success of Tupac-II and in his view Project Karachi would be counterproductive to his grand plan. However, Lashkar-e-Taiba (LeT) vetoed Imran Shah Malik and decided to go ahead with the attack.

Nausheen, Imran Shah Malik's pretty wife answered the doorbell to welcome her husband, who had come back home from Abbottabad after two days.

Imran loosened his necktie and enquired about the whereabouts of their son, Aban.

"Ever since he has come back from the United States, he is busy with his MacBook. His love is either his engineering project or this little toy. " Nausheen smiled and started to move to the kitchen. "I'll tell Aban to come downstairs and prepare tea. Would you like to have some *kebabs*?"

"Aha! Why not?" Imran smiled sheepishly and moved to his study to check the latest report. He was expecting an important call from his brother at 07:55 pm PST (Pakistan Standard Time) to get information on whether Project Karachi was to go ahead as per the LeT plan or if it would be aborted, as Imran wished so desperately.

The phone rang. "The LeT boys have landed at Colaba in Mumbai. As per plan, they will split into different groups. However, Hafiz Muhammad Saeed has made a slight change in target since his commander has held back two of his men. The new target is the Governor's House and Sena Bhawan instead of the Mumbai Police Headquarters. As for the rest, the plan stands as it is."

Imran sounded worried, "What if the Hindustāni authorities catch them?"

"No option. As per the LeT code, they will have to follow their ideology and lay down their lives for *Jihad*."

"Absolute rubbish! I never approved such an atrocious plan. I told Hafiz not to fall into the trap of al Qaeda since Pakistan will gain nothing by this mayhem. Instead, we'll have to face flak from Western countries. Hindustān will gain an upper hand and cry foul. However, Hafiz wouldn't listen to me."

"Well, he doesn't listen to our government either."

"Does the Government of Pakistan know about it?"

"Yes. They were informed a few minutes ago."

"What is their take on it?"

"They have asked LeT to abort the plan and call back their men. But LeT says they never look back. So, the government has no option but to play dead."

Imran Shah Malik took a deep breath. "How could Hafiz Saeed not understand that he is putting Tupac-II in jeopardy? What was the need for inviting world attention when you have something so big to bargain with the Hindustāni dogs from a vantage point?"

"When I was with Hafiz Saeed, he mentioned that Tupac-II is still embryonic. It will take a lot of time and it needs a lot of preparation. Moreover, its success is not guaranteed."

"I guaranteed everything. If it works out according to my plan, I'll bring the Hindustāni government to its knees. If they don't agree to our demand, the destruction that the world will see will reduce 9/11 to a mere footnote in the annals of history. The only thing I need to take care is to keep al Qaeda out of the loop."

"al Qaeda is very much on the scene after Saeed al-Masri attended the meeting at Chitral."

"How do you know about the meeting?"

"The al Qaeda people told me a bit about it. But I don't know the finer details."

"It was a top-secret meeting. Wait for some more time, brother. I'll tell you about it soon. I told Hafiz Saeed not to invite the al Qaeda to the Chitral meeting. But he said that such a complex plan required a great deal of logistics and international support. According to him, without al Qaeda, Tupac-II will always remain a distant dream. He seems to be playing into their hands and cannot dissociate himself from them."

"Hafiz Saeed can't take the risk of antagonizing them either. Even if he wants to get rid of al Qaeda, it's too late, brother. I think they are now completely involved."

"How can you be so sure about it?"

"My dearest brother, trust your ears. If information about a top-secret meeting has reached me, then you should know what I mean."

Imran Shah Malik stopped to consider, "Why doesn't everyone understand what al Qaeda will ultimately do to Pakistan? One day, each one of us is going to repent this error of judgment. Hafiz Saeed will then know that al Qaeda never belonged to anyone. Truly speaking, not even to the Taliban!" He continued, "Anyway, tell me if any al Qaeda member was present in the meeting at the mosque?"

"Yes."

Imran Shah Malik was appalled, "Hafiz Saeed always plays into al Qaeda's hands. He has allowed them to interfere in this matter too?"

"He didn't invite them. Perhaps al Qaeda wanted to watch every move of LeT. al-Masri wanted his men to be present in the mosque. So, Hafiz could not do much. No one dares to go against them."

"If you remember, I went against al Qaeda and I promise that I will do the same again and again."

"I'm worried, Imran. Don't depend on anyone, not even Hafiz Saeed. Be alert. What if al Qaeda goes after you?"

"I'm neither holding up, nor keeping cover, brother. But can someone explain why are they hiding like a sly fox in some cave? Why are they living at the mercy of our tribal leaders? Why don't they come out into the open? Are their top leaders scared of death? Why do they send their Mujahideen to fight a losing battle and then leave them in the wilderness to live like hunted animals who ultimately die horrible deaths? But if their top leaders ever come out in the open, it's my promise that I'll make them realize that how a Pakistani can sort out things in seven minutes, things the Americans could not figure out in seven years." After a pregnant pause, Imran Shah Malik whispered, "Where are you, brother?"

The man at the other end laughed. "Nemogram. Back in my den."

"You were always an enigma. I still don't know what you do and for whom you work? Tell me, are you leading some Mujahideen group?"

"As always, you are so straightforward, my dearest brother. So here is a candid reply for you. I don't work for anyone. I work alone."

"What's your mission?"

"Chase al Qaeda."

"For what?"

"Nukes."

A wide smile spread across Imran's lips, "Everyone knows how desperate al Qaeda is for a nuclear bomb. And my brother, a one-man army, is chasing al Qaeda for nukes? It seems that the plot has already thickened." Imran laughed out loud, "Well, we'll talk about it when we meet. But I know what my brother can do. At day's end, he sits with Hafiz Saeed and he is back in his den before the new day dawns. After sundown, he gives me pinpointed information about what will happen in Mumbai. Yet he never tells me how he gets such vital information or who his contacts are?" Imran breathed in and continued, "Though you are younger, but looks to me that you're my older brother even though you work alone."

"I'm still the same man, who used to play with his nephew Aban. I still feel my Aban's soft touch. It has been years since I met him. Only I know how much I miss him. Give him my love." After a long silence, Imran Shah Malik heard his brother say, "You have never been to Nemogram, have you?"

"No, I haven't. But why do you ask?"

"The place has Buddhist monasteries. One may experience a divine nirvana here."

"Are you a Buddhist convert now?"

"I'm a true follower of Islam."

"Good."

"Yet I respect all human beings."

"Seems like I am talking to a Sufi saint." Imran Shah Malik expressed amusement. "Only this dervish walks around, armed with an AK-47. A wizard of geopolitics, a virtuoso of all-source information and a fakir! Sounds interesting. I haven't seen you in years. I wonder what my brother looks like now."

"You will get all your answers when you come to Nemogram?"

"Insha Allah!"

"I'll wait for you. *Khuda Hafiz, bhai.*"

The line went dead. Imran Shah Malik called a few more numbers and got confirmation of what he feared most. He sighed deeply. Thinking about the inevitable, he stretched out on his reclining mahogany chair and shut his eyes. Sleep evaded him as he shuttled fitfully between sleep and wakefulness.

After a little while, he answered the door when he heard a mild knock. Nausheen smiled. "Aban is waiting for you. He has got a movie ticket for 'Twilight' at DHA Cinema."

"I can't go tonight."

"But why? You know Aban will go back to America after Eid al-Adha. Shouldn't we all spend some time with him? Ever since he has come to Lahore, you have been very busy with your work. Why can't you relax in your retired life?"

"Only Allah will decide when I'll call it a day. Till then, I'll work for my country. Anyway all of us will go to the movie tomorrow."

"I know this tomorrow never comes. Why don't you understand? He is our only son and only Allah knows when he will come back again."

"I told you not to send him to America. We all know how difficult it is for Pakistani Muslims to live in America after 9/11. The Americans treat each one of us as spies and consider every Pakistani a perpetual threat to their existence. After the black September day, everything has changed. It will never be the same again for us. The Americans can't stand us and the irony is that our government can't ignore them. "

"It was you who wanted to provide the best education to Aban."

"Our engineering colleges in Pakistan are not bad. I studied in Forman Christian College in Lahore for a few months before joining the armed services. The college is proud of its alumni: former Prime Minister of Hindustān Inder Kumar Gujral, President Pervez Musharraf and the Foreign Minister Shah Mahmood Qureshi. The list is long. One of Forman's faculty members Prof. Arthur Compton conducted the bulk of his research on cosmic rays here, for which he received the Nobel Prize. I was member of the Undergraduate Mathematics society and know how good they are."

Imran pointed his finger to an image hanging on the wall, "He, Swami Ram Tirtha was a Mathematics genius. I have never come across anyone better than him. He was a proud member of our undergraduate society in Forman College and trust me, our entire alumni still hold him in the highest regard."

"Aban says getting a decent job in Pakistan is not easy for civil engineers. The companies pay them poorly."

"Does he really need that much money? He is a descendant of the Nawab of Dir and heir to a vast dominion. "Imran Shah Malik looked blankly at the ceiling and slowly turned his attention back to Nausheen. "But I know him. He thinks the same way as

I do. He will prefer to earn by toiling and lead a decent life rather than spend sleepless nights in a castle with his inherited wealth. Make him understand that many multinational construction companies operate in Pakistan. He can always come back to our *watan* after his studies and find a deserving job."

"Don't you think Aban will be a better person, if he stays in a cosmopolitan milieu?"

"The Americans are no different from the rest of the human race. They too are prone to exploiting life for selfish gains. The Supreme Court of the United States declared that the Native American Tribes and their land is a sovereign nation. Right under the nose of the authorities, drug peddling, flesh trading and smuggling are rampant in these 'sovereign nations'. All this goes in the name of culture, respecting other cultures. And the very same Americans bomb our tribes without understanding the 'otherness' of our culture." After a pause, he said, "Rather, the world is one."

"Still, why force him? Let him choose his own path."

"I know my son too, *Begum*. I know that right from the beginning he wanted to study in the Ivy League. He worked hard to get admission to one of the finest programmes. So, I never interfered. Today also if he wants to complete his education at Cornell, I will never force him to come back. However, if you ask me for my opinion, then I would want my child to return after he completes his research paper. I would love to see him prosper on his native soil and live among his own people in ease and peace."

"Still…"

"No questions."

Nausheen observed her husband's hand shaking violently

and scratching his right thigh. She had seen this for many years. Whenever her husband was under extreme emotional stress, it would happen invariably. In these times, the best thing was to leave him alone to deal with the situation.

A shrill voice echoed from the living room. "Come down, Mom."

"Call me *Ammi*. Don't imitate those Westerners."

"Come at once!"

Nausheen's eyes widened when she saw Geo TV flashing the report of the Mumbai attacks. "How could they? Why?"

The question remained unanswered as Aban and she watched the events unfolding before their eyes: mindless killing at a busy railway station, a gruesome bloodbath inside two five-star hotels, a chilling carnage in a café, a morbid massacre on the streets of the Mumbai and a ghastly butchery inside a Jewish Centre.

"Where is your *Abba*?" Nausheen turned her gaze to Aban, who held his head in disbelief.

"He's left."

Meeting at Connaught Place

THE MACABRE MUMBAI attacks happened in the late evening hours of November 26th, 2008.

The same afternoon Sundaram Iyer had gone to attend a meeting with the officers of the Central Water Power Commission at Sewa Bhawan, New Delhi. In the evening, he asked his chauffeur to leave the car keys with him, as he would be late.

Sundaram drove his car to Connaught Place and steered into the parking lot of M-Block, in front of the famous Variety Book Depot. He walked leisurely to the Lalit Intercontinental Hotel at Barakhamba Avenue and entered the Presidential suite, booked by a Dubai pharmaceutical company. Sundaram's three accomplices were eagerly waiting for him. He greeted them and asked each of them to power off their cell phones and to remove the batteries. With all cell phones dead to the world, a satisfied Sundaram asked Somashekhar Rao to turn off the television as well.

Somashekhar Rao obeyed, returned to his seat and blurted out, "How come you could not prevent the Indian Government from cancelling our contract, Sundaram?" The disenchanted Managing Director of the Progressive Architecture and Construction Company Ltd. of Hyderabad demanded answers from Sundaram Iyer.

"They say that the project cost has overrun because of non-performance by your company. You know the Hydroelectric Corporation is quite miffed with the project delay. "

"What about the ten million dollar bank guarantee that they have already encashed?"

"Calm down, Mr. Rao. You have already moved the Indian Council of Arbitration for resolving your commercial dispute. Your lawyers can always point a finger at the environmentalists, who have been hindering your work. Isn't it natural that your work gets affected for reasons beyond your control?"

"We put forth the same argument, but the metropolitan judge brushed aside our point of view."

"I'll talk to the Law Secretary. Let's see if he can be of any help."

"Everything has a price, my dear Iyer."

"Who knows that better than I? Forget about the company's revenue? What will you gain even if your company gets the money back from the government? Perhaps a few words of hollow appreciation! That's not an incentive in this cruel world, my dear friend." Sundaram chuckled. "Therefore, tonight we are going to finalize the issue in a way that will please all of us. In fact, none of you will need to serve anyone. What I'm going to tell you will make everyone sufficiently well-off."

"How much?"

"Five million dollars for each one of you!"

Somashekhar Rao nodded and Sundaram turned his attention to Parag Nanda, who seemed to be lost in his own world. "What's bothering you, Parag?"

"I'm worried about the Intelligence Bureau, which is making a mountain out of a molehill. They are exaggerating my role in the Israeli Barak Missile deal." The impatient Parag Nanda, who had always lived in the lap of luxury, could not take 'no' for an answer and so wanted a quick fix solution. "Why don't you put in a word for me to the Defence Minister and if possible the Prime Minister and get things sorted out?"

"That's out of the question. You know both are impeccable. They are not going to interfere in the work of the IB."

Parag Nanda was visibly fidgety. He picked up his glass of scotch and drank it in one large gulp. He quickly poured out another shot and stubbed out his cigarette with the other hand.

Ignoring the young Nanda's grumpiness, Sundaram Iyer continued, "Tell me if you will be able to get our remaining consignments of explosives through the Nepal border."

"That is another big problem. After the accession of a communist government in Nepal, diplomatic relations with India have taken a steep downturn. The Indian government doesn't count on inimical Nepal anymore since it is not cooperating with the extradition of the Naxalites and the Maoists, who have taken refuge inside their country. The IB and R&AW have even resorted to snatching terrorists from Nepal without taking their Nepalese counterparts into confidence. Nepal, in turn, has adopted a very hostile posture. Their Central Customs Authority is not clearing anything from its check posts even though we take care of its interests."

"Surprising!"

"Laughable too. They say fake currency notes have flooded India. So, the customs people don't trust our cash. They want payments in Euros or dollars and that too everything in advance."

"Bizarre! Anyway, talk to the Director General of Nepal Customs. You can always declare your consignment as some innocuous item like steel. I don't see why his men at the border will not clear it?"

"Even if they do so, it will raise suspicion on the Indian side."

"Why?"

"Nepal doesn't produce steel."

"Think out of the box. You may even forget the Nepalese route. More importantly, you cannot declare the consignment as UNDEX. That's the point, isn't it?" Sundaram said blandly.

"We don't need UNDEX, the underwater explosives, my dear friend," Somashekhar Rao cut in.

"Why?"

"It won't cause the intended deluge that you have planned. Even though, the explosion will create a massive water-dome in the reservoir, causing water surface shockwaves to hit the wall of the dam with tremendous force, it will still not be sufficient enough to cause a large rock-pile dam to fall."

"Well, it will create wide cracks inside the masonry and steel panels and then it will not be possible for the weakened foundation to hold it for a long time. The massive backwater pressure of the reservoir will crumble it."

"Nothing will happen. I'm a structural engineer and I know how big structures like dams take care of cracks. They withstand severe earthquakes and don't collapse like a house of cards. The enormous weight of the sand and earth of the gravity dam will quickly fill up the crack. Any porous opening disappears in the blink of an eye."

"What if we carry out successive explosions one after another? Will it not be sufficient to cause dam failure?"

"Each successive explosion will amplify the height and the strength of the waves. Even though each of them will weaken the various segments of the dam, still it cannot tear the dam apart."

"What is the solution then?" Sundaram seemed to be worried, as his grand plan seemed to be falling apart piece-by-piece.

"Resonance, my dear, resonance," said Somashekhar Rao, "It is one of the most striking and unexpected phenomena in physics, which can cause bridges to collapse, aircrafts to turn to dust and buildings to come crumbling down. Think if the sturdy Broughton Suspension Bridge in Britain could give way due to the resonance created simply by the rhythmic steps of marching foot soldiers, imagine the magnitude of devastation that a bigger resonance can create. *Tabla* maestros and opera singers have been known to shatter glass to smithereens with their mesmerizing beats and shrill high-pitched notes."[1]

Somashekhar Rao poured wine in a plain wineglass and pinged the glass with a teaspoon. He observed the sound attentively and then walked over to the System III Sirius Turntable at the far corner of the room. He chose Luciano Pavarotti's opera

---

1   Broughton Suspension Bridge in Britain and Angers Bridge in France gave way because of resonance when the frequency of the bridge harmonized with the rhythmic steps of marching foot soldiers. The forced resonance of the wind caused the Tacoma suspension bridge to collapse, simply by providing an external periodic frequency, which matched with the natural structural frequency of the bridge.

performance in *bel canto*. He mounted the LP, gently lowered the stylus and turned the volume knob, increasing the echo and hum. Nothing happened at tenor and countertenor levels, where the intonation alternated between two extremes. He then slowly turned the knob in the opposite direction, slowly reducing the sound to a very low volume, and waited.

Every one of them watched tentatively, holding their breath. When the vocal chords of the artist let out a bass-baritone, a large crack spread from the top to the base of the wine glass to the rim, shattering it into tiny shards of glass.

Somashekhar Rao walked pompously from the music deck to his awed audience. He chuckled, "Resonance of a Simple Harmonic Motion is the only thing that is capable of flattening the entire planet. A well calculated resonance could even split the planet into two."

The Additional Inspector General of the Central Industrial Security Force then spoke up, "I won't allow any of your reverberation unless you accept my terms."

Sundaram was upset, "We had a deal."

"I never agreed to anything. And you've not paid my previous dues yet."

"What dues?"

"Well Mr. Iyer, you know the Deputy Commandant at the dam doesn't work under my jurisdiction. Another officer of my rank has jurisdiction over the region. But then, I had to carry out the assigned work against all odds. When the Indian Government received a specific terror threat on dams from western intelligence, the Director General called for a meeting in Delhi. After a lot of deliberation, I convinced the DG to allow us to place the security post at a faraway place on the reservoir and upstream of two rivers. He agreed. To implement it, he assigned the work to me. Then, I had to work out everything to the last possible detail. I knew that I couldn't carry out the sensitive work, if the Deputy Commandant posted at the dam oversaw it. So, I managed a five-day training program for the DC. When he left for the training at NIS Academy in Hyderabad, we started our operations. After that, we had to complete the entire work within those five days. It was tough job to place explosives right under the nose of constantly tracking satellites. You know that the government has placed the dam in a highly sensitive zone. Every forty-five minutes, the satellites routinely take pictures. After erection of temporary sheds, my men had to justify the sounds of drilling machines. Transporting and then placing those explosives in the bore was not the only task at hand. My men had to connect all explosives with the timing device, and synchronize the frequency with the Ku-Band satcom. We hid the VSAT antenna on top of one of the temporary tin-sheds of the security post. In spite of all these odds stacked against our team, we pulled off the impossible. In fact, the VSAT is presently catching National TV programmes and a few satellite radio stations. You can tune into the desired frequency even remotely, sitting on your comfortable couch, and detonate these explosives right from here. I hope, my dearest friend, you understand now that what we did was surely not a happy- baby-nappy-changing job."

Sundaram Iyer smiled back, "Brilliant! Now tell me what happened to the temporary security posts?"

"They are still there, guarded by the CISF personnel. And the poor guys don't know what lies right beneath them."

Sundaram Iyer tried to underplay the swaggering AIG. "Terrific job. How much is your past due? I want to clear it."

"A million dollars."

"A million?" Sundaram Iyer was taken aback.

"Yes, Mr. Iyer. I've to cough up a substantial amount to the naxals of Bengal."

Sundaram Iyer looked worried, "Naxals are not experts in handling high-grade explosives, which can create a blast of such magnitude. The massive hills will stand tall. I think you have gone all wrong."

"Check your facts properly, Mr. Iyer. Never ever underestimate the naxalites. Many of them have worked in the open cast mines, handling explosives that can literally move mountains. Blasting small knoll and tor is a daily affair for them. Their explosives are highly sophisticated. If our calculation goes right, all three hills will crumble down into the reservoir, one by one, and amplify the waves into gigantic waves."

After thinking for a long time, Sundaram Iyer asked, "How much do you want for the next assignment?"

"Ten million dollars, my friend."

"Ten million!"

"Of course. You know that before joining government service, I swore allegiance to our constitution."

"So with greenbacks, you will change your loyalty." When the officer did not reply, Sundaram Iyer continued, "What if the Tupac-II people don't agree?"

"I'm out then. Tell them not to count me in."

"You do know that a government job is transferable, don't you?" Sundaram Iyer talked tough.

"My voice will echo everywhere in the world, Mr. Iyer. The media is ever ready to sink its teeth into a juicy piece of gossip. And this is a real story. Anyone can get a good price if he has a story to tell the world. If I drop a bit of a hint, they will chase me till hell freezes over."

Sundaram Iyer nodded.

The AIG pulled out a miniature memory chip from his pocket and continued with his wordplay, "Well! I can put this chip inside my cell phone and activate it as a transponder. You know very well that I can blow up all three hills at this very moment, don't you?"

"I know how capable you are. Now, hand over the transponder frequencies of the VSAT and the trigger sequence of the explosion."

"It has a very small executable file, which contains a few codes only." The AIG handed the miniature memory-chip to Sundaram. "The Ku-Band frequencies are mentioned in a small file. These few lines of written code can move a hill and tramp down the valley. Very interesting, isn't it?" The AIG chuckled.

"What about the abort sequence?"

"That's in the same file. Tell your boss to transfer the contents to his customized watch. He can initiate the trigger sequence as and when he wishes, but he will have to conform to a perfect timing schedule in case of the abort sequence."

"I will advise you one last thing though. Hold on to your horses till they are ready for the final race."

The AIG nodded.

The meeting was adjourned. Still unaware of the Mumbai attack, while going back to Connaught Place to pick his car, Sundaram was worried. "Why should one close the barn after the horse has already bolted?" he said cryptically.

As Sundaram walked out, two things haunted him: 'Resonance' and 'Not to count me in'.

A waiter of a well-known restaurant *Kake da Dhaba* and his *paanwala* friend, who were engrossed in late night chatter, casually watched a man entering a swanky Internet café.

The neon signboard of the café boasted, "Open 24 X 7".

Backup

A CAR FOLLOWED Imran Shah Malik's glossy black Mercedes Benz. The minute Imran turned right on PMG *chowk*, bullets started to spew forth from the car that was following him.

The bulletproof car of Imran Shah Malik bore the brunt of a few shots. However, the rear glass shattered completely when a grenade landed near it and exploded. His highly secured cell phone which was on the dashboard fell on the floor and was beyond anyone's reach under the front passenger seat. Imran fumbled, trying to pull it out, but could not. He stepped hard on the pedal, speeding down on N-5 or the New Grand Trunk Road towards Shahdara. Left with no choice, Imran activated his car phone and called his son, "Listen carefully, Aban. Go to my study and create a backup of my computer data right now. Leave for the US by the earliest flight. Once you reach the US, I will tell you what you need to do next."

Imran Shah Malik's car veered sharply to its left, as a bullet burst the rear tyre. Although it sustained the impact, it was enough to send it off balance. Riding the wave, Imran allowed the vehicle to enter a narrow by lane.

"What was that sound, *Abba*?" Aban's voice hollered into the instrument.

"The boys are lighting up fireworks." Imran laughed.

"I think…"

"Stop sweating the small stuff, son. I have been hearing these noises since I was as young as you."

"I'm worried, *Abba*…"

"Take it easy, son. Never ever mention this to *Ammi*. She will panic unnecessarily. "

Aban kept quiet.

"Someday, I will explain everything." The father disconnected the line.

He turned his car towards Landa Bazar. After crossing two blocks, Imran Shah Malik steered his car to a backstreet and swiftly killed the engine. He walked leisurely on to an adjacent alley, crossed a Hindu Temple and vanished into the darkness.

Aban tried to log onto his father's Mac Pro, but it was well protected by a 256-bit random cipher text password, cleverly hidden in the shadow hash function generator. He immediately understood that it was a kind of one-time pad cryptograph. So, even if he succeeded in deciphering it, the merciless machine would present millions of possible password permutations. He knew that if he keyed in even one wrong password out of the million possibilities, the key generator would deliver another million combinations.

As if mocking at a helpless man, the emotionless machine seemingly waited for an input.

Aban just sat there, staring at it. He remembered what his father had warned him about when he was to leave for the US for the first time. "Life is not a gamble. So, never opt for a shortcut to make decisions. Gambling machines churn out all possible combinations, except the jackpot integer. Casinos around the world have perfected a fail-proof-system, ensuring that only the house wins."

"Ever since man learnt how to count numbers, the old and the wise have been warning the younger generation that no one can ever win a bet based on the numeral digit. A game of dice, *teen patti*, *matka*, video poker lottery tickets, Russian roulette are the means of the devil to lead men astray."

Pointing towards the racecourse, he had continued, "The fate of Greyhound racing, sports betting, match fixing, arbitrage betting, lay-bet, options and futures, although not strictly based on numbers, are still decided by the devil and the demon."

"Right from the time of the primates and primitives, man knew how to design codes and ciphers, perfecting both for encryption and decryption. A tool for both man and machine, the skill became just another ritual of gambling, capable of forcing the world to teeter on the brink of extinction," he had concluded.

Aban recalled everything that his Abba had said that day. However, the situation was completely different now. *Abba* had asked him to take a backup of his computer.

"Could it be possible that trying out all the different combinations to find the password to his father's computer was nothing more than a game of dice?", wondered Aban. "Ought he to look elsewhere to find the key?" He tried to call his father, but the phone went unanswered. He tried calling up the car phone but in vain.

Aban brought out his MacBook and backed-up all his important data in a zip drive. After partitioning his hard disk, he connected both Macs. He rebooted his father's computer and executed a carbon copy cloner program to replicate the entire hard disk into the hard disk of his own MacBook.

Little Hog Cay

BACK FROM THE Intercontinental Hotel, Sundaram Iyer watched the television coverage of the Mumbai attacks with eyes wide open. His admiration for his mentors in Pakistan grew by leaps and bounds. After all, they had pulled off a near impossible feat.

He sipped his scotch and closed his eyes. If the grand strategy of Tupac-II worked out entirely, he was going to retire and live peacefully in a private barrier island, Little Hog Cay, in the North Bahamas. Once relieved from the humdrum of a boring life in office and an unexciting wife at home, he would do nothing but sip exquisite wine with half closed eyes and play golf every now and then.

Iyer already had a Pakistani passport and a top plastic surgeon of Dubai had promised to change his looks forever. The front company of Hussein Pharma was to deposit a princely sum of money, which would be abundant for a luxurious and indulgent life.

Sundaram Iyer sipped his scotch again and closed his eyes as his mind wandered off to replay his wild sensual fantasies.

Eyes shut, he found himself in his private massage parlour of his palatial home in Little Hog Cay Island. The gorgeous Venezuelan concierge helped him out of his clothes and ushered him into the sanctum sanctorum of the parlour. The most beautiful women from Sweden and sugar girls from Puerto Rico took over, gently and softly. However, he could not waste time, since he had invited a few princesses to his island. The reverie continued with uninterrupted fervour and the story continued to grow in his mind. The guests arrived in the afternoon. He imagined gesturing his men to escort his guests to their exclusive suites. After a while, handsome young men knocked at the doors of the suites. These able-bodied men then performed the ritual of gently lowering the young women into a bubbly bathtub.

The beautiful nymphs stepped out of the liquid, their bodies dripping wet. Their friends helped them out and wiped the 'mermaids' with large silk kerchiefs. The ensuing fire baptized the damsels, making them ready for more rituals.

The sexy sommeliers played gracious hosts to the hilt. They enticed the ladies with their extensive knowledge of wine and food combinations, played seductive tricks and entertained them with erogenous tickles, teasing and titillating them to keep the fire alive. When evening fell, lilting Persian music filled the air. The chilled wine tingled the nerves of all present, but then the warm glow of the candlelight immediately arrested the sensation, inflaming passions to unthinkable heights.

Sundaram Iyer came out of his psychedelic world and abruptly spoke in cold calculating tones. "I will handpick my personal secretary. How can I forget that this woman spurned my advances when I went to Europe the first time? My bunny girl from the Mediterranean may be piping hot, tingly and spicy, but I have all the money in the world to shower on this Miss High and Mighty."

Iyer planned to lie low for a decade and then, in his new avatar, pursue his long-standing hobby of lobbying for big business houses, arbitration of big stakes on money, politicking on sensitive issues and occasional liaising with government officers. Even though these activities were fraught with danger, he just could not live without those old habits.

Taj Mahal Hotel

ABAN CAME BACK to the living room and found Nausheen still watching television. The media was airing minute-by-minute accounts of death and destruction. A television commentator was reporting from Hotel Taj Mahal at the Gateway of India, Mumbai. His camera operator panned on to a window from where the NSG commandos were rescuing many guests using a ladder.

The camera zoomed in and Aban's face lit up, but soon became anxious when he spotted a young girl who showed up at the window. "Oh God! What the hell is she doing there?"

"Who is she?" Nausheen looked surprise.

"She is Juhi. She studies at Cornell. We know each other."

"How much?" Nausheen's interest spiked up.

"Not much. A bit." Aban turned his gaze away. "I need to talk to her. She must be feeling terrible."

"Hold on, Aban. It is not a good idea to dial Mumbai at this time. The Indian intelligence agencies must be monitoring each call from Pakistan."

"To hell with them! I'm concerned about her. I don't care what they think." Nausheen wanted Aban to understand the danger, but he would not listen. "Her father is the Indian Ambassador to the US. Nothing will happen, *Ammi*."

"I'm really worried for you, my son. The situation is quite messy. You may be inviting big, big trouble."

Aban found himself trapped in a tight spot. He had to heed his father's warning and conceal the fact from Nausheen that he had heard gunshots in his father's car. He was also worried sick because his father's phone went unanswered and Juhi was caught up in a life and death situation.

"*The sweetest joy, wildest woe is love.*" Aban struggled to avoid his mother's prying eyes while he called Juhi several times. However, it seemed the cell phone networks were clogged.

Nausheen could clearly see the fretfulness in her son's eyes. She drew closer to Aban. "Don't do anything that your father would disapprove of."

"Someday, I will explain everything to *Abba*." Aban turned his gaze away from his mother. Fervently, he tried one more time and the line connected. Aban ran to his room, escaping his mother's probing eyes and cocked ears.

However, Nausheen heard a few sentences, "Hi sweetie. I was scared to death when I saw you on television…"

Nausheen stood in silence in the living room, feeling shut out of her husband's and son's lives. The disquieting sound and the gory pictures on TV did not interest her anymore. Exhausted, Nausheen opened the window and stared blankly into the darkness that had spread outside.

Bugged

THE INTELLIGENCE BUREAU of India (IB) had mounted surveillance on the elusive Imran Shah Malik for the last two years. To their utter frustration, he was too hard to pin down because he never left a trail of his movements, not even accidentally. There were no lapses on his part.

Although a few laptops and an iMac at home were connected with Airport Extreme Base Station, the Mac Pro of Imran Shah Malik's study room was entirely isolated from the outside world. It was never connected to the Internet and so was not accessible to anyone intending to ping into that computer. He had taken extreme care to turn off any sharing: file, printer, Xgrid, screen, web, remote login, everything. He preferred to use USB keyboard and mouse, instead of the latest Bluetooth version. The Bluetooth was always turned off. The Ethernet port was never wired. He loved to work on an ultramodern machine in the most archaic way. Perhaps, one could say, the most modern way!

Imran Shah's cell phones and landline phones were highly encrypted and therefore completely inaccessible. The IB personnel could eavesdrop only on the droning hum of the phones that were kept on constant tap or wiretap. They had planted the most sophisticated bugs in his home, but nothing was of any use.

The Indian agents were even more frustrated because whenever Imran Shah Malik drew close to the bugs they had planted, he would recite divine Pashto poetry or hum melodious classical music with a perfect blend of *raag* and *taal*. Clearly, he found it amusing to mock his Indian 'friends'.

Though he was fond of Ghazals, which spoke of idealistic lovers pining for each other unto death, he would sing old Punjabi songs with soothing tunes; spanning over a wide range of moods: the joy of living, the rains, sowing, harvesting seasons and what not? He hummed the love legends of Heer Ranjha, Sohni Mahenwal, Saifu Mulk and the many tragic tales told in those folklores, all aimed at misleading the Indians, who sat listening with wide earphones, hoping to catch even a minor aberration on Imran Shah Malik's part.

However, the story of the car phone was entirely different.

Imran Shah Malik's young driver constantly chatted with his fiancé over the car phone. It was also a free means of communication for the driver's friends: the gardener, the cook, the *dhobi*, the milkman and the fruit seller who frequented Imran's house on a daily basis.

The Indian officer, who was deputed in New Delhi, to listen to conversations on Imran Shah Malik's phone, cursed the day he had joined the IB. He often begged his seniors for a transfer from the post because all that he got to hear day in and day out were the driver's sleazy words, his fiancé's coy giggles and the gardener's constant bickering with his wife - a mother to eight children, whose voices were forever present in the background.

The overriding concern of the *paan*-chewing cook was to open a tea, samosa and boiled egg stall and then later on construct a small roadside *dhaba* of his own and to hire cooks and waiters. He would then sit at the cash counter and watch sitcoms through the day and occasionally scold the waiters, even if they worked well. At night, he would take home a few rupees to please his pesky wife. Most of the money would be spent on the maid, with whom he was madly in love. He would shower the *Mohtarma* with red lipstick, snow powder, talcum, *alta*, glass bangles and most importantly, slip a gold ring on her finger. This had been on his mind from the very first day he had seen her in Imran's house. He instantly knew that she would never refuse his advances. Oh! That night would be a different night. But he had no money to fulfil his dream. For this, he would have to keep abreast of the loan and the interest rates that were made available from the local *sahukars*, the moneylenders.

The *dhobi* nursed a childhood dream of washing the silvery glad rags of the Sheikhs and Shaykhahs of Dubai in the basement of their stunning castles. *Insha Allah*, after serving those 'dumdum nobles', and 'gorgeous czarinas', the day would not be very far off, when he would be back to his fatherland, wearing his best bib and tucker! He would then employ another dhobi to wash his spotless white togs and black ties!

And since he was a washerman, he had a very sound idea of the kind of clothes that the rich and famous wear. However, his imagination could not travel beyond wearing pants. And since *hawai chappals* or rubber flip flops had always adorned his flaky feet, the idea of slipping shiny shoes over his scaly feet had never ever crossed his fuzzy mind. So he would end up in his imagination, wearing designer clothing, paired with *hawaiis* and stepping out in style from an Air Emirates flight from Dubai to Lahore.

But entry into Dubai was only through 'pushing', the term used for illegal immigration and for this constant networking over the phone with illegal immigration agents, their cronies and his Dubai-based cousins was crucial. Moreover, what could be better than the free car phone that lay idle all day long and when any ISD call was beyond his means. Hence, the compelling need to use the neglected car phone!

The milkman was the occasional Hindu that one found in Pakistan. Since all his relatives lived beyond the borders, he was ever on the lookout to get in telephonic touch with them. His most recent fad was to buy a *Kajri* cow from the Sonepur *Mela* with a row of bells tied around its neck and hot pink and crimson tassels around its horns. Along with this, he was also consumed by a heart-rending desire to offer its milk at the *Jyotirlinga* in Baidyanathdham before coming back to Pakistan. The IB Officer was occasionally rewarded with the fruit seller's enquiries regarding price fluctuations at the Mughalpura Fruit Mandi of Lahore.

The reason why all these people risked their necks to use the master's car phone was the fear of fat bills, that the infidels or the personnel of billing department of those 'morons', the telecom companies, slapped on these *'Allah ke bande'*, the chosen men of God. Allah, who had created all men equal, had also created the cell phone. Then, why the bills!

How the beleaguered IB officer wished Imran Shah Malik had secured this car phone line too!

But for once, on that fateful night, the IB officer was excited. His eyes lit up as he heard Imran give instructions to Aban. He noted down Aban Malik's number and flagged it immediately. Euphoric, he emailed the relevant information to Siddhartha Rana, the Joint Director of IB.

"Imran Shah Malik has asked his son Aban to backup his computer and leave for USA tomorrow. The cell phone number of Aban Malik is +1..."

He got an instant reply, "Send in the entire transcript and voice file."

Noida Driveway

IN DELHI, THE head of the banned fundamentalist organization SIMI (Students' Islamic Movement of India) received a call from Pakistan. He noted down the Hyundai car licence plate number and called his trusted men to carry out the task.

The thoroughly inebriated AIG of the CISF staggered out of the Presidential Suite humming the classic *'Na jao saiyan chudha ke baiyan...'*, the haunting Meena Kumari song. He fumbled and fell as he walked across the lobby. Groping his way across the well-lit lobby, the AIG somehow managed to pass through the glass door of Lalit Intercontinental Hotel. He then flashed his car parking ticket at the valet captain.

When his car pulled up at the porch, he dug out his wallet, ripped out a fistful of thousand-rupee notes, and shoved the tip into the hands of a bewildered celebrity, who had just got off from his burnished limousine. While the valet gave the AIG a quizzical look, the superstar gave him a steely stare. He slapped the money on the valet captain's desk and walked away.

The AIG pushed hard to get his burly body inside his sleek car and sat confidently behind the wheel. Like every self-possessed carouser, he did not put his seat belt on. He engaged the gear and pressed the pedal hard. The muffler puffed out thick black smoke and the vehicle sped jumping several traffic signals.

There was no sign of life on Golf Road in Noida. The AIG slowed his car down and veered to his right when a truck headlight pierced his eyes. He steered left, but the truck headed straight towards him. Frantic, he pressed the horn repeatedly. The next minute, all was silent.

The steering wheel had broken into his front ribs while the truck zipped past in the opposite direction and stopped. Gasping for breath, the AIG wanted to shout out for help, but not a word passed from his lips. He groped for his cell phone on the passenger seat.

The phone connected and his wife answered. "I love you, honey." he whispered hoarsely.

"Where are you?"

"Listen very carefully. Tell the Director General of the CISF that Project Karachi was only a trailer." He strained to take a deep breath, but his lungs seemed to give away. "Tell him that the Jihadists of Pakistan have initiated Tupac-II."

"What is this 'To Pak to?"

"I don't have time. Also tell the DG that the Indian agent of the Pakistani Jihadists is Sun…" The AIG's voice drifted into nothingness. He struggled to inhale, but his lungs, filled with blood blocked out all air.

"Who is Sun…?"

The eyes of the AIG riveted on the two men, peering closely at him through the glass of car windows. His lips moved. He gulped, exerted all his enervated energy, but only red plasma emerged. "Help me," his eyes begged.

Two bullets pierced the AIG's brain and the sound boomed into the instrument. While one of the men busied himself snatching the AIG's gold chain, Rolex watch, diamond ring, and other expensive stuff kept in the glove box, the other picked up the cell phone. He heard a screaming female voice, "Why don't you speak? What's happened to you?"

The man whispered nonchalantly, "We killed the bastard. Come to Golf Road and cry over his body, baby."

Mumbai Police Headquarters

THE RAPID ACTION Force, the Marine Commandos, and the National Security Guards cordoned off all attacked premises in Mumbai. Operation Black Tornado kick-started in full swing.

The Police Commissioner of Mumbai called an important meeting of the senior officers of Mumbai Police, the Intelligence Bureau and the Research & Analysis Wing (R&AW) to coordinate and strategize the further course of action. A few high-ranking officers dashed from New Delhi to Mumbai in a special aircraft. The roads were cleared from the CST Airport to Marine Lines. Some fire engines and ambulances had to wait until the entourage zipped past *Mantralaya* towards the Police Headquarters. The red beacons on their vehicles flashed through in the gloomy night, while the sirens pierced the sombre silence.

The Additional Director of R&AW initiated the discussion, "A few minutes before these terrorists landed at Colaba, one of our technicians, who was monitoring satellite transmissions, picked up snatches of conversation between the assailants and their handlers in Pakistan."

The Police Commissioner of Mumbai had a bone to pick with the other officers. He sounded dejected. "The Pakistanis are always a step ahead of us. As per my information, they chose phone numbers from an online phone directory and made random phone calls all over India with an aim to overwhelm our listening devices. This has been going on for the last several months. Precise information of this attack got lost in the cacophony of plenty. We missed out on the crucial cues. I asked my research wing to check out the approximate numbers of calls made from Pakistan to Mumbai. You will be surprised to know that there were more than a thousand new calls every minute."

"What type of calls?"

"It seems the Pakistanis are using some autodialing software, which picks up telephone numbers from the database of online yellow pages, connects to the caller, speaks about some market products and then goes dead."

"Six months back, we had some information about an attack on a few Mumbai hotels and other sensitive locations."

"We know your Signal Intelligence agency intercepted a few calls originating from Pakistan, but nothing specific came out of it. They keep talking about one impending attack or another with the intention of hoodwinking us. Their Cellcrypt software with its unique code is also ahead of our snooping system."

Siddhartha Rana, the Joint Director of IB and the youngest participant in the high power group interjected, "Sir, let's not waste any more time and start intercepting calls originating from the terrorists to their handlers in Pakistan."

The Police Commissioner of Mumbai nodded and connected his line to the electronic intelligence room of the Mumbai Anti Terrorist Squad (ATS). He asked the technician to record the conversation between the six hatchet men and their handlers in Pakistan. The technician right away tapped all calls originating from or terminating at the towers of Cuffe Parade, Colaba and Nariman Point. A few minutes later, he pointed out to the Police Commissioner that most of the calls originating from Pakistan were made using Chinese cell phones, which did not have any IMEI numbers. Hence, the caller's identity could not be established. Though he could intercept calls of Thuraya Satellite and Blackberry phones, he was unable to record the voice data of the phones since the data exchange among the phones was highly secured. The Police Commissioner immediately spoke to the Home Minister in Delhi. The Minister promised to talk to the Attorney General of the USA and to seek the help of the FBI to start decrypting the phone conversations.

Siddhartha turned to the Police Commissioner, "Sir, that still may not be enough. We need to tap and audit trail all phone calls from the area under attack."

"We have only one mobile passive interception van, equipped with 32-channel listening devices. Therefore, we can send it to one spot only."

"Please have it moved to the Trident Hotel. I'll try to work out something at other locations."

The meeting continued for a few more minutes and was adjourned when the Police Commissioner left for Cama Hospital to oversee operations there. Disconcerting reports kept pouring in from Cama Hospital and CST Railway Terminus.

Two terrorists had gunned down the Chief of the ATS, Hemant Karkare, one of its finest officers and two senior police officers Vijay Salaskar and Ashok Kamte.

Siddhartha left Police Headquarters for the Taj Mahal Hotel. He instructed his officer to get different cell phone companies to provide a gateway to the backbone network of the Intelligence Bureau.

Siddhartha was horror struck when he saw the menacing black fumes rising from the domes of the Taj Mahal Hotel. It sickened him to the core almost as if he was watching smoke rise up from the funeral pyre of the heart of India's culture. It was an attack that had charred something into much deeper than just the edifice. Suddenly, he was jolted out of his trance by the uninterrupted gunshots and intermittent grenade explosions inside the hotel. One valiant fire fighter had climbed the ladder set against the window of a room and was struggling to douse out the soaring inferno. NSG Commandos were frantically trying to go inside from the side entrance but had to retreat many times in order to dodge the indiscriminate firing of bullets by the terrorists. Some brave ones entered from the guest room windows, facing impending death.

The soothing dim light of moon and the tranquil waves of the Arabian Sea were in complete contrast with the mayhem created by a few jihadists.

Siddhartha Rana powered on his laptop and clicked on the Spycell Phone tapping software. Thousands of call records filled his screen. Most of the calls were domestic and a few were to USA, UK and various other countries. He clicked on the menu and filtered calls originating or terminating at: Pakistan, Jordan, Yemen, Somalia, Saudi Arabia, and a few other Islamic countries.

Soon, he had all the phone numbers and the ids of the owners, who were active in the vicinity of the attack.

Amongst what seemed like debris in the form of numbers, one call caught his attention. When he checked the call data record, he was surprised to find that a caller from Pakistan was trying to call Juhi Shergill, an Indian, using a US cell number. He fed the number into his software. Relationship trees and clusters of phone calls of the suspected numbers sprang up on the screen.

The American number was not getting through because of congested networks. Siddhartha racked his brain as the US number appeared to be quite familiar. He checked the email, *"The cell phone number of Imran Shah Malik's son Aban Malik is +1…"*

Through his software, Siddhartha Rana assigned a gateway through a dedicated spectrum and pinged a fake call to the phone of Juhi Shergill. As soon as he did that, a bug got embedded in the target phone electronically.

Siddhartha's laptop beeped and started to record the conversation between Juhi and Aban.

"I've been trying to reach you since I saw you coming out from Taj Mahal Hotel in a television live feed. Are you all right?"

"Yes, darling. It all started when I was dining with a member of the European delegation on the rooftop at Souk restaurant. In the din, we got down to the first floor, where a hotel staff directed us to the room from where we made our exit. It's pretty horrible over here."

"I can understand. Did you talk to your father?"

"Yeah, he told me to come back to DC. He has already spoken with the MD of Air India. I'll be boarding tomorrow."

"I'll be boarding PIA too."

"When do you reach JFK?"

"Around afternoon."

"Good. I will be there two hours before that. I'll wait for you in the Air India Maharaja Lounge."

"But that's on the departure concourse of Terminal-4."

"Well, that's where my father has arranged for me to be."

"How could I forget that my mademoiselle, the daughter of an Ambassador, is a virtual princess!" Aban teased.

"See you, sugar." Juhi hung up.

"Aban, the son of Imran Shah Malik, the retired Chief of ISI…" Siddhartha's mind was abuzz with rapid thoughts that flooded him as the facts began to come together. "Juhi, the daughter of the Indian Ambassador to USA! "

"Everything seems to be rather knotty!"

Photo Studio

ONE DAY AFTER the Mumbai attacks, a man named Shalim Amīr Khan approached Advanced Photo Studio and Digital Color Lab, near Subzi Mandi. He asked the owner to quote his price for video recording and capturing still pictures of the entire area: the topography of mountains, the catchment areas of the rivers, the contour map of the lake and snapshots of T1 to T4 shafts of the Great Dam.

The wary owner was skeptical, but when the visitor told him that he wanted to deliver the pictures to a film producer in Mumbai, the studio owner was excited. He quoted a price of fifty thousand rupees and asked for four days' time to get everything ready. The visitor specified that he would require high definition video and ultra-high resolution still-images burnt into DVDs. Shalim Amīr also made it very clear that he would copyright the contents to protect the exclusive rights of the film producer and so the photographer should not keep any copies of the footage.

The owner sensed that something was not right. He therefore, enhanced his charges to one lakh rupees.

After Shalim Amīr Khan left the studio, the owner stuffed the money into a secret cavity to escape the probing eyes of the regular visitors of the revenue department and the police. He picked up his camera and camcorder and left his shop. The dam was not very far off.

Meanwhile, Shalim Amīr Khan drove his car to the CCR Tower to meet the *Mela* Officer. He asked him for video footage of the *Ardh Kumbh* of 2004. The officer directed him to the Media Centre. The media officer proudly handed him all available video footage and made an earnest request to include his name in the credit roll of the documentary film.

Shalim then drove along the Upper Ganges Canal Expressway. The next destination was the holy city of Mathura. Shalim stopped at a street in Aligarh, where a Sufi singer and his flute maestro mesmerized a small audience. Shalim chose a corner and sat quietly on the ground, occasionally voicing his appreciation. In silence, feeling both happy as well as numb, Shalim slowly got up and opened the door of his car. The driver steered the car to the Grand Trunk Road, where a signpost read -- Kanpur.

During the long and winding drive, Shalim enjoyed delicious Punjabi food at the roadside *dhabas*. *Golas,* made of shredded ice, topped with multicoloured sweet syrups reminded him of home. He could smell the Balochistani scent in tandoori food on the roadside dhaba, which was no different from the aroma of the *Dilli* Biryani of Lahore. The freshwater fish that he bought from the markets of Karachi tasted no different from the mustard *rohu* that he had relished in Kolkata many years ago.

Many times, during that journey, he regretted that the two

countries could not live peacefully. But everything changed, as painful memories that had lasted with Shalim for many years came back, "Why did the *Hindustānis* cut Pakistan into two pieces?"

Finally, Shalim reached the place from where he had started. He drove to the Digital Colour Lab one more time, collected the cassettes, memory disks and DVDs and returned to Jolly Grant Airport. The late night connecting flight from Delhi to Mumbai was running behind schedule. So, as soon as he boarded a Jet Airways flight, its deep leather couch was enough to cuddle him into a dreamless slumber.

Next morning, Shalim Amīr Khan met the owner of Crest Telefilms Entertainment Ltd in Filmistan, Mumbai. He handed over the script and media contents to the owner and instructed him to leave one soundtrack blank. This, he said, would be mixed afterwards. He paid up an upfront amount of fifty thousand dollars after the owner promised to get everything ready within six months.

During a long solitary walk in the bylanes of Linking Road and S.V. Road, Shalim Amīr Khan stopped at a few places. From Andheri to Bandra, he paused to appreciate the humble Jarimari Temple as well as the ostentatious Bohra Mosques. Within a distance of a few thousand yards, the imposing St. Peter's Church stood close to the unpretentious Sri Guru Singh Sabha Gurudwara.

"Which one is more true -- unity in diversity of culture or diversity in unity of religion?" Shalim wondered and checked into the luxurious Orchid Hotel, near the domestic Airport.

There was no direct flight from Mumbai to any city in Pakistan. Therefore, his natural choice was to reach Lahore via Dubai.

Tired, he hit the bed and slept like a log.

FBI at JFK

SUITE 241, BUILDING 75 at JFK International Airport, New York is a busy office of the FBI Resident Agency. Special Agent Robert McLean received hundreds of requests from all over the globe every day. An untiring man and ever willing to oblige, he had earned rave reviews from intelligence agencies around the world. His penchant for anonymity had made his task easier.

Robert Mclean stood glued to the television, absorbing every detail of the Mumbai attack. His uncanny ability to analyse a complex situation was set in motion. He firmly believed that learning the tricks, tacks and tactics from one's opponent and using the same stratagems, plot and strategies against the opponent was a truly successful way of conducting a counter-terrorist operation. His mantra was to turn the tables on the perpetrators through the perpetrators themselves.

The same afternoon, Robert McLean got a call from Siddhartha Rana. In the past, both of them had coordinated to solve transnational crimes. Siddhartha Rana gave him the telephone number of Aban Shah Malik and asked Robert McLean to get Aban's complete profile from the FBI database and also do a background check at Cornell. "Aban is travelling by the PIA flight from Lahore tomorrow and will be landing at Terminal-4," said Siddhartha.

"Don't worry, Sid. My agent will tail him and try to find if he has something interesting up his sleeve." Robert McLean was prompt as usual.

"That won't be easy. He will be meeting the daughter of the Indian Ambassador. If she accompanies him, you need to watch out for diplomatic protocol."

"Our airports officers frisk even cabinet ministers, if it's a question of our national security. The children of diplomats hardly enjoy any privilege."

"Try to keep things as low key as possible. It would be good if it's an undercover operation."

"Wait a minute, Sid. For an undercover operation, I'll need a formal official request from your government."

"I'm stuck in Mumbai and so it won't be possible for me to go to Delhi and get formalities done."

"I understand, but I can't be of much assistance. We cannot carry out any undercover operation unless we have sufficient reasons to justify it. If our congressional representatives and senators, so much as sense something, they will simply go public and attack us. In addition, all the hard work of a dedicated officer will go up in smoke since these politicians will earn free brownie points. Moreover, the media has been hounding American agencies after the Guantanamo Bay exposé. I'm sorry, Sid. I can't act on a mere oral request."

"Even if a Pakistani has something interesting in his MacBook, Bob?" Siddhartha put a bug in Robert McLean's ear while he went on to explain everything he knew.

"Got it!", said Robert succinctly. The operation was on.

Crematorium

THE ADDITIONAL INSPECTOR General of CISF was put on the pyre at *Antim Niwas*, a crematorium in Noida. A few days later, his wife went to Block No. 13 in CGO Complex at Lodhi Road, New Delhi to call on the Director General of CISF and tell him everything her husband had told her just before he had been shot dead.

When she had left, the DG was lost in thought. "How could the AIG know about the Pakistani Project Karachi?" However, the DG could not make out anything of the phrase 'Tupac-II'. For him it was '*To Pak To*', with no meaning at all.

Another problem was the incomplete name of an Indian Agent, whose name started with Sun... which could have been anything; first name: Sunand, Sunay, Sunder, Sunil, Suneet, Sundri, Suneeti, Sunita... or last name: Sundaray, Sunitha...He tried his best to untangle the threads, but was at his wits' end because he did not even know whether the person was male or female. '*The Indian agent of the Pakistani Jihadists is Sun…*" kept ringing in his ears. When he could not make any more headway, he rang up the Director of IB and told him everything he knew.

The Laptop

AIR INDIA FLIGHT AI 101 landed at Terminal T-4 of JFK in the afternoon. A tired, but radiant Juhi completed the formalities at the Customs and Border Protection special desk, which dealt with the diplomatic Red Passport.

Juhi then walked towards a retail shop 'New York Fashion'. She picked up a pair of dazzling Zegna Centennial limited edition cufflinks for Aban and proceeded to the Maharaja Lounge. There, she sank into the sofa and sipped hot coffee as she waited.

Pakistan International Airlines Flight No PK 711 landed two hours later. US Custom and Border Protection cleared Aban. When he crossed the Homeland Security barrier, an FBI officer flashed his identity card at him and whisked him into the lounge, where Agent Robert Mclean was waiting in anticipation.

Robert McLean politely asked Aban to boot his MacBook. Aban obeyed the order. The operating system booted and asked for the username and password before logging-in. Aban entered the username Imran Shah Malik and stopped dead.

"Enter the password." Robert demanded.

"I don't know it."

"Why?"

"Only my father knows it."

"Whose MacBook is this?"

"Mine."

"How does your father have knowledge of the password of your MacBook while you claim you are unaware?"

Aban tried to clarify, but Robert McLean was unwilling to listen. The last thing that Robert McLean was willing to do was to trust a young Pakistani, carrying a MacBook, unable to feed in his own password. He asked Aban to follow him to his office. Aban requested Robert McLean to allow him to make a call before he left. Robert McLean took a deep breath and nodded. Aban called Juhi.

Juhi was perplexed by the sudden turn of events. She quickly explained the situation to her lawyer, who advised her to be patient and bide her time until the FBI divulged exactly what they wanted. When Juhi reached the FBI Residency Office, she found Aban signing some papers and handing them over to an agent. She expressed her desire to meet the Agent, but the officer stopped her and instructed her to wait in the adjoining chamber.

Robert started interrogating Aban, "Where did you purchase this MacBook?"

"From eBay."

"When?"

"A year back."

"Where do you go to college?"

"Cornell School of Civil and Environmental Engineering."

"Graduate or undergraduate?"

"Graduate."

"What's your area of specialization?"

"Environmental and Water Resources Systems Engineering."

"Something to do with city water supply."

"A bit more than that. My research papers are about the environmental impact of big dams." Aban sighed heavily.

"When are you submitting your research paper?"

"Before Christmas."

"Is your work complete?"

"No."

"How much of your research work is still to be finished?"

Aban brooded for a while, "More than half."

"Is this vacation time in your school?"

"No."

"Why did you go to Lahore?"

"My mother wanted me to visit her."

"Why?"

"She said she was feeling lonely."

"So you went to Lahore to make your mother happy."

"Yes."

"Tell me the password."

"I don't know."

"Mr. Malik, your story is complete trash. You say you bought this MacBook through eBay and logically you must have the data of your research paper in it. And you say you don't know the password."

Aban kept absolutely mum, as he saw no point in arguing with the officer. The officer continued, "You have to submit your research paper before Christmas and your school is not closed for vacation. Still you are jockeying around in Lahore. You don't inspire any confidence, Mr. Malik."

Robert McLean recorded Aban's statement and declared, "You are under arrest."

When Robert McLean came out of his room, Juhi hurried up to him, "Sir, can you tell me what's going on?"

"The matter is serious. I'm afraid I can't tell you anything right now."

"I know Aban. He is a simple guy."

"This is a matter of national security and I suggest you leave this place now."

Juhi came out, but decided to wait around the Residency office instead of leaving the terminal. After a while, Aban, handcuffed, and accompanied by Robert McLean and two other officers came out of the room. His eyes met Juhi's fleetingly. Juhi's blue eyes remained fixed on Aban, who walked slowly as the officer exited the JFK terminal.

Juhi could barely hold back her tears when she dialled her father's number.

"Where are you, my little doll?" The delighted Ambassador was quite over the moon.

"At the airport."

"Why? Your flight landed four hours back."

"I'm in love with a boy, dad."

"Great! That's wonderful, my little bird. Is he the reason for you being tied down at the airport?"

"Yes."

"Oh! Come home quickly and bring him along, so that your mind is not stuck with him while you are here."

"Dad…"

"Is the boy with you?"

"The FBI has arrested him."

The Intelligence Bureau

OPERATION BLACK TORNADO finished when the last terrorist was shot down at the Taj Mahal Hotel, Mumbai. The terrorists had massacred one hundred and seventy three people, ruthlessly bumped off three senior police officers of the Mumbai ATS, cold-bloodedly shot dead a Major of the NSG and liquidated dozens of cops and commandos. More than three hundred people were grievously injured. Many battled for life while a few became incapacitated for life. A few lucky ones got away with simple first aid.

They had inflicted an eternal everlasting wound on the vibrant city, something that would bleed for a long, long time.

Siddhartha Rana went to Delhi to brief the Director of IB about all the leads pertaining to the Mumbai attack. When he mentioned that the FBI wanted to interrogate Juhi, the Director became uncomfortable. "You shouldn't have got the daughter of our Ambassador involved."

"I agree, sir. I told Robert to leave her alone. But he doesn't seem to have ears."

"What is making him so hard-nosed?"

"He says Juhi claims to be the girlfriend of Aban. On the day of the Mumbai attack, she was in the rooftop restaurant of the Hotel Taj Mahal. She managed to escape without so much as a scratch, when others even from the second and third floor, could not make it. As soon as she came out of the hotel, a Pakistani national called her on her cell phone. They have arrested the same caller, Aban Malik. According to Robert, the whole series of events is like smoke and mirror, raising sufficient suspicion in the minds of the FBI." Siddhartha went on to explain everything he had heard from Robert McLean.

"Any lead on his father, Imran Shah Malik?"

"He's disappeared."

"How could he?" The Director appeared upset with the recent setbacks. "We asked R&AW to provide us with his complete profile. Have we managed to get hold of his computer ip addresses? Didn't their agent in Lahore gather information regarding all his recent activity? What of the bugs planted in his house? I have instructed our agents at Lahore to shadow him all the time. Still he escaped? Quite surprising!"

He instructed Siddhartha Rana, "Get in touch with Sundaram Iyer and ask him if he can throw some light on all this. I know the Director of the CBI had assigned a related case to him two years back. However, the CBI closed the matter. Try to find out the reason."

"I'm sorry sir, but I think the IB should examine the case on its own without attracting the attention of others."

"Why?"

"Luckily, we got a small opening when Mr. Malik talked with his son on his car phone." Siddhartha put in plain words everything he knew and then continued, "However, we still don't know what's in his computer. And, for the time being, I don't want to share the contents of the computer with any other agency."

The Director sighed. He raised his eyebrow and directed, "Then, Mr. Rana, I want you to take up the entire case, bunch everything up and try to get something out of it."

"Sir!"

"I'll have to talk to the Foreign Secretary regarding Juhi and also to Ambassador Shergill. Otherwise, it might escalate into a diplomatic disaster."

"Indeed, sir. I have a nagging feeling that there is more to the Mumbai attack than meets the eye. We need to act, or else we will never know what's brewing in Pakistan."

"What do you suggest?"

"I'll have to go to the US"

"Not now. There is one more puzzle." The Director gave an account of every detail to Siddhartha: about the bumping off of the AIG of the CISF, the indecipherable name of a person's name starting with 'Sun…' and some bizarre phrase '*To Pak To*'.

Siddhartha came out of the Director's office and went to his room. The truth, it appeared was hidden behind several manifestations of falsehood.

Wandering

IMRAN SHAH MALIK wandered all over Pakistan and travelled to India a few times. He deliberately steered clear of everyone except his enigmatic brother, who, one day showed up in front of Imran, unannounced.

Imran's brother assured him that the Government of Pakistan or ISI had no role in the shootout. Surprisingly, both LeT and al Qaeda had expressed complete ignorance of any happening of this sort too. So, Imran's enemy still remained a mystery.

His brother also suggested that Imran remain in hiding for a few weeks until the matter settled down. Although Imran's brother was aware of Aban's arrest, he did not disclose it, thinking Imran might end up doing something that would endanger his own life as well as Aban's. He wanted to work out a solution on his own.

Imran Shah Malik was himself preoccupied, as he had to tie up a crucial loose end. He had not instructed Aban to securely erase the file from his computer when he had told him to make a backup of his computer.

Imran wrote a letter to Nausheen, mentioning that it would take a few days more before he could visit home. He mentioned a date and a time late at night, when Nausheen was to power on the computer and connect it to the Internet through Apple Airport Extreme Base Station, which was highly secured by a WPA2 Enterprise wireless security.

Imran's brother, disguised himself as the regular milkman, and visited Nausheen's home in Lahore. He handed over the letter. Both talked briefly and the 'milkman' left.

On the date mentioned in the letter, Nausheen powered on the computer and switched on the Base Station. The computer booted and demanded a password. As soon as she keyed-in the alphanumeric code, the computer screen came alive. She turned on the Wi-Fi connection.

Far away, in the Business Centre of Karachi Sheraton Hotel, Imran Shah Malik remotely accessed the home screen while playing with a computer keyboard. He downloaded a text file containing a few codes and transferred it to a hidden memory chip in his customized watch. He uploaded a few files from his home computer to a cloud account. He then securely erased the files of his home computer and typed the shutdown command.

Hours before the computer had gone into a deathly sleep, it had already transferred the ip address, the password, and the username to the Systems Office of the IB in India. A miniature program silently got embedded in the OS X Leopard operating system. The program collected data in the background, encoded and zipped the contents, and silently transferred them to the intended destination—the server of the Intelligence Bureau office of India.

Triangulation

SIDDHARTHA RANA REQUISITIONED the telephone numbers of the AIG of the CISF, who was shot dead on the Noida Golf Road. He asked the telecom service operator to provide the details of the movement of the officer on the day of his death.

The telecom company extracted each of the tower positions, which had caught the AIG's cell phone network on the fateful day. The AIG had stayed home for the entire day and then from Noida, driven over the Kalindi Kunj Bridge, turned to Mathura Road and finally arrived somewhere near Connaught Place. At the Connaught place location, his cell phone had caught the signal from three towers at different points of time during his three-hour long stay: a tower on Oriental Bank of Commerce, another near LNJP Park, and the third on Bhagwan Das Road.

"A person on some secret mission needs a secluded place. Restaurants now-a-days are too crowded. Some innocuous apartment could be an option. However, the most probable location would be a hotel room, where the hidden truth may be easily buried," thought Siddhartha as he spread the map of Delhi and concentrated on the Connaught Place area. He took out a pencil and a scale and joined all three places. A triangle lay bare before him. "What would be the best position for a cell phone to catch the network from three different positions of a triangle?" He was thinking aloud, "The median!"

When he calculated the median, it pointed to one place — Lalit Intercontinental Hotel.

Nausheen

ONE AFTERNOON, NAUSHEEN dozed off and dreamt about Aban when he was a toddler. Aban was on his father's back, tapping Imran's shoulder as if Imran were some Arab steed. On the weekend, in their small Rawalpindi apartment, father and son frolicked the entire day until little Aban got tired and slept. In the next sequence, Nausheen was running after Aban to get him to have his milk and a meal, but he was as ever raring to go on with the next game, and the next, and the next. Moreover, his father was ever willing to invent ingenious and imaginative games for his son.

Then Nausheen saw herself pushing a stroller in Ayub Park. Suddenly an old man, with a long flowing beard, lifted Aban from the stroller and sprinted towards the War Hero Monument. She wanted to run after him, but her legs failed her.

Nausheen woke up in a cold sweat, "Where is Aban?"

A mother's instinct told her that something was wrong.

She had already tried to contact him on his cell phone, but it was switched off. She then spoke with Aban's professor and a few students. They confirmed that Aban had not been seen on campus and were unaware of his whereabouts.

Nausheen wanted to get in touch with her husband, but his phones did not respond. She went to her bedroom and opened the drawer, hoping to find some clue. If only she could find the US addresses from where Aban had written the letter to her, then she might be able to trace him.

In one of the letters, Aban had written, "Dear Ammi, I'm fine. I'm sorry I could not drop a line. My friends and I are doing the Dirt Bike Cross-country Race from New York to Duluth and back. Right now, we have just crossed the stunning Delaware Water Gap. The gorgeous sight of the Delaware River cutting through the huge ridge of the Appalachian Mountains is out of this world. The biking is great and we are having a good time. In our next leg of the journey, we will meander all along the Great Lakes and also cross the cities: Cleveland, Detroit, Michigan, Chicago, and hike across the beautiful countryside. We will be back in Cornell after a week. Pray to Allah for my bike-team's victory…"

Nausheen sighed, "Oh Dear! This boy prefers his bike to his *Ammi*."

She found another email from the Dirt Motorbike Racing Company, inviting Aban to participate in the winter race. The contest was scheduled for two days after Aban had left for the US.

Nausheen called up the company to enquire about her son. The company promised to call her back if and when they had any news.

She waited.

In the meantime, the company received a message from the FBI. Finally, Nausheen received a call from the company, telling her not to lose sleep, stating in the most enigmatic terms that her son was on a great journey.

South Block

The Director of IB went to South Block to see the Foreign Secretary. He explained the situation to the Secretary and how the FBI was dragging Juhi, the daughter of the Indian Ambassador to the USA, into a controversy.

The Secretary was worried. He asked his PA to connect to the Under Secretary for Political Affairs of the US Department of State. After explaining everything to the officer, he hung up.

The Secretary turned his attention to the Director of IB, "The situation seems to be messy. The FBI has already reported the matter to the Secretary of State, stating that they will need to call the daughter of the Ambassador for questioning. They say that Juhi may throw light on the Mumbai attack, since she is in a relationship with Aban."

"Sir, the riddle is full of twists and turns. We still need to join many missing dots: the AIG's murder, Mr. Malik's instruction to his son to take the backup of his computer to the US. Aban's closeness with Juhi seems to be just the tip of the iceberg. There is certainly more underneath. The AIG mentioned something 'bigger' than a certain Project Karachi. However, we still don't know what it is and what could be bigger. Then, there is this '*To Pak To*", which we have not been able to decipher.

"What do you propose then?"

"I think our Foreign Minister should talk to the US Secretary of State. He should talk to the Director of the FBI to keep us in the loop. I'm sending my Joint Director, Siddhartha Rana, to New York in order to coordinate the investigation." The Director went on to explain every lead in the case.

"The Foreign Minister is in the meeting of the Cabinet Committee on Security. Once he is back, I'll ask him to work out the nitty-gritties."

Lalit Intercontinental Hotel

Siddhartha Rana reached the Lalit Intercontinental Hotel and went to the front desk. The reception staff escorted him to the spacious chamber of the General Manager.

Siddhartha showed the photograph of the AIG to the General Manager and wanted to confirm whether any staff member had seen him. The GM called the Concierge and asked him to help Siddhartha.

The Concierge took him to the Maître d'hôtel and asked him the name of the servitors and butler, who were on duty on 26/11. The list was more than one hundred names long. The manager called up each of them, one by one, in his chamber and showed them the photograph.

One of the butlers recognized the AIG as he had attended the visitors and was rewarded with a handsome tip. "Yes sir, there were four people in the Presidential suite."

"What time did they leave?"

"Just before midnight."

"On the same day."

"Yes."

"Did anyone stay the night?"

"No. All of them left."

"Are you sure?"

"Yes sir. I went for clearance to the room the minute they left since the next guest was to arrive in half an hour."

"Can you describe what they looked like?"

The butler recalled everything that he could. Siddhartha noted down each description and then asked the butler to report to his office the next day so that the graphic experts could draw a fairly accurate sketch of the three remaining people.

Siddhartha went back to the office of the GM and asked him to get the video footage captured by roof-mounted cameras at: the Lalit Luxury Lounge, near the Presidential Suite, elevators, along with any other place from where the guests might have entered or left the hotel between nine pm and midnight on that day.

Siddhartha once again called the butler and asked him to go through each of the images and try to recognize the people. The Butler concentrated on each footage, frame by frame, while Siddhartha wondered if he should have caught a flight to New York, instead of solving a murder mystery and dwelling upon some unknown Project Karachi.

He turned to the GM, "Who booked the Presidential Suite?"

The GM extracted the details from his computer terminal, "Hussein Pharma Ltd. of Dubai."

"Who are they?"

"They are our corporate clients."

"Any telephone number or business card of the company?"

"Oh yes," the GM printed out the details and handed it over to Siddhartha.

"Can I use your computer?"

"My pleasure, sir."

Siddhartha typed the web address of the company. The site mentioned that it was an export company that specialized in bulk drugs. Siddhartha visited the 'contact us' web-link and found telephone numbers, names of executives and email ids and a Post Box Number in Dubai. There were links for placing export orders. Nothing looked unusual.

Siddhartha Rana rang up the registered number of the company. "Sir, I'm calling from Lalit Intercontinental Hotel, Delhi. There is excess payment of bill by your company. Please let me know where the hotel management should send you the cheque."

"That's not needed. Please charge it to your staff welfare fund."

"We don't do such a thing, sir. It's against the policy of our company."

"Let it remain as a credit in our company's ledger account." The line went dead.

Siddhartha seemed to have hit a dead end. Except the AIG of the CISF, who had been captured by the camera, the butler could not find any of the other three persons in the video footage.

Siddhartha asked the GM, "Are there any other exit points, where you don't have any video camera?"

"No, sir. As per the new government guidelines we have to monitor every visitor and guard each point."

"Oh!" Siddhartha sighed.

The Butler cut in, "If someone uses the fire exit, we don't have cameras there."

"Isn't the exit guarded?"

"It is. But an inferno doesn't strike every day. So, that is an excellent place for the security guys to doze off."

"Who knows," thought Siddhartha, "India may have to pay a big price because someone chose to snooze!"

Miram Shah, North Waziristan

SUNDARAM IYER RECEIVED a telephone call from Miram Shah in North Waziristan, Pakistan. "We received a message from the Director of Hussein Pharma. He says that his company received a late night call from the Lalit Intercontinental Hotel in New Delhi. We crosschecked with our Indian Agent, who confirmed that IB officer Siddhartha Rana is snooping around. The AIG officer's murder seems to be his area of interest."

"This is surprising since a murder normally interests the police and not the IB."

"Then try to find out why he is poking his nose around."

"I will. However, you should also convey this to the Shura members of Tupac-II."

"Right."

"Have you told Aban's parents about his arrest?"

"No."

"Why?"

"I talked to Saeed al-Masri. He says we are not supposed to mention the arrest since Imran may hit the panic button."

"Do you still have access to 65th Street?"

"Do you mean the office of Consulate General of Pakistan in New York?"

"Yes."

"Mr. Sundaram, you should know that we have access to every place on this planet."

"Did your man approach the top?"

"For what?"

"Aban."

"We are not interested in him."

"Why did the FBI arrest Aban Malik?"

"We know only a little bit."

"Tell me."

"See tomorrow's newsflash."

"Why can't you tell me?"

"I'm not authorized to. Sleep tight and you'll know everything before tomorrow sundown."

"Still…"

"Listen very carefully. In our kind of work, we never ask too many questions. We just execute what we are told to and put it into operation. Your AIG expected too many answers. You know what happened to him? My dear friend, *Shabba khair*."

Ajmal Kasab

ON 26/11, MOHAMMED Ajmal Amīr Kasāb created mayhem at Mumbai railway station CST gunning down close to fifty people including women and children. He also killed four police officers at different places and sprayed indiscriminate bullets on the streets, while fleeing in a Skoda vehicle with another assassin, Ismail Khan.

The police at Marine Drive received information about the duo and they put up a road barricade at Girgaum Chowpatty *naka*. The Skoda stopped fifteen metres before the *naka* and steered to take a U-turn. The car hit the road-divider and came to a standstill.

Kasāb and Ismail fired at the policemen. The policemen returned fire and shot Ismail Khan dead. Kasāb lay motionless, playing dead. When an officer with a baton approached him, he pumped five bullets into the officer. The lion-hearted officer, instead of falling, continued running towards him, and clung to Kasāb's AK-47. Kasāb continued firing without any mercy. Other police officers then captured the frenzied assailant.

Onlookers gathered and started to beat up the assailant. The police somehow controlled the situation, and rushed to Nayar Hospital with the injured police officer and Kasāb. The doctors declared that the police officer had been 'brought dead'.

In the other room, Kasāb pleaded with the doctors, "I don't want to die. Please put me on saline."

The doctors gave Kasāb painkillers. Outside the emergency room, the officers of the police department and other investigating agencies waited to interrogate Kasāb. However, the doctor declined any access to the patient until recovery.

While condolences and promises for cooperation from all countries were pouring in, Pakistan went all out to deny involvement of any Pakistani national or organization operating from their soil. They even claimed that it was the handiwork of Indian Intelligence Agencies executed with the sole purpose of maligning the image of Pakistan.

Two days later, when interrogators started questioning Kasāb, a senior ATS officer received a call from Siddhartha Rana, asking him to extract categorical answers on Project Karachi from the 'gentleman'.

Though Kasāb was unaware of 'Project Karachi', he spoke about the involvement of the ISI and LeT and narrated how the terrorists, during the attack, constantly received instructions from the Lashkar control room, which was setup in the locality of Quaidabad, Karachi. He also mentioned how other terrorists and he himself were given commando-like training in the jungles of the Kashmir valley along with marine training in the Mangla Dam of Pakistan.

The officer sent a copy of the interrogation report to Siddhartha, who kept wondering if there was a connection between the Mangla Dam training, Project Karachi, the brutal butchery of the AIG officer, and the still mysterious 'To Pak To' operation.

The hunt to unearth the truth was on, but many questions remained unanswered.

Swat River

DURING THE FESTIVAL season of Eid al-Adha, on 7th December, when people were shopping in the Qisakhawani area of the Peshawar Market, a bomb detonated inside a car parked outside a Shia mosque. A man, who chose to remain anonymous, told the Reuters News Agency that it was a suicide bomber targeting the members of the local tribal council.

Later in the day, another news agency claimed that a few people had abducted the informer and taken him to Nemogram in the Swat Valley.

In the valley, the video recording started. Imran Shah Malik was on his knees in prayer. When he lifted his head, he saw four men pointing AK-47s at him. His hands shook and he started to scratch his right thigh nervously.

The men tied Imran Shah Malik's hands behind his back and covered his head with a black cloth and retreated to their position.

The automatic tracking MT tripod of the camera spun, following the direction of the four men and focused at the firing squad. They inserted the magazine, placed the selector at the automatic middle position, pressed the stock latch, aimed at the sight and rested their fingers on the triggers.

The camera slowly swivelled and zoomed in. The focus was on Imran Shah Malik. The stunning valley resounded with the sound of the bullets.

From the high cliff, Imran's body fell into a deep gorge. The cool current of the river quickly swept him into the gushing water cascades of an almost vertical waterfall. His body hit an outcrop of a hard rock and the impact tossed him up in the air. Once again he plummeted down, scrapping against the mossy rocks. A funnel-shaped whirlpool pulled him inward into a deep constricted bore.

Several copies of the video recording were made and sent to T.V. Stations and newspaper offices. The ruins of a Buddhist Stupa and monasteries clearly visible in the backdrop confirmed that the incident was recorded on the banks of the Swat River.

Reuters got a special message, "*No one dares to deal a deathblow to our tribal council.*"

A senior ISI officer visited Nausheen to convey the condolences of the present ISI Chief. Many of Imran Shah Malik's colleagues, relatives, and friends from the neighbourhood assembled at the house, expressing their deepest grief. A heart broken Nausheen was inconsolable. At that time, the grief-stricken woman just wanted one person beside her – her son, Aban.

A few hundred miles away, Sundaram Iyer watched the video in silence and remembered the chilling words, "Never ever dare to ask too many questions. Implement whatever the *Aka* of Qaeda tells you."

Encryption

AS SIDDHARTHA RANA watched the cold-blooded murder of Imran Shah Malik, he was both rattled and alarmed. He needed to go to the USA as quickly as he could. He asked the systems expert to reach his office immediately and left for the office himself. The System Expert was waiting for him. "Did you download everything from Lahore?"

"Yes sir."

"The password?"

"Yes. Our keylogger captured each of the keystrokes."

"Good. Did you check the mails and files?"

"There is not much except one large file."

"What's that?"

"It would not open. It's password protected."

"Did you take a crack at it with our brute password breaker program?"

The system expert pointed his finger to a small window on

the screen, "See the progress bar, sir. It's been almost ten hours and still our supercomputer has no idea of the secret code."

"Our system can decode even a 256-bit encryption. Why is it failing?" Siddhartha was vexed. "Did you try Ŏ, the big O notation, the big theta Θ or the big omega Ω?"

"The computer made several exhaustive key searches and every possible combination that it could, without a single hit. This is the first time that a password has failed this system. Frankly speaking, this is a unique system of password protection, and in my view, it's completely unbreakable."

"Why is that?"

"Instead of the alphanumeric keywords, the file seems to be protected by an image password made up of several smaller images."

"Image password!" Siddhartha was surprised. "I know people are trying to develop doppelgänger, where a ghost password remains on the cloud and never remains inside the computer. One has to download it with sophisticated Unix commands and only then does the system boot. However, I've never heard of an image password."

"The National Institute of Standard and Technology of the US Department of Commerce has developed this. It is a very recent system, where the 'secret words' are a combination of images, each of which should be dragged into a grid. Once the correct images fill up the grid, it turns into a theme. The procedure is known as salting. The file unlocks after authentication of the theme."

"Did you try different combinations of images?"

"Mr. Malik seems to be an avid photographer and a connoisseur of all types of art. He has snapshots of flowers, nature, wildlife, clips of historical places, countless portraits and god knows what else!"

"How many images are there?"

"More than a hundred thousand." The System Expert leaned and clicked on the keyboard, "To be precise 2,09,71,52."

"Interesting. It's two to the power twenty one."

"Exactly 2^{21}. He seems to be not only a computer expert, but also adept with mathematical numbers. The results can run into sextillion or one thousand trillion of possible combinations in a 2X2 grid if a modified image file becomes the password."

"Can't our supercomputer find it in another twenty four hours?"

"I don't think so, sir. We don't have any program that can break an image-password. Even the cryptologist of the National Security Agency of the USA doesn't enjoy it. That is why the American government is not very comfortable with this concept. They treat it as a security risk and have not ratified it for putting it into common practice."

"Then, who can take a shot?"

"We can try the father of the program, the NIST. They may be able to work out some solution."

"It's not that straightforward. We usually think of the US Special Army as the most secret organization of America. But in reality, the Department of Commerce of the USA is the most enigmatic. It just doesn't divulge any details. After all, it has to protect American commercial interests in today's competitive world."

The System Expert gave Siddhartha a blank look. Siddhartha smiled and patted him. "Anyway, give me a complete shadow copy of the downloaded files, any unusual emails, and flag germane details that you think could be important."

"I'll compile everything in about two hours."

"Good. I want it before I board my evening flight. "

Massachusetts Avenue

THE ASSISTANT DIRECTOR of the FBI of the Washington Field Office sought an appointment with the Indian Ambassador and after confirmation reached the Indian Embassy at Massachusetts Avenue.

"Good to see you, Director. What can I do for you?"

"Mr. Ambassador, our New York office wants to question your daughter, but she is not responding to our call. We tried contacting her on her cell phone and also at Cornell. She is not there. We will appreciate it if you could help us reach her."

"Officer, she is in DC. But if your inquiry is about the arrest of a Pakistani gentleman, then I'm afraid she doesn't have anything to say. I don't want her to be put through the wringer and get into trouble because of some Pakistani lout."

"I appreciate your feelings, Mr. Ambassador. But we have a request from the Indian Government to grill the Pakistani boy. And it is your intelligence agency, which has found that he was in contact with Juhi at the time of the Mumbai attack. We believe that it couldn't be a mere coincidence that Juhi was at the Taj Mahal Hotel at that very point of time."

"Acquaintance between two young people, studying in the same school, is nothing new and has nothing to do with nationality. Many people from different countries are in the same campus and share many common things. And for your information, she was with a European Delegation when the Mumbai attacks begun."

"I have the same opinion as yours. But Juhi has to come to our office at 4th Street for a very short time. It will only help to clear her name."

"I suggest that the FBI send her a questionnaire. I will ensure that she replies to each of your questions candidly without concealing a single fact."

"This is not the way the FBI works, sir. We need to record her statement and sign an affidavit."

"Then come to my home. I'll see what best I can do for you. By the way, the Under Secretary of State rang me up and gave his word that there won't be any diplomatic disaster. So, I suggest that the FBI keep this information very confidential."

"It is my word of honour, Mr. Ambassador, that it will be held in the strictest confidence."

"Thank you, Director. Send your officer home this evening. Juhi will co-operate. By the way what's the name of the boy?"

"Didn't Juhi tell you?"

"No."

"Why?"

"She reserves the right to tell or not tell her father anything strictly according to her wishes. I never question her wisdom."

"He is Aban Malik."

"Is he the son of Imran Shah Malik?"

"How do you know him?"

"Just a guess. I saw in the newspapers how Mr. Malik was snuffed out. I believe it's not the work of western intelligence."

"The Government of Pakistan is looking into the matter."

"Don't forget to see me after you see Juhi. Let this cat out of the bag. I'll tell you more about Mr. Malik."

Long Battle

SIDDHARTHA ENTERED THE Director's room. "Sir, I've to go to New York. The situation has turned grave after Imran Shah Malik was shot today."

"What about your progress at the Lalit Continental Hotel?"

"Still groping in the dark. The butler who attended to the four gentlemen will visit our office tomorrow and help the graphic expert to draw their sketches. I think we may be able to recognize some of them. When I'm back from the US, I'll see how to proceed in that matter. One more interesting fact has come to my notice. Hussein Pharma of Dubai booked the Presidential suite in the hotel. I've sent orders to our agent in Dubai to verify the profile of the company and get back to me. I'll keep you posted about everything."

"Anything else?"

"I need two hundred thousand dollars from our secret fund."

"Two hundred thousand!"

"Yes, sir. We may have to fight a long battle for the young man."

"Why should we get involved for a Pakistani?"

"I think he holds the key to Indian security."

"Is he a security threat?"

"Maybe just the opposite."

Zia-ul-Haq

THE ASSISTANT DIRECTOR of FBI and two senior agents reached the Ambassador's stately home in the evening. The agents greeted the Ambassador and then expressed their wish to see Juhi. The Assistant Director waited in the living room.

The agents expected Juhi to be fidgety, but found her poised and confident while answering their thorny questions. Soon it was over and as Juhi signed the paperwork, one of the agents remarked, "May I suggest something to you, Ms. Shergill?"

Juhi nodded.

"If you know what is good for you, keep away from this Aban Malik."

"I hope you people do not harm him any more than you have already done," Juhi could not hide her ire.

The agents stood up, thanked Juhi and left the room. "We'll be back, young lady," The officer chewed his words under his breath.

The Ambassador saw the agents off and then came back to the Assistant Director, still sitting in his living room.

"I'd now like to have the Imran Shah Malik story you mentioned." The Assistant Director's tone was brusque and business-like.

"Try and recall the assassination of the President of Pakistan Zia-ul-Haq in a plane crash in the late '80s," the Ambassador began. "After witnessing a US Abrams tank demonstration in Bahawalpur, the President came back to the BHV airport. An officer presented a crate of mangoes to the President, when the President was to board his C-130 Hercules. The mangoes were spiked with VX gas. The President was seated in his air-conditioned VIP capsule with the American Ambassador and the head of the U.S. Military aid mission. When he showed the mangoes to his American guests, boasting how good Pakistani mangoes were, the VX gas escaped and the nerve gas finished them all off. It then dispersed and reached the cockpit. The commander, the first officer and the flight engineer, although not choked immediately, suffered extreme twitching and sweating, followed by severe bronchial constriction. It was so swift and intense in its action that the crewmembers were overcome by drowsiness before they could send out a Mayday signal. The plane flew erratically for some time, nose-dived and exploded on the ground. The officer, who had presented the mangoes, was to accompany the President, but had excused himself and joined a top-ranking Army officer in another flight, which took off a few minutes before the President's Hercules. They witnessed the crash and loud boom from the other aircraft, but did not bother to help. Instead of returning to Bahawalpur, their aircraft headed straight for Islamabad. That officer did not join in national mourning, when the Senate Chairman announced the President's death. He did not attend the funeral ceremony of Zia-ul-Haq. Do you want to know the name of the officer, who presented the mangoes to the President?"

Without much to speculate, the Assistant Director shook his head.

The Ambassador continued, "Then you don't need to be a rocket scientist to know how capable that gentleman is. Even the US is aware how he, with the help of the Pakistani army, obstructed the crash investigation carried out by a high power inquiry commission. To sabotage the investigation, he stated that both America and India were behind the President's killing."

"How could he accuse these countries without substantial proof?"

"It was just a ploy to divert attention. The deception and false emphasis misdirected the investigator on a red herring chase. The plot was to deliberately confuse each and every one of us. This gentleman stated that the complex Afghanistan problem was the reason for the assassination of the President. These countries wanted a regime which would act according to their wishes."

"How did you know about his involvement in this stratagem?"

The Ambassador laughed, "It's not mere coincidence that I know so much. I was then posted in Pakistan as First Secretary of the Indian High Commission. Rumours were abuzz everywhere and conspiracy theories were rampant in every corner of Pakistan. Friends of mine told me several stories. Some facts cropped up from hearsay and gossip coupled with real accounts, and all of which led to this man."

The officer nodded and the Ambassador stated matter-of-factly, "Don't lose the bigger picture by paying far too much attention to small things. I think none of you is seeing the forest for the trees, officer."

The Ambassador smiled, "Do you think Mr. Imran Shah Malik is so naïve as to involve his beloved son in such a dangerous mission?"

New York

Siddhartha packed his gear and headed straight to the Indira Gandhi International Airport. He checked into the Executive Class of the non-stop Air India flight, which was long, but smooth. It landed at JFK in the morning. After immigration clearance, he briskly walked out of the lounge and went to the Residency office of the FBI.

"What can I do for you, Sid?" asked Robert McLean.

"Bob, I'm here for Aban."

"What could the Indian Government want with a Pakistani national?"

"What if I tell you that I have the password, which you have been trying to crack for many days?"

"Not a big deal, Siddhartha. We'll unravel it eventually."

"Then you will be able to enter the MacBook, but will never gain access to an all-important file. No one in this world can break this uniquely protected password." Siddhartha explained to Robert McLean everything about the image password and salting method.

Robert McLean's eyes widened in awe, "So, you think there could be a lead in that file."

"Indeed, Bob. We've analysed all other folders and documents and there is nothing much to show except thousands of files."

"There may be hidden files too."

"True, but all hidden files are system files. There are no email exchanges either. A few of them may interest the Pakistani government, but not us. What is important is just one file."

"So, Mr. Aban Malik must be aware of the contents of this file?"

"Let's see how much he knows," Siddhartha responded.

"Let's go, Sid."

"Where?"

"To 26 Federal Plaza, our downtown Field Office."

Ravi Road

TODAY WHERE A bustling timber market stands on Ravi Road in the majestic city of Lahore, a few film studios stood in the late '20s. One of these released the first Indian talkie 'Alam Ara'.

However, the partition of India and Pakistan left the Lahore film industry in a complete shambles as most of the actors and artistes left Lahore for better pastures in the new-fashioned city of Bombay and to live through the traditional charm of Calcutta. Today, not even a single film-related signboard finds a place on this road. However, a few descendants of the artistes and performers of yore have lived to tell their tale. They have tried their best to carry on the time-honoured traditions of myths, rituals of legends and the saga of folklore.

One of them happened to be a master of mixing and combining audio and video clips in such a way that even the best professionals of Hollywood would have envied him. Everyone called him Master-Mixer. Yet he had to fight for a living as he hardly got any work from the dying Pakistani film industry.

Qualms of conscience did not let him leave his motherland, but this only added more misery to his already arduous life. He dubbed a few English documentaries in Urdu, but did not find a single taker since what interested liberal and the so called progressive people were pirated Hindi Bollywood movies and xxx rated Russian blue films!

He then decided that the time had come to down the shutters of his office once and for all and try his *kismet* in some other business venture. However, he was soon forced to reconsider his decision since a few days later, a person visited him with a proposal worth five lakh rupees.

He looked with a lot of interest to what was handed over to him. The first video clip was about the joint aerial operation, codenamed 'Indus Viper 2008' by the Pakistani Air Force and the Turkish Air Force. The clippings showed F-16 fighter aircrafts of PAF and TuAF taking off from Sargodha Air Force Base in the Punjab province and flying in combat formation towards Tarbela Dam to the north east of Lahore.

In the second scene and setting, the Indian Sukhoi-30 and Jaguar took off from Dehradun AFB and soared towards the mountainous region of the Great Himalayas.

A thirty-one minute documentary of History Channel was the third part. It was about the calamitous collapse of South Fork Dam near Johnstown, Pennsylvania, which had drowned thousands.

The Master-Mixer grinned, "These moving pictures must be protected under copyright. Won't that create a problem?"

"Don't lose sleep. We'll take care of it."

"What the hell should I do with these?"

"Sequence it and mix it all up the way I tell you."

The agent explained everything to him. When he had finished, the Master-Mixer asked, "What should be the length of the movie?"

"Not more than ten minutes."

"Do you want this to appear absolutely real?"

"Beyond a shadow of a doubt."

"I'll charge ten lakhs."

"What if someone still claims that it is not authentic?"

"If you want that even the best professionals of Hollywood should not be able to point out even a single frame as *faux*, I'll charge twenty."

"Done. How much time will you take?"

"One year."

"That's too much."

"In this real world, this time is less, my dear brother. I have to work for hours and sometimes for days on each frame. And there are thirty frames per second."

Both men shook hands. The deal was on.

Forget

JUHI WENT TO sleep, but woke up in the hush of the night when she had a bad dream.

In her dream, she was with a few friends and Aban, visiting a picturesque fjord, surrounded by steep hills and a dense forest. One of Aban's friends dared him to swim across the water. Others rode a boat to cheer the duo. Suddenly, a surging oceanic wave unbalanced the vessel carrying Juhi, plunging her into the icy water below. Since Juhi did not know how to swim, she started to drown, occasionally thrown up by the force of buoyancy. Spotting this, Aban turned back, pulled her out and pitched her safely into the craft before resuming the race. As soon as he began catching up with the contestant, he found himself trapped in a swirling whirlpool that kept sucking him down. He lashed around, trying to get out of the vortex; but the more he struggled, the deeper he sank.

Juhi watched in horror. She wanted to save him, but could

not. She tried to move and jump into the water, but her limbs refused to budge and her hand gripped tightly on to the balustrade. Her friends watched petrified, but unable to move as though transfixed by some invisible force.

Suddenly the merry-makers seemed to forget the present and moved onto a different time, laughing and singing, sailing their boat to the shore.

Juhi was left all alone in the middle of the lake, stuck in the roots of the mangrove trees that looked like long-limbed apparitions of ancient origin.

She woke up in cold sweat. The moonlight streamed through the window and lit up her beautiful face. She quickly made tea in her kitchen, hoping that it would steady her nerves. When it did not, she knocked at the door of her father's bedroom, hesitantly.

"Are you still awake?" The Ambassador was mildly surprised.

"I had a terrible nightmare."

"Relax, my sweet doll."

"I'm worried about him. It has been almost a week and there is no news of Aban."

"I'm concerned about you, my darling. I can't do much for Aban. We cannot even provide consular access to him since he is not an Indian citizen."

"Can't you talk to the Ambassador of Pakistan?"

"That will make matters worse. There is a procedure for consular access. The Ambassador will have to send a written official communication to the office of the US Attorney General in the Department of Justice. Depending upon the sensitivity of the matter, they may or may not grant consular access. The request will travel over many official desks before reaching the highest up. Worst of all, Aban may get exposed to the media and the outside world and that will compound his difficulty. If the Government of Pakistan has forgotten about the son of a very high-ranking officer, then I see a major problem."

"What problem, dad?"

"Someone has chosen not to set the young boy free."

"Why?"

"Maybe his father was the reason. However, I can't say this with certainty. In fact, I don't know. Only time will unravel the mystery."

"Don't scare me, please."

"This is the way the opaque world works, young girl."

"I don't agree. There has to be someone, who would want to see Aban walk free."

"Let's see."

"What should I do then?"

"Forget him."

26, Federal Plaza

SIDDHARTHA RANA **and** Robert McLean reached the Field Office of the FBI at 26, Federal Plaza. The elevator zipped to the 23rd Floor and both walked to the Criminal Division. A special agent, who was handling Aban's matter, brought out the case record.

Robert McLean went through the document. "Has he been photographed and his fingerprints taken?"

"Yes."

"Was he ever involved in any crime as per our database of Information Service Division?"

"No."

"Any lead on his MacBook."

"The Cryptanalysis and Racketeering Records Unit gave it their best shot, but without any success. We then sent a cloned copy of his hard disk drive to NSA. We still have to hear from them."

"That won't be needed. I have the key," Siddhartha joined

in, and explained how the IB could gain access to Imran Shah Malik's computer.

Robert asked the special agent to bring the MacBook. Siddhartha entered the password and the laptop accepted the credential."

"Which is the file that is protected by an image password?"

"Surprisingly it's not like a normal file, but a morphed image of Túpac Amaru II, a descendant of the Incas of Peru. He is a mythical figure, who rose against the Spanish rule. Peruvians still adore him for his valour." Siddhartha clicked on the image, and a 2X2 grid opened. "This grid is the password. We need to place four images in the grid such that they represent a single theme."

"We can have a go with the images in the computer file."

"Our systems expert has already tried using the decoder. It seems the four images are not in this computer. I believe that they are stored in some removable-media like a pen drive or scandisk. Mr. Malik must have been dragging the image from them into the grid."

"That should leave traces on the hard disk."

"It won't since these images get temporarily loaded into the flash-memory and disappear when the computer shuts down."

"We can still try since the password image files are nothing, but bytes of 0 and 1 in computer machine language."

"True. But each image file has millions of bytes. Even if we try different combinations, the best of the supercomputers in NSA will take thousands of years to decode this image-password."

"What's the solution then?"

"Magical words." Siddhartha smiled, "Open sesame!"

"What?"

"What a computer cannot do, a man can. Free Aban."

Divers

CONTRARY TO POPULAR belief, the Pakistani community living in Britain are not very well off. In fact, they rank second poorest after the Bangladeshis. They have not fully assimilated into British society and the Brits don't fancy them either.

A majority of the Pakistani emigrants to the United Kingdom are from the Punjab province and the Kashmir region under Pakistani occupation. Half of them come from Mirpur in Kashmir, where the Mangla Dam stands today. Their social customs are orthodox even by Pakistani standards and they do not mix with white men and women. In spite of the British Government's efforts to enrol their children into 'white schools', only a handful of them send their children to school. A low standard of education compels them to work as manual labourers. They live in ghettoes and can barely support their families. Such an appalling situation has given rise to a perpetual hostility against the United Kingdom, the United

States and their allies especially after their troops marched into Iraq and Afghanistan. That there is no love lost between these *'Pardeshi Britons'* and India is no secret. Pro-*Azadi* slogans for the liberation of Kashmir echo in their ghettoes and resonate in other Islamic countries.

The Jihadists always look for such men to carry out their nefarious plans in Europe, America and India. The British government also holds a view that half the terrorists in Britain have their roots in Pakistan.

The architect of Project Tupac-II knew that he would find many disgruntled youth, willing to take up Jihad with a little bit of indoctrination and oodles of dough. The city of Plymouth is one of the recruiting hubs.

Shalim Amīr Khan found a diver working for Her Majesty's Naval Base of Davenport in Plymouth. An expert in retrofitting of operational submarines and a trained hydrographer, he was the only one who could dive more than two hundred and fifty meters with SCUBA.

As luck would have it, the diver was a dissatisfied man too. Compared to the lesser skilled *'white diver'*, he was paid much less.

A hundred thousand pound bait was enough for the diver to shift loyalty from 'Her Majesty' to an anonymous man. With half of the money paid as advance, he fancied starting a diving school and employing his childhood buddies, who were fighting abject poverty. He would then make sure that all his acquaintances would be reasonably rich enough to take care of their progeny and next of kin.

He needed to apply for a month's leave from his work, but had to wait for the right opportunity. First, he had to visit Interdive

Services Ltd. in Plymouth and enrol in a training program on the use of underwater explosives. Though the training course was offered all around the year, the month of July, when the sea would be stormy, was the perfect period to get trained for the deadliest operation designed in the chronicles of man.

Shalim Amīr Khan assured him that an appropriate and well-timed arrangement with a famous Mumbai Scuba Diving Club would be made. All he had to do was to dive and dive deep when the time came.

FBI Field Office

THE FIELD OFFICE of the FBI in New York drew up a report, seeking authorization to free Aban, and sent it to the FBI Headquarters in Washington DC. Since the arrest of Aban was linked to the Mumbai attack, the FBI wanted an undertaking from the Indian Government that they had not found or established anything against Aban. Siddhartha signed the document on behalf of the Indian government.

Within two days, Aban was a free man.

Siddhartha took custody of Aban and left the FBI office. As the lift descended, Aban's eyes grew moist. Siddhartha patted him reassuringly.

Aban wanted to call his mother and Juhi, but Siddhartha asked him to put it on hold till Siddhartha spelled out the complexities involved in the course of events.

They rented a cab and reached Central Park and settled down to talk. The caress of a gentle breeze and the soft touch of the fresh grass was enough for a worn-out Aban to close his heavy eyes and sleep. Siddhartha let him be for some time. He could not afford to hurry things up since what Aban was going to hear from Siddhartha would be life altering.

Anthony Tindall

AT THE HEAD OFFICE of the FBI in Washington DC, Special Agent Anthony Tindall had worked day and night to unearth the perpetrators of the Mumbai crime. He had deployed eight agents from Los Angeles and many technicians to glean information from cell phones, satphones, Internet data and GPS used by the terrorists and their handlers. All leads led to Pakistan.

It became obvious that Hafiz Saeed had instructed his trusted man Abu Yakoob to set up a temporary control room at Quaidabad, situated between Malir Cantonment and Jinnah International Airport in Karachi. Three days prior to the attack, the higher-ups of LeT took over the control room and then installed and commissioned modern equipment: Satellite Phones, laptops, LAN wires, TV sets, dish antenna, GPS navigation system, and many other gadgets and gizmos.

The handlers setup VoIP network in the name of Kharak Singh. It ensured that the communication between the terrorists and their handlers was routed through Callphonex, USA, and thus could not be intercepted by any intelligence agency in real-time.

They had even registered fictitious email accounts in Karachi. A very interesting pattern of accessing email accounts came to light. Emails were never sent, but were simply saved as drafts. All that the terrorists had to do was to access the saved draft through the known username and password of these email accounts, log out and implement the instructions mentioned therein. Security agencies could not trace these messages, since no emails were ever exchanged.

Abu Kahafa, another handler called all the ten boys into the control room and demonstrated the use of the GPS system. Hafiz Saeed delivered a brief sermon to the young boys and then left the control room. Another man asked the boys to board a mini Van, which was waiting outside the control room to take them to the boat at the pier of Karachi Fish Harbour.

The GPS data showed that Dara, one of the terrorists, piloted the boat called Al-Husseni from Karachi Fish Harbour in Pakistan to Porbandar, Gujarat in India. Another clue came from a Thuraya satphone, bearing the number +88216 55526412 and IMEI No. 352384000408640, proving beyond doubt, that they had hijacked and boarded an Indian fishing trawler 'Kuber' in the high seas. The satellite phones communicated through INMRSAT base station at Pune as well as in Karachi.

The terrorists slew the four crewmembers of 'Kuber' and forced the Captain, Amar Singh Solanki to navigate the vessel to Mumbai. Before disembarking in a rubber dinghy, a few miles from South Mumbai coast, they slit the captain's throat.

A scrutiny of the phone transcripts showed that the handlers in Pakistan had instructed the terrorists to kill everyone -- innocent people, political leaders, foreigners and celebrities. Two handlers were Pakistani Army Officers—Major Sameer and Sajid Mir-- who visited the control room regularly to ensure a smooth operation. The hardcore radicals goaded the young terrorists in Mumbai to gun down as many Jews as possible with their chilling message, *"If you cut one Jew to pieces, it will be worth eliminating fifty people."*

The other messages were quoted in Annexure-VII of the official dossier of the Home Ministry of India. Siddhartha Rana went through each line, word by word and encircled a few important ones.

At Taj Mahal Hotel, the first transcript:

A handler from Pakistan, "There are three Ministers and one Secretary of the Cabinet in your hotel. We don't know in which room."

One of the terrorists in Taj Mahal Hotel, "Oh! That is good news. It's the icing on the cake."

"Find them and then you can get whatever you want from India."

"Pray that we find them."

"Do one thing. Throw one or two grenades at the Navy and police teams, which are outside."

"Sorry. I simply can't make out where they are."

At Taj Mahal, the second transcript:

Another handler from Pakistan, "Are you setting the fire or not?"

The terrorist, "Not yet. I am getting a mattress ready for burning."

"What did you do to the dead body?"

"Left it behind."

"Did you not open the locks for the water below?" A reference to MV Kuber was made.

"No, they did not open the locks. We left it like that because we were in a hurry. We made a big mistake."

"What big mistake?"

"When we were getting into the boat, the waves were quite high. Another boat came. Everyone raised an alarm that the Navy had come. Everyone jumped out quickly. In this confusion, the satellite phone of Ismail got left behind."

At Nariman House, the first transcript:

From Pakistan, "Brother, you have to fight. This is a matter of prestige for Islam. Fight so that your fight becomes a shining example. Be strong in the name of Allah. You may feel tired or sleepy but the Commandos of Islam have left everything behind: their mothers, their fathers, their homes. Brother, you have to fight for the victory of Islam. Be strong."

However, one Pakistani cell number 0321-5023113 was baffling. Terrorists were in touch with an untraceable person. The SIM card was issued on a fake identity carrying the address -- G-9/2, Islamabad. Surprisingly, the call record showed that the phone kept shifting from one place to another in Pakistan during the Mumbai attack.

The FBI prepared a report and sent it to the Home Ministry in India. The Ministry sent it to the Director of IB for further analysis. The Director called up Siddhartha, "I'm sending you the email of the report received from the FBI. One number is worthy of note."

"Understood, sir. Will get back to you."

"What are you doing?"

"Sitting in a park."

"What for?"

"Waiting for the boy to rise and shine."

Smallest Machine

THE GUINNESS BOOK OF WORLD RECORDS mentions that the smallest submarine was fabricated and assembled by Pierre Poulin of Canada having a displacement of six hundred kilos. In the year 2005, Poulin made a successful official dive in his submarine in the Quebec Lake.

The Tupac-II mastermind was not interested in anything that could attract media attention. Making contact with a man with a Guinness Record under his belt would be too dangerous.

A Russian from St. Petersburg, who had built a personal submarine and got it registered as a boat by the Russian Boat Registry was of greater interest to them. The submariner had planned to dive in the Gulf of Finland and remain underwater continuously for a week on his journey from Russia to Finland and back while attaining a maximum speed of eight knots. He claimed that his state-of-the-art submarine was quite silent as the battery driven motor, rotating the screw propeller, hardly produced any sound. He was certain that no sonar could detect her presence since she was truly a stealth machine.

Shalim Amīr Khan approached the Russian and asked him to fabricate a completely new submarine that could carry a payload of five hundred kilos of underwater explosives. He wanted certain additional features like remote operation, contour mapping of underwater surface, and a robotic hand, which could place the payload at any desired location and a special feature to self-destruct at the destined time after it completes its work.

"I'll have to take permission from our Russian authorities as your specification does not fall under the 'Boat' category." The Russian was sceptical.

"We are not planning to get it registered."

"Sorry, gentleman. You've come to the wrong place."

"What if we pay half-a-million dollars in hard cash?"

"What if I get caught? I'll have to cough up more than a million dollars to the authorities?" The Russian laughed, "Russia is not cheap anymore."

"We'll take care of that situation."

"Why should I count on you?"

"You know the rebel group, the LTTE of Sri Lanka also assemble submarines at a very low cost."

"Those are just wet subs, my dear. They don't have navigation aids and hardly one in ten has ever resurfaced after filling its water ballast tank. They simply dive and sink forever. If you want to send your men to their watery graves, that's not a bad idea."

"Tell me how much do you want?"

"Two million dollars in hard cash. All upfront."

"How much time will you take?"

"A year."

Shalim Amīr Khan promised delivery before nightfall. The two men shook hands. When Shalim Amīr Khan left, the Russian poured out a large glass of vodka for himself and busied himself on the drawing board.

Sheep Meadows

ABAN OPENED HIS eyes and found Siddhartha hanging up a call on his cell phone. "I want to call *Ammi* and Juhi."

"There are a few things that I want you to understand before you talk to them," Siddhartha explained everything he knew and finally told him about the gruesome killing of Imran Shah Malik by an unknown Mujahedeen group, which had yet not claimed responsibility. The purpose of killing was also not known.

Tears welled up in Aban's eyes. "*Ammi* is alone. I want to go back to Lahore."

"I'm sorry, Aban. But, you can't go to Pakistan right away. The FBI will not allow you to leave USA. I've signed the undertaking, wherein it's mentioned that you need to seek permission from them before you make that move. I think your life may be in danger in Pakistan too."

"Why?"

"As per our understanding, your father worked for ISI and

was close to Hafiz Saeed, the Chief of the LeT," After a pregnant pause, Siddhartha continued, "We believed that he was close to al Qaeda too."

"He'd be the last person on earth to have any association with al Qaeda. He hated them."

"But try to appreciate the situation. By this time, the ISI and LeT are probably aware of your release by the FBI. As a result, you are double trouble for them."

"What should I do then?" he asked in a helpless voice.

"Listen to what I'm saying." Siddhartha explained about the image-password and the possibility of some key images in some removable media. "Unless we get the removable media, no one in this world can open that file. Therefore, I want you to go to Lahore and get that missing media."

"But you said the FBI won't allow me to leave USA."

"There could be a way out. Go back to college and complete your research paper. I'll return to India. But before that, I'll work out the details with the FBI and the Ambassador."

"Ambassador of Pakistan?"

"No. The Indian Ambassador." Siddhartha explained everything that had to be done.

"I can't do this. It's too dangerous."

"Let me tell you one more fact. We have yet to unscramble the meaning of *'To Pak To'*. However, I have a sneaking suspicion that this weird phrase may put millions of lives in danger; where and how, we still have to figure out."

"What phrase did you say?" Aban asked.

"*To Pak To.*"

"I've heard about Tupac-1 from my *Abba*. He hated President Zia-ul-Haq and his half-cooked Tupac programs."

"Tupac? Tupac-1?" Siddhartha wondered. "Oh! Now I understand. This *'To Pak To'* is actually Tupac-II. The phonetic of this phrase *'To Pak To'* and axiom 'Tupac-II' never struck us."

Aban listened.

"But why did your father hate President Zia-ul-Haq? We presumed that he was close to Zia."

"He was never close to the dictator. He could not stand Zia as *Abba* always believed in a democratic government. *Ammi* told me she still remembered how much *Abba* refused food for almost two days when Zulfikar Ali Bhutto was hanged. My father had always opposed military rule since the Army could never deal strategically with intricate political situations. He was sure that military rule, one day, would destroy our country."

"This appears paradoxical. Our intelligence has a completely different perception of Imran Shah Malik. They believe he masterminded the Kargil operation."

Aban laughed, "Indian intelligence has failed to notice a very important fact. After General Pervez Musharraf assumed power, the first casualty was no one, but *Abba*. I'll give you the reason. Perhaps, he was the only one, who could speak against the General and his military rule, even though he was holding the top position in the ISI at that time."

"He must have been an audaciously brave man."

"He was. And he always wanted me to be as brave as a lion."

"So, I think the lionhearted boy will accept my proposal."

"Let me think about it."

"There is no hurry. Take your time. But never ever mention this to anyone; not even to Juhi, and for that matter, to your *Ammi*."

Siddhartha wrote his secured cell phone number and handed

it to Aban, "If you decide against my proposal, you may choose not to call me. If you are in, just send me a short message, 'Santa. Come home this Christmas'."

Aban nodded. "Can I talk to *Ammi* and Juhi now?"

"Why not? And now it's time for me to make a move."

Khalil Deek

ONE THING THAT bothered Shalim Amīr Khan was the selection of explosives. He had watched many real video images of demolition of buildings and knew the potency of the powerful explosives C-4 and HNIW. The attractive name of Her Majesty's eXplosive (HMX) brought a smile to his lips. However, he knew from his vast experience that he had no chance of procuring it since military grade explosives was not available among his known contacts. Underground operators did not have sufficient quantities of these extremely regulated explosives.

As per international agreements, each and every explosive needs to have a detection taggant or marker, which should produce a distinctive vapour signature after a blast. In case of a terrorist blast, this vapour signature can be sniffed out by both dogs and specialized ion mobility spectrometers even if as little as 0.5 parts per billion is left as residue in the affected surrounding.

Shalim Amīr Khan therefore ignored military explosives and turned his attention to others that could be as devastating as any of these if a proper technique was used. He knew that al Qaeda had already brought into play an explosive to bring down the Khobar Tower in Saudi Arabia. However, the blowout left behind telltale signs at the mise-en-scène and the investigating agencies could zero in on the source of the explosives. Hence, for Tupac-II, he would not use such things that would leave a signature for detection after destruction. He knew he could not take triumphant credit for his feat, when the time came.

A seven thousand-page guide, entitled *Encyclopaedia of Jihad* was recovered from the home of Khalil Said al-Deek, aka Joseph Adams, when the Jordanian Police arrested him. Enquiries conducted by the police revealed that he held dual US-Jordanian citizenship. He had gone to America to study computer science and having lived in Los Angeles for sufficiently long years, he became a naturalized US citizen and worked as a computer engineer. As a privileged American passport holder, he visited Peshawar in Pakistan several times without raising an eyebrow. There, he came in contact with Osama bin Laden, who encouraged him to learn explosives techniques to add to his specialized knowledge, thus creating a deadly cocktail.

After his arrest by Jordanian authorities, he was imprisoned for seventeen months on the charge that he had hatched a plot to bomb Queen Alia International Airport, Amman on the eve of the millennium. After a year-and-half, he was out of jail and promptly left Jordan for North Waziristan to meet Osama bin Laden.

Al Qaeda planted a story that they had killed Khalil Deek and his wife, who was expecting her fifth child. They cited the reason that Khalil Deek was a spy, working for the Jordanian Authorities. The Pakistani army and the ISI also claimed that he had been killed in a raid, but his body was never found.

Khalil Deek moved to the hidden caves in the Hindukush Mountains, in the safe-haven of the al Qaeda. Here he turned into an expert in bomb making. He could now turn a packet of cigarettes, chocolate bars, toothpaste and hairbrushes into deadly devices.

Naturally, Shalim Amīr Khan contacted Khalil Deek, to complete project Tupac-II. After setting aside military grade explosives, Shalim Amīr Khan discussed other alternatives with Khalil.

Khalil responded, "According to me, semtex is the best option."

Shalim Amīr Khan nodded while Khalil Deek continued, "Remember what the investigator of the ill-fated Pan Am Flight 103 said in its official record, '*Only 312 grams of semtex tucked into a Toshiba cassette recorder felled the huge Boeing 747 like a winged mallard*'. The beauty of semtex is that it looks like brick and feels like Play-Doh. You can roll it into any shape. And we should not forget the Vietnamese defeated the American's C-4 with the same semtex during the Vietnam War."

"That's right. In fact, two properties of semtex 1A are very important. It retains its elasticity even when subjected to a wide temperature range and it is waterproof. Thus, semtex is a perfect choice for an underwater blasting."

"But from where can we get it?" Khalil Deek was not sure of the current status of availability of semtex.

"As per my information, the Czech company Omnipol exported seven hundred tons of semtex to Libya. The President of Libya, Colonel Qaddafi supported every terrorist and radical organization: the PLO, Red Brigades, Black September and the Irish Republican Army. He sold semtex all across the globe: from Manila to Belfast and from Slovakia to Chile. But our safest bet lies with our most trusted friend in the Palestine Liberation Organization. I know where the PLO is hiding it." Shalim Amīr Khan gave pinpointed information.

"But what about the detection signature?"

"The taggant agent was added to semtex only after 1991. All semtex produced before that is without any detection signature."

"When did Omnipol export semtex to Libya?"

"In late '70s and early '80s"

"So, the Omnipol explosives will not leave any signature." Khalil Deek sounded jubilant. "But the bomb will require other components too."

"True. And the good news is that you can buy the components from local supermarkets."

Khalil Deek nodded while Shalim Amīr continued, " Tell me how much time will you take to assemble the product?"

"Less than a year."

"Terrific." A smile spread on Shalim Amīr Khan's lips, "And semtex can be rolled into any shape."

"Absolutely. What shape do you want?"

"Fishes."

"Which one?"

"*Hindustāni* Hill trout and mahseer."

"I haven't heard of these species."

"Their Hill Trout is the Snow Trout and the mahseer is Hamilton type."

Khalil Deek grinned. "I'll paint the red bricks with the colour of these fishes. Just show me their pictures."

Part-II

Year 2009

Extradition

THE OFFICIAL TENURE of the Indian Ambassador in the USA came to an end. The new Ambassador joined just before Christmas. Juhi finished her under graduation, but did not enrol for a Master's.

The Boeing 777-200LR took off from Newark Liberty. She wondered when she would come back again to the land of opportunity. Had she taken the right decision at the most important juncture of her life? Would she ever meet Aban or were Aban and his memories, a dream she had left behind in the Cornell campus?

Juhi was jolted out of her reverie when the aircraft hit an air pocket. She wanted to remain in her dream, but that was not to be.

Back in Delhi, the Ambassador took up residence in Defence Colony, New Delhi. He was a busy man even after retirement. He played golf at the Delhi Golf Course, spent afternoons at the

India Habitat Centre, and still found time to read the books of his favourite authors. Off and on, he would also be invited by different organizations as their Chief Guest. He also became a panellist on foreign affairs in a television channel.

Juhi associated herself with an NGO working for the UNEP sponsored 'Billion Tree Campaign'. Both Aban and Juhi kept in touch with each other, but both were busy with their work.

Aban wanted his *Ammi* to visit America, but every time she applied for a US Visa, the American Consulate in Pakistan rejected her application. Aban could not go to Pakistan until the FBI approved of his travel. Hands tied, he felt completely helpless. He would turn taciturn while talking to his mother on the phone and stare blankly into space. He felt helpless when she sobbed on the phone and whenever he received an email from her. Focusing on Academics became difficult. Even though he had to submit his research paper on 'Water resources system simulation' before the Christmas vacation, he just could not do it. His professor granted him a three-month extension and extended it once again for a fortnight, when he failed to meet the deadline. But it took almost six months of evaluation and constant improvement, before his professor finally approved the paper for publication.

A few days later, he opened his email program and typed, "Santa! Come home this Christmas," and clicked on the send button.

A week later, an FBI officer met him and asked him to sign a few documents. He seized Aban's passport and the laptop. He was arrested and produced in 65B District Court, which exercised jurisdiction over Ithaca.

The District Attorney presented the call log of Aban's cell

phone. It showed several calls made from Lahore to Mumbai on the day of the Mumbai attack. The Mumbai Metropolitan Magistrate had already sent a summons for Aban and the Indian Government had requested Aban's extradition to India so that he could be tried before the Mumbai court.

Aban hired a lawyer, who tried his best to defend his client. The lawyer raised a very valid ground, requesting the court to rethink whether the United States of America could extradite a Pakistani citizen to a country other than that of which he held a citizenship. As per the extradition treaty between the two countries, a national could not be extradited to a third country, in this case India, where a court case was pending against him.

After a lot of deliberation, the Judge reserved judgment, instructing both the State and Aban to be present in the afternoon. The judge retired to his chamber. He received a call from the office of the Attorney General.

The court trial was leaked out to the media, which came running to cover a story of the Mumbai blast accused. In the afternoon, the court pronounced that if a terrorist act had taken place anywhere in the world, where an American citizen was killed, it would be deemed as an Act of Terror against America. Since American citizens were also victims of the Mumbai attack, Aban could be extradited to India, irrespective of Aban's Pakistani citizenship.

Two Indian officers signed a warrant for Aban's extradition. The FBI handed Aban to them. When they came out, media people surrounded Aban and the Indian officers.

One of the reporters directed his salvo at the Indian officer, "Sir, could you please tell us if Mr. Aban Malik is directly involved in the Mumbai attack?"

"When the matter is subjudice in an Indian court, we are not authorized to make any comments," was the terse response.

Aban shouted, "The *Hindustāni* agencies are trying to fix me. I'm innocent. This is a deliberate set up against all Pakistan nationals."

The camera flashed and captured many images of Aban being shoved into a rented car.

The car sped to JFK Airport.

Plastic Surgery

A PRIVATE COSMETIC surgery hospital on Al Wasl Road, Dubai, offered a complete makeover solution, using a combination of a cutting-edge laser non-surgical procedure and the more conventional maxillofacial surgery.

Shalim Amīr underwent the procedure in July 2009. He revisited the hospital for minor corrections. The laser technique was sufficient to remove small anomalies.

When he came out of the hospital, he was sure that no one could ever recognize him, not even his own family members. Committed to a cause, he was even willing to disown his roots as a descendant of the Nawab of Dir. He was not worried about losing the enormous wealth, which he was to inherit from royalty. He was a satisfied man.

He rechecked his new passport arranged by a trusted friend in Dubai. He had already made several trips to Russia, the Gaza strip, Egypt, India, United Kingdom and many other countries during the last one year.

The next day, he went to the Indian Embassy. The Visa Consul was impressed with his profile and took no time to stamp a multiple-entry visa.

His chauffeur took only an hour and half to drive the Rolls-Royce Phantom Coupé from Dubai to Abu Dhabi. Finally, Shalim Amīr checked into the luxury suite of Emirates Palace. He reconfirmed the schedule with Hussein Pharma about the arrival of a few others. He was to board a yacht with his Indian guests along with Saeed al-Masri, the financial chief of al Qaeda, the following day.

Telephone Number

ELEVEN MONTHS HAD passed, but the Indian Intelligence had not been able to unravel the mystery of Tupac-II. The images drawn by the graphic experts with the help of the butler of the Intercontinental Hotel were not sufficient. The name starting with *Sun...* was still a mystery. The telephone number 0321-5023113 was untraceable and also nothing worthwhile was coming in from Indian Agents in Pakistan.

Siddhartha Rana had co-ordinated with several Indian law enforcement and intelligence agencies: R&AW, CBI, the State intelligence, ED and DRI. He was also in constant touch with the international agencies: CIA, MI-6, FSB, Mossad, BND, ASIS, DGSE and Interpol. Although some plots of the Mumbai attack had started to get unravelled, none of the agencies were even remotely aware of Tupac-II.

Finally, in October 2009, an Indian agent in Pakistan rang up Siddhartha Rana, "I've got some very interesting facts about the mysterious number 0321-5023113. As per the Pakistani telecom department, there is no STD code 0321." The caller gave Siddhartha some analogous codes: 07321 of Liaqatpur, 05321 of Khar in Pakistan that did exist. "The last three digits 321 are common STD digits for both the places. However, my hunch is that it should be Khar, in the Federally Administered Tribal Areas (FATA) of Pakistan, near the Afghanistan-Pakistan border."

"Why do you think it is Khar?"

"Till recently it was one of the strongholds of al Qaeda. I can feel it in my bones that al Qaeda is involved."

"Oh!" Siddhartha sighed.

"This number was used very frequently till the Mumbai attack. I got hold of the shopkeeper, who issued the SIM card. However, the shopkeeper had a very vague recollection of his features. He divulged that he had sold the SIM card to some Gilani. I tried to trace Gilani, but could not. Later on, when I analysed the call record, I found that on 13th March 2007, this phone was powered on at Chitral Airport in Pakistan. It caught the signal till a bridge on the Kunar River on Chitral-Masjud road. After four hours of complete silence, the cell phone started to catch the signal once again when the owner of this phone returned to Chitral Airport. Of course, he switched it off again when his flight took off. Now, the plot thickens here. Four other cell phone numbers followed the same pattern. All caught the network signal till the same bridge, went silent for few hours and again caught the signal from the bridge to the airport. The phone number 0321-5023113 was used for the last time at the JFK Airport, New York. All cell phones became completely silent when the Pakistani Government and the FBI started to investigate. However, one cell phone is still in use."

"What's that number?" Siddhartha was getting excited.

"The number is…"

Siddhartha wrote down the cell phone numbers on a sheet of paper. "Interesting! One of the cell numbers seems to have been issued by an Indian telecom company." Siddhartha was thinking aloud, "This cell phone number is a highly-secured number, issued only to the officers of the intelligence department: R&AW, Military Intelligence and IB. Even the records of these numbers are not kept with the telecom companies. The government of India has a long-term arrangement with the telecom companies, who are paid one-time service usage charges for five years. The DCS-1400 series encrypted calls cannot be monitored or intercepted by any authority since a single dedicated spectrum belonging to the military bandwidth is used."

The man continued, "There is another twist to the story. After a long period of silence, this number is active today once again. I traced that the same number has called a person, who has checked into the Hotel Emirates Palace in Abu Dhabi."

Siddhartha was surprised as to how this man in Pakistan could trace an encrypted call. He asked, "From where did he call Abu Dhabi?"

"Indira Gandhi International Airport, New Delhi."

"Where is the present location of the person?"

"Don't know. The line went dead. It seemed as if all traces were swallowed up by the Persian Gulf."

Siddhartha contacted Robert McLean and provided all the details he had got from this man from Pakistan. "Get some information on Gilani. And I need the help of the FBI office in Abu Dhabi to chip in."

Camcorder

A young woman boarded a yacht at Dubai Marina Yacht Club Canal. She was allowed only her purse and a cell phone while she had to undergo a strict security check. She checked into her room in the lower deck and waited.

Even though no one had boarded the yacht except two security personnel guarding it at the pier, she had to tread very cautiously.

Her voice trembled when an FBI Agent called her, instructing her to retrieve the camera from the small fishing net, hooked to the fiberglass hull. She quickly erased the incoming call number and moved to the intended location.

Wiping away the cold sweat from her hands, she pulled out the rope attached to the fishing net, retrieved the camcorder and moved towards the conference room. She shuddered to think what would become of her if she were caught. Those men would tie the heavy anchor around her neck and let her find a silent place in the abyssal depths of the ocean.

She entered the conference room to find a central location above the conference table for mounting the camcorder. A French chandelier hung above the table. Unable to find a proper location, she moved to a corner to carry out her work.

She pulled out her lipstick and turned the bottom knob to exactly match the 3 O' clock position. A knife popped out from the tube. She cut a small piece of the wooden panelling of the roof and placed the camcorder inside. Only a tiny aperture lens, connected with the night-shot enabled camcorder, peeped out from the tiny hole, almost invisible to the naked eye and ready to capture everything happening at the conference table. Its wide-angle lens and variable aperture could be panned and zoomed remotely from another room.

She turned the lipstick knob in the opposite direction. The lipstick turned into glue. Even though she applied the glue with finesse to fix the wooden panel, she was not sure that anyone could identify the difference between the tampered and the adjacent panels.

To reassure herself that no one could pinpoint the difference, she applied the age-old technique. She shut her eyes tightly and randomly followed a zigzag path and moved in a circular motion. She went to each corner to identify the cut panel. She could not make out any difference.

Finally, she somehow connected an HDMI connection to her Blue Ray Disk Roaster.

Custody

ON THE BREAKING NEWS' segment of every channel in India, Juhi watched Aban's helplessness before the media, "*The Hindustāni agencies are trying to fix me. I'm innocent. This is a deliberate set up against all Pakistan nationals.*"

On the other side of the globe, the Chief of the Cabin Crew of the Air India flight continued with the mandatory announcements while the aircraft taxied to the runway. The aircraft took off from the JFK airport and Aban closed his eyes.

The Mumbai Police took custody of Aban when he arrived at CST, the international airport terminal of Mumbai. They produced him before the Special Anti-terror Court, which remanded Aban to the police custody of the Mumbai Crime Branch for fourteen days of custodial interrogation to discover his links with the masterminds of the Mumbai attacks.

Siddhartha reached Mumbai and briefed the Police

Commissioner about Aban and handed over a confidential memo to the Police Commissioner. The Police Commissioner, in turn, asked the investigator Crime Branch to hand over a copy of the case records to the IB.

After fourteen days, the Police produced Aban in court. The media, which had gathered outside in large numbers, was not allowed to witness the court proceedings. The court started the in-camera hearing. Before the judge, Aban's lawyer vehemently pointed out that no case could be made out against Aban since there was not even an iota of evidence, which pointed to his involvement in the Mumbai attack.

When the judge asked the prosecution to file the evidence to the contrary, it failed.

The court set Aban free, stating that the arrest was made on the basis of exaggerated hearsay.

When Aban came out of the court premises, the waiting media surrounded him. One of the reporters jumped out of the barricade put up by the police. His cameraman focused on the man of the moment, "Is it true, Mr. Aban Malik, that you made a call to Mumbai on the day of Mumbai attack?"

"Yes."

"Did you talk to someone who was in the Taj Mahal Hotel?"

Aban nodded.

"Can you tell the name of the person?"

"No."

"Were you in touch with one of the terrorists?" Another newshound jumped in.

"I'll not react to your rhetorical questions."

"Why?"

"I've disclosed the facts before the court."

At this point, Aban's lawyer cut in. "My client reserves the right not to respond. If you want an answer, get the certified copy from the court."

The Police whisked Aban away. Siddhartha was waiting. "You'll have to go to Delhi," he said.

"Why?"

"As per the procedure, the Indian authority can hand you over only to the High Commission of Pakistan. Someone from your family or any acquaintance, who can produce valid credentials, will be required to identify you before the First Secretary. After that the High Commission will take your custody as a Pakistani National."

"Who will visit India to identify me?" Aban wondered. "The Indian High Commission in Pakistan will never give a visa to our family members."

"Don't worry. I'll do something. Someone will definitely come for identification. After the formality, you can go back home. But you'll have to wait till tomorrow when your lawyer gets the certified copy of the court order."

Aban nodded and Siddhartha left in another car.

The next day, a Mumbai police officer escorted Aban to Delhi. The High Commissioner of Pakistan was furious with the treatment meted out to Aban. He lodged a formal protest with the Ministry of External Affairs, which promised to look into the matter. A man from Nemogram visited the Pakistani High Commission office in New Delhi and identified Aban. Aban tried to recognize the man, but could not. The man signed on the papers and left.

The man contacted Siddhartha Rana from the garden outside the High Commission. He wanted to accompany Aban to

Lahore, but Siddhartha Rana strongly advised against it, stating that it would be too dangerous.

The man quickly left the High Commission office and went straightway to Indira Gandhi International Airport. He booked a ticket on Air Emirates to Peshawar via Dubai.

The High Commission arranged for a ticket for Aban, who reached Allama Iqbal International Airport, Lahore two days later. The Pakistani media contingent was eagerly waiting for him. They needed to cover the story of the atrocities carried out by *Hindustāni* agencies on an innocent Pakistani citizen.

When Aban reached home, he was due for another shock. Nausheen had not come out of the grief of the loss of her husband. She would occasionally sit in some corner of the house, staring blankly at the wall for hours. When Aban hugged her, one evening the dam holding back her tears burst.

She would not let Aban out of her sight even for a moment. Even if Aban wanted to go to the backyard, she would beg him to come back, fearing that gunmen would bring him down as they had his father.

Aban took her to the doctor, but the treatment did not alleviate the condition much. Nausheen was becoming more and more possessive of her only son. She could not afford to lose him.

Each day was getting tougher for Aban too. He had repeatedly watched the video recording of his father bending on his knees, praying to Allah, his wrists tied up, head covered with a black cloth and the sound of AK-47s resounding in the valley. His eyes always stopped at the scene where his father's hand shook violently, scratching his right thigh. He knew from childhood that when his father was under tremendous pressure, he instinctively reached for his thigh. As a child, Aban used to be frightened of that sight, but had slowly learnt to leave his father alone whenever it happened.

* * *

Aban could see in his mind's eye the trauma his father would have faced before the bullet tore into his body. The horrible incident would not leave Aban even in his sleep. In his dream, it would repeat itself every night and Aban would wake up in a cold sweat when the dream ended with the sound of bullets.

He tried to investigate why his father's body was never found, but whenever he asked the Police and the ISI, they gave the same answer that they could not identify the exact location. When Aban pointed out that the location could be matched to the Buddhist Monasteries in the background of a swelling runnel, pat came the Police reply, "Will a body still be floating in the water after so many months?"

To this argument, Aban had no counter-argument, and the questions remained. "Why would someone kill him? What did his father do to have been deprived of his life in such a gruesome manner?" There was nothing that Aban could do except seek the truth.

He rummaged around every corner of his home including his father's study to find some clue. He read his father's letters, emails and diaries, but could not get any lead. The image file of Túpac Amaru II always mocked him. He tried several combinations to open the file, but could not.

"Was he killed because of this image file?" There was no one to resolve his conflicts, "Where are those four images? How will those mysterious images unlock the password?"

Yacht

AN EIGHTY-SIX FEET VIP Yacht sailed from the Dubai Marina Yacht Club Canal. Even though the Gulf Craft brand of the luxury yacht was fitted with laser lights, a DVD player, satellite television connection, iPod docks and LS V10 Bose Music system; Hussein Pharma, while booking the Yacht, demanded a Blue-ray-disk player and a powerful Mac Pro to be made available to its distinguished guests.

Although Shalim Amīr Khan did not approve of the presence of any unknown person, Hussein Pharma had acceded to the request of its Indian guests and arranged for a few pretty women. One of the women boarded the yacht in the early morning to oversee the arrangements, the others followed after a few hours. They could rest for some time in the three lower deck cabins reserved for them, later they would have to get ready for the show. The smouldering barbecue grill and the cold vintage wine created a contrasting atmosphere.

After departing from Marina Beach, the yacht sailed towards Atlantis the Palm. The Captain steered to port and the yacht responded to the command. It pitched in the northwest direction towards the open blue briny deep. Within half an hour, it cruised beyond the territorial water limits of the UAE and anchored in the international waters of the Persian Gulf.

Three speedboats docked with the yacht one after another. The boats dropped off the passengers, turned back and faded away into the horizon within minutes.

Sundaram Iyer went inside a small cabin on the upper deck to meet another person. Shalim Amīr smiled at the guest. Sundaram was friendly, "Welcome aboard, Shalim Saheb."

Shalim Amīr got straight to the point. He asked Sundaram to provide him with the minutest details of the Deputy Commandant of the dam: his way of dressing, the way he walked, what his voice sounded like softly or when he shouted in a harsh tone, details about his family members, their lineage, details about his dog or other pets, his likes and dislikes and anything else that anyone could imagine.

"I will get his 360 degree profiling done. I'll also tell my contact to prepare a DVD and send it to you."

"No need for that. It is dangerous. Just pay him a courtesy call and befriend him. Visit his home. Stay in the small town for a few days. Everyone relishes a nice meal, but opens up only after a few drinks. And, I know how much you love drinking all night. But for heaven's sake, you control your craving at least for a few days in his company. Let him take your place. So, you drink less and watch more. If you follow this, you will have everything you ever desired."

Sundaram Iyer nodded and turned his eyes when he heard

the footsteps of other persons joining them in the room. Somashekhar Rao looked exhausted since he had had to undertake a quick tour of the dam site and board the flight to Dubai the very next day.

"It was tough to come all the way from the dam to this awesome ocean?" Sundaram Iyer laughed.

"Still it's tempting when so many gorgeous women are around," Somashekhar Rao grinned.

No one noticed when Saeed al-Masri stepped inside the room and overheard them. "Let's get down to brass tacks," The usually calm Saeed al-Masri could not hide his ire.

A lull came over the room, as no one dared say anything before the first in hierarchy of the financial wing of the al Qaeda. al-Masri, on the other hand, looked a little ill at ease in the presence of an unknown man. He turned to Sundaram Iyer, "Will you introduce our new friend?"

"He is part of our team and will play a major role on the day of deliverance." Sundaram Iyer smiled, "He is Shalim Amīr Khan." Sundaram Iyer went on to explain his role.

"Welcome to our world, Amīr Bhai." Al-Masri was all heart. He then turned to Somashekhar Rao, "Can you tell us about your simulation?"

"Let's go to the conference room. We've set up the equipment in that room."

"Why not here?" A tiny doubt crept in al-Masri's mind. "Anyway switch off all the lights in the conference room."

"Why?"

"After living for many years in pitch-dark caves, I'm more at ease in dark surroundings."

Somashekhar Rao pulled out a Blue Ray disk and loaded it

into the player. "Before I start the simulation, let me tell you a little bit about it."

Al-Masri approved and Somashekhar continued, "We all know that if a water body is bound from all sides, it has a definite characteristic of natural vibration. To understand it in a better way, I visited the Mount Olympus water park in Wisconsin Dells, USA, which is known to be the Water Park Capital of the World. It gave me insight into how walls of waves of more than nine feet could be created with very little energy. I went to the park's Poseidon's Rage, where I met the operator. He showed me four air jet-pumps, which release compressed air every ninety seconds to bring up a new wall of water. I requested him to puff out the compressed air after an interval of seven seconds just to see what happened. I paid him a bit and he obliged."

"Why seven seconds interval?" al-Masri interjected.

"I calculated the area of the surf pool and evaluated how much time the first wave would take to travel to the far end and come back to its original position. It was exactly seven seconds. When the compressed air pushes the incoming wave at the precise interval, the nine feet waterfront became thirteen feet. The third release elevated the wall to twenty seven feet."

"Hold on. The nine feet wall rose by four feet only in the second burst, but the third gust raised it by another fourteen feet. How is that possible?"

"This happened because the third surge synchronized with the frequency of the pool. The resonance of the pool took it to that high level."

"What will happen if you fire the fourth burst?"

"That will break up the height of the water wall."

"Why?"

"Because that will kill the resonance of the pool and water."

Al-Masri smiled in appreciation. "How can you do this to a very big pool?"

"Oh! You mean the big lakes? Once we determine the exact contours of the water body, we calculate how much time it will take for a wave to travel from one front to another and return. If we amplify the oscillating wave, the same effect will occur."

"Can you do this to the biggest manmade lake?"

"The world's largest manmade reservoir is Lake Kariba in Africa. The water volume is more than one hundred and fifty quintillion gallons. It would be almost impossible to make that enormous volume of water to sway back and forth in simple harmonic motion."

"Then what type of inland water body is suitable?"

"Any backwater storage, which rests in a deep canyon and holds just the optimum amount of water."

Al-Masri nodded. However, he still had his doubts. "Has it ever happened in reality that waves have been created by the resonance of the pool, in the way you have described?"

"Not exactly. But every reservoir, bay and sea is affected by seiche."

"What is seiche?"

"Though imperceptible to the naked eye, a standing wave of extremely long wavelength oscillates to and fro in an enclosed water mass. This is a seiche. The time period of oscillation depends on the length and depth of the body of the water. For a bigger but shallower lake, the time period may be hours. But, if the lake is deep, the time period is a few minutes only."

"How tall is the water front?"

"It's not more than a few feet in a large lake."

"A few feet will do nothing," al-Masri was getting fidgety, "Seiche is good for nothing. It won't even move a stone."

"What if the seiche amplifies to a wall of several hundred feet?"

"How will you do that?"

"I'll show you in the simulation." Somashekhar Rao smiled and leaned to press the play button of the disk player.

Clue

ALTHOUGH TUPAC-II was still an enigma, Siddhartha did not have much time to weigh it without further leads. For many months, he was deeply involved in unraveling the Mumbai attacks, thread-by-thread, trying to uncover Pakistan's role in it.

Many breakthroughs were achieved during the year 2009. The Indian government furnished evidence and testimony to Pakistan: call records, GPS data tracking records, the details of DNA samples of the terrorists, the items found in the fish trawler Kuber, and several other corroborative evidence. One of the disturbing facts was about the explosives signature of the grenades used by the terrorists. The manufacturer was China's state-owned company Norinco.

The Pakistani plan of passing the buck on to al Qaeda or the Bangladeshi Islamic jihadist group and to hide the role of Pakistani State Actors in hatching Project Karachi fell flat on its face when India provided Pakistan with the intelligence inputs gathered by western countries. In January 2009, the Pakistani Information Minister accepted the nationality of Ajmal Kasāb as Pakistani. A few days later, the Interior Minister confirmed that the Mumbai attack was indeed planned in Pakistan. The pressure of USA, UNO and western countries started to mount on Pakistan to arrest the key players of the conspiracy.

Some information was received by global intelligence that Pakistan's terrorist outfits were planning to attack other important coastal cities from the seaside, this time using underwater explosives and small submarines.

"Underwater explosives and submarines? Something big must definitely be on their mind." Siddhartha concluded after pondering for a long time.

Missoula Flood

SOMASHEKHAR RAO CLICKED on the simulation, but in a flash pressed the pause button. "Gentlemen, I'll first show you a video of an unprecedented destruction caused by a megaflood before running the scientific simulation of dam failure."

The simulation began. After a brief introduction of megaflood in the western part of North America, the movie started.

The massive Cordilleran ice sheet blocked the mouth of the Clark Fork River and caused the water to backup and submerge the city of Missoula.

The scene cut and the camera pointed to a highlander, running atop the highest peak of a mountain. With bated breath, he watched the breaking of the ice dam, unleashing a megaflood of biblical proportions. The flood plowed ahead and created havoc in the Columbia River Gorge in no time.

The highlander, who watched massive waves, towering thousands of feet high moving at great speeds with a deafening noise and approaching him, he stood thunderstruck. The giant wave scoured and stripped the topsoil, cut deep canyons and coulees in no time, randomly depositing hulking boulders at different places. The gargantuan water then turned into a colossal vortex, spiraling with tremendous velocity. It drilled the hard rock and sunk into the belly of the earth. One vortex followed another. The water poured in from three-mile high cliffs into deep gorges.

With the last scene of the biggest waterfall in human history, the movie ended.

"How big is our lake?" asked al-Masri.

"Big enough to bring doomsday to the entire plain."

"Upload this file to our remote server too."

Hafiz Saeed

ABAN STARTED TO post in blogs, detailing the atrocities inflicted on him during his custodial interrogation and the torture meted out to him by Indian agencies. He began to contribute to Jihadist literature. A Karachi-based literary agent got in touch with him to write his story in book form. Private FM channels broadcast his interviews. Aban told the radio-jockey about his future as a Jihadist, willing to work tirelessly for the liberation of his Muslim brothers all over the world and do everything to alleviate their suffering. Television crew lined up in front of his home to interview him and he obliged each one of them. These television channels projected Aban as a warrior against Israel, aiming to liberate Palestine from the clutches of Zionist rule. Aban was getting famous day by day, hour by hour and minute by minute on his way to becoming a living legend.

Slowly, a few Islamic ideologues started to make contact with Aban and he would invite them home to talk of strategies to free

Kashmir from *Hindustān* and Afghanistan from the American led armies.

In one of the mornings, Aban declared before a famous newspaper reporter that he would not mind picking up the gun to serve the greater cause of Jihad. On the same day, a man from LeT asked Aban to meet him at Jamia al-Qadsia mosque in Chowburji, Lahore.

On Friday afternoon, Aban drove to the university road and parked his car in front of the mosque, situated in the heart of the city. He spread out his mat and waited for the person, who had promised to see him.

At the end of the evening prayer, the Qazi of the mosque announced that Hafiz Muhammad Saeed was going to deliver a sermon to the devotees.

While his followers listened to Hafiz Muhammad Saeed in rapt silence inside the mosque, outside policemen with machine guns stood guard and bearded security men frisked all those, who entered the prayer meeting place. Hafiz Saeed's voice echoed not only inside the mosque, but also blared through the loudspeakers, spreading out to a radius of several miles. A few techno savvy people recorded his speech, word for word, in their digital voice recorders.

Hafiz Saeed spoke with complete conviction. "God has promised to make us Muslims a superpower if we follow the right path. Our rulers are the slaves of America and have sold their conscience for a few dollars..." With his calm and serene demeanor, he continued, occasionally coughing in between and taking deep breaths.

A man came and whispered into Aban's ear. Aban stood up and followed him. On the first floor, they entered an air-conditioned room, with majestic marble floorings and a gorgeous floral ceiling. A plush divan was placed on an Iranian carpet, slightly away from a deep leather settee. The escort asked Aban to make himself comfortable and wait.

After a while, Aban heard several footsteps. Hafiz Saeed entered, but stopped his followers at the door. He asked one of his men to bring dry fruits and *sherbet* for the guest.

The door was shut. Aban stood and bowed before the bearded man.

"Please be seated, my son," Hafiz Saeed said in his deep, profound voice.

"Was it you who called me?"

"Yes."

"What holy service can I offer?"

"First let me explain why I called you. I'm aggrieved about your father's death. I sent my condolences to your family."

"Unfortunately, I was not in Lahore. I could not visit my *Ammi*, as the FBI would not grant me permission to leave America."

"I know everything. Let me continue, son. You may not be aware that your father always stood for the just cause of Pakistan. He is a martyr."

Aban could not resist, "But it was our men who killed him without showing any mercy."

"I'm still not sure who killed him."

"Why was his body never found?"

"We sought the help of the Pakistani army to retrieve his body. However, before we could reach the place, the Pakistani Army ditched us. The Americans pressurized them to intensify army operations against the Taliban in the Swat valley."

Aban clutched his hands together "Where?"

"Nemogram."

"Nemogram," Aban said under his breath. "I've heard this name. I don't remember exactly, but *Abba* used to mention it." Aban racked his brains to find the connection between Nemogram and his *Abba*, but in vain.

"Because of America, the bully, Pakistan has banned our organization. So, we had to withdraw our men from Swat Valley and concentrate on other assignments. Now we have to be very discreet in our modus operandi. For this, we have restructured our organization LeT and renamed it JuD, the *Jama'at-ud-Da'wah*. During the day, our men carry out charitable work and after sundown they carry out the divine work."

"What divine work?"

"Jihad, my son, Jihad!"

Aban nodded and Hafiz Saeed continued, "I also want to know what happened to your father. So, get to the bottom of it and come back to me with the truth. Serve your motherland, my son."

Aban bowed one more time. "Tell me what else I will have to do."

"Join us."

"Anything for you."

"If I ask you to kill *Kafirs?*"

"I'll not blink."

"What if Kafirs are your family members?"

"Kafirs are Kafirs!"

Hafiz Saeed expressed amusement, "I will tell you when the time comes. You will certainly know who the Kafirs are. Till then write whatever I say. Post them to western media. And carry out the unfinished work of your *Abba*."

"What work?"

"Tupac-II."

"What's that?"

"Time will tell you everything. For the time being, I have a very small request for you. You are trained as a civil engineer. You've submitted your papers on the environmental impact of big dams. Your simulation model of Lake Mead is a unique presentation."

"How do you know about my simulation model?"

"Don't be in a rush, my son. Right now, we want you to do only a few calculations for us."

"What kind of calculation?"

"Calculations regarding the contours and resonance of a dam."

"Dam!"

"Yes." Hafiz Saeed's eyes twinkled.

The Wave

It was nighttime on the yacht. The Chief Steward laid out a sumptuous dinner. However, to his surprise, no one visited the dining room. On request, he asked the maître d' to serve tea and kebabs to the guests inside the conference room.

With every passing hour, Sundaram Iyer's urge to move to his suite and enjoy the company of the gorgeous girls grew stronger, but he was too scared to express his craving in front of the dreaded al Qaeda man. For the time being the best option for him was to limit the discussion to 'Giant Waves'. He turned to Somashekar Rao, "I have a very simple solution to our plan. Why not repeat 9/11 and let the dam crumble down?"

"Please understand that it won't make any difference. Even if we get the biggest passenger aircraft, say for example an Airbus 380 or the heaviest aircraft *Antonov Mriya* and let it hit the dam, it will still not come down."

"How can you say that when much smaller aircrafts caused

the two huge towers of World Trade Centre to tumble down like a pack of cards?"

"We all know that the twin towers didn't collapse because of the impact of the aircraft. The truth is that the burning jet fuel of the aircraft melted the weakest structure of the columns. The connections between the floor trusses and the columns of the building broke within minutes of the impact. When the floors detached from the main structure and fell onto each other, it quickly exceeded the load that any one floor was designed to carry. It then initiated a progressive pancake-collapse. But the same thing will never happen in a big dam since the temperature of burning Jet Fuel will not be sufficient to melt steel. Only a gaping hole of a few feet wide on the concrete lining would be exposed and that won't be sufficient enough to cause the structure to collapse. Even if we assume that it collapses, it will only be after several hours, giving sufficient time to the engineers to empty the dam with a regulated flow of water."

"Let's create something like a tsunami then."

"If we bomb the hillside of the lake, huge chunks of earth and rocks will suddenly fall into the water and displace it, creating a massive tsunami. Yet we know that the biggest tsunami, which hit Vajont Dam in Italy, was not sufficient to break it. And Vajont was a more fragile dam than this dam. In the '60s, heavy rains around Vajont Dam triggered a landslide. Millions of cubic metres of earth and rock fell into the lake. The landslide displaced gallons of water, creating a two hundred and fifty meter giant wave. The wave overtopped the dam, and flooded many villages, killing about two thousand people. The village, just beneath the dam, suffered damage from the 'air displacement'.

However, except the top masonry, which got washed away, the dam's structure remained intact."

"You mention that our tidal wave will be a few hundred metres only. Then how will that break this dam?"

"You see there is a difference between what happened in Vajont Dam and what will happen in this dam. In case of Vajont Dam, a solitary tidal wave struck the dam. More importantly, the tsunami generated only a surface wave. In our case, the whole lake will move in simple harmonic motion, causing a cascade of tidal waves hammering the wall of the dam with tremendous force, thereby weakening the structure progressively. Here we have an added advantage. The dam is hollow in the midsection. So, at a particular point of time, even the hollow portion of the dam will start resonating with the same frequency as that of the water of the lake. The centre of buoyancy will shift both upward and downward, making the dam more vulnerable to the successive hammering. A very different kind of destructive water-pancake effect will be created."

"What if that won't still be sufficient?"

"Don't forget that an unnoticed oscillation in a big lake can create both a tremor and a quake. It has happened in southern India when the Koyna dam was the reason for a devastating earthquake. Another is Lake Kariba, where more than twenty earthquakes have occurred."

"I want a sure-shot option."

"You have already planned to place explosives at the toe of the dam. Combine the effect of the seiche, the simple harmonic motion of waves creating giant waves, explosives at the toe and most importantly the resonance of the hollow portion of the dam. I don't think anyone in this world can save the dam.

al-Masri was thinking aloud, "We'll need more explosives." He picked up the phone and connected to Hafiz Saeed, "Tell your friends to arrange for more semtex. Tell him to contact Khalil Deek and ask him to redo his drawing." After a pause, he continued, "Now we want two submarines and two explosives-trained divers."

"Why two? One is sufficient," asked Shalim Amīr.

al Masri chose not to respond.

Ajmer Sharif and Pushkar Lake

AFTER MEETING HAFIZ SAEED, Aban returned home. Nausheen answered the door. "Where have you been since noon? I have cooked *keema* and *Kashmiri pulao* for you."

"I have to go to Nemogram in Swat Valley, *Ammi*."

"Why?"

"In search of the truth. I want to know what happened to *Abba*."

"Don't mention to anyone that you plan to go there."

"Why, *Ammi*?"

"Someone will come to receive you at the airport. You will get the answer."

Aban nodded. Nausheen stared at Aban for a long time, without saying anything. She went to the kitchen and brought back the meal that she had prepared.

"I'm not hungry, *Ammi*."

"If you eat, I'll tell you a story. You know most of them. But there are many things, which I have never told you."

"I was very young when I accepted the *Nikahnama* of your *Abba*. At that time, your *Abba* had just joined Foreman Christian College. He was a very bright student, an extraordinary sports person, an amazing swimmer, extrovert and very talkative. He qualified for the prestigious Pakistan Military Academy Long Course examination and joined military service. The Military Academy Passing out Parade at Kakul, where he was awarded the best commissioned officer, is still alive in my memory. As Second Lieutenant, he was subsequently posted in the Eastern Command during the 1971 War between India and Pakistan. When Pakistan lost the war, the Indian Army captured him and imprisoned him as a POW, prisoner of war. After six months, Pakistan and India signed the Simla Agreement and one of the important clauses of the agreement was to release all the POWs on both sides. In the meantime, the new government of Bangladesh demanded that India extradite two hundred Pakistani army personnel so that they could try them in their military court for war crimes. However, since the Indian government had promised Pakistan that it would pardon all of them, the Indian government refused the request of Bangladesh. Almost everyone returned to Pakistan except a few, including your *Abba*. The reason was that he had earlier fought with someone in the Alipore Central Jail in Kolkata for the rights of the POWs as per the Geneva agreement. Somehow, he landed in a remote area of Bangladesh. The hostile Mukti Bahini kept him hostage for five long years. One day, he managed to escape. He jumped into the Bay of Bengal and dived many metres below, staying underwater for a very long time till the Bangladeshis were convinced that your *Abba* had sunk into the sea or a strong undercurrent had sucked him into his watery grave. So, they did not wait for his body. Your *Abba* was a fighter and after a long ordeal, he came back to Pakistan. He was admitted to Military Hospital at Rawalpindi, and it took him almost two months to recuperate. After he was discharged from the hospital, he contacted me.

But he was a changed man. Your grandfather took him to the Army General and he was properly reinstated in the Pakistani Army with full honours. Though he was conferred Hilal-i-Jur'at for his act of valour, he remained a man unto himself. He stopped sharing his deepest thoughts even with me and though I could sense that he was under immense stress, he would never tell me anything. Days passed, years went by, but your *Abba* remained the same. I tried my best to get him out of his shell, to no avail. I went to every mosque, met *maulvis* and *Qazis*, anyone who could give me a solution, but nothing came out of it.

Even a decade after our marriage, we had no child. Doctors of the Central Military Hospital told us that there was nothing wrong with either of us. Still, I had three unexpected miscarriages.

In the mid '70s, the government of India changed and the new government embarked upon confidence building measures between India and Pakistan in a big way. Getting a visa and traveling to India became easy. One of my friends, who was married in India, and settled in New Delhi, invited me to visit India.

I wanted your *Abba* to accompany me, but he flatly refused. He always said that he would go to *Hindustān* only to watch India split into two, the same way India had divided Pakistan into two in the 1971 War.

I didn't feel comfortable with his extreme views, where hatred breeds hatred. You know it very well, my son.

I went to Delhi, from where my friend took me to the Dargāh Sharīf in Ajmer to offer my prayers to the Sufi saint Khwāja Mu'īnuddīn Chishtī. I prayed for a child. In the afternoon, she took me to a nearby place called Pushkar, where the holy lakes of the Hindus stand. My friend told me that it was the only place, where Brahma is worshipped and so quite unique for the Hindu religion. While I was walking around the lake, I felt as if someone was calling me from behind. When I turned, I found no one. I was tired and so sat on a bench and didn't know when I fell asleep. In my dream, I saw a Hindu God, who told me that I would be blessed with a son within a year. This child would not only make me proud, but also the whole human race.

When I woke up, I heard the evening 'arti', being performed in the nearby temple. I went out of curiosity and saw a four-faced Hindu deity, sitting in a crossed leg position in the aspect of creating the universe. To my utter surprise, he was the same God, who had come to me in my dream. This was Brahma, who as per Hindu belief, is the Creator-God. I bought one of his photos and have always kept it close to me.

You were born in the same year and I named you Aban, which means water. The reason is the water of the Pushkar Lake."

Aban quietly went near his mother and rested his head on her lap. Nausheen stroked his hair lovingly.

"My son, the four symbols, held by Brahma, in his four arms tell us about time, the causal waters from which the universe has emerged, knowledge and the sacrifices to be adopted for sustenance of various life-forms in the universe. It's not very different from what our Islamic scriptures tell us."

Bugging

SOMASHEKHAR RAO CONTINUED with the simulation, explaining the particle-particle collision technique, the waveform equations, a little bit of hydrological engineering and finally a real-life modelling of a dam crumbling because of hammering by successive giant waves, falling one on top of the other.

Saeed al Masri had a question, "Is the reservoir capacity sufficient?"

"At FRL, Full Reservoir Level, it's several billion cubic meters. The bulletin of the Central Water Power Commission of India says that the expected reservoir level would be eighty-five percent. As per my calculations, this is precisely what I need; neither too big nor too small, but just enough to bring a cataclysm, beyond what anyone can imagine."

"Extrapolate your simulation and show us the result."

"For safety reasons, this simulation is in my laptop. I'll not run it on the computer of this yacht," Somashekhar said and fed some data into his program.

The simulation began.

A dam crumbled and a giant wave, five hundred metres high leaped in the downstream, gaining more and more height while passing through the narrow path of the canyon. Moving at a tremendous speed, it engulfed town after town, village after village

The simulation ended after showing the aftermath of the megaflood -- an unimaginable devastation affecting thousands of square miles of luxuriant land.

While Somashekhar Rao smiled with satisfaction at his achievement, Sundaram Iyer smacked his dry lips. al Masri felt a compelling need to drink a glass of water and Shalim Amīr heaved a sigh of relief. The stark details of destruction shown in the simulation seemed to explode to life and become a living reality for all the viewers. It chilled them to think that the calm sea was potentially a gargantuan monster, ready to devour tiny morsels like boats, buildings, trees and men across which the giant would spread out its arms.

Shalim Amīr broke the silence, "Upload the files to our remote server."

al Masri croaked, cutting in, "No. This file will not be uploaded anywhere. Let it remain in the laptop." Pausing a little, he said, "I think we should confirm the date of deliverance."

"The date will be the death anniversary of the philosopher-saint Ramana Maharishi. I have a special reason for the choice." Shalim Amīr responded. "Coincidentally, the place, which will initiate the destruction, bears testimony to another interesting historical fact. Another great saint took *samadhi* at the same place and attained ultimate Nirvana. Both time and place are in perfect synchronicity with each other." He smiled. "Cannot be mere coincidence!"

In another room, the young woman listened intently to everything being said. She recorded the conversation and had taken care to copy through a Wi-Fi connection to the computer. A blue ray disk roasted the grand show of the Megaflood through a parallel HDMI connection to a Blue Ray Disk recorder.

She contacted the attaché office of the FBI in Abu Dhabi and briefed a Special Agent about everything.

The Special Agent asked, "Could you get a photograph or a videotape of any of these men?"

"No sir. After they arrived by different boats, they met in the small cabin, where we didn't expect them to assemble. So, we hadn't bugged the place."

"Why didn't you take their photograph, when they were moving from their speedboat to the yacht?"

"The Chief Steward wouldn't allow any of us to come to the deck. He confined us in a suite on the opposite side of the docking station."

"What happened next?"

"All of them moved to the conference room, where somebody switched off all the lights. I ran the camcorder, but the film is all grainy."

Before sunrise, three speedboats docked once again with the yacht and the two men vanished into the darkness as quietly as they had come. While one speedboat returned to Marina, the other sailed northwest to Abu Dhabi.

One boat was still docked at the yacht. In two suites, five big-sized suitcases, full of high denomination US dollars, still lying in a corner, were to be picked up and deposited in Dubai. They kept lying there while Somashekhar Rao and Sundaram Iyer enjoyed the company of the gorgeous girls. The young woman disembarked from the Yacht when it docked and headed straightway to the secret location in Abu Dhabi.

When one of the boats neared Abu Dhabi, Shalim Amīr Khan made a call, "Our worst fears seem to be looming large. Al-Masri wants more explosives now along with two submarines and two divers."

"Understood. If al Qaeda has decided upon a plan, no one can stop them."

Shalim Amīr Khan spoke in his leonine voice, "I can."

"You cannot, brother."

"I will. No questions."

Stranger

THERE WAS NO direct flight from Lahore to the Swat valley. Aban's travel agent Himalayan Odyssey booked a connecting flight of PIA from Islamabad to Saidu Sharif, the capital city of Swat District.

A person with a placard was waiting for Aban. The first thing he did was to ask Aban to switch off his cell phone.

Aban tried to recognize the person, who looked somewhat familiar. He was the same person, who had visited the High Commission of Pakistan in India to identify Aban.

Aban tried hard to obtain a clue about the identity of the man, but failed. The man with a long white beard wore dark sunglasses that hid almost half his face. The man showed Aban a letter written by Nausheen, mentioning Aban's visit. Aban recognized his mother's handwriting, read it and gave the letter back to the stranger.

In an unchaperoned land, under the shelter of a man, who

looked kindhearted, Aban felt uncomfortable with a stranger. Aban opened the door of the Hummer while the stranger took control of the steering wheel.

The Hummer rode over the rugged mountain, crossed many rivers and runnels and reached the Buddhist Monastery after a two-hour drive. Aban's escort asked him to get down, as the vehicle could not cross the Swat River since the bridge over it was too narrow and there was no further road beyond the torrent of runnels gushing to meet Swat.

He took Aban to the same spot where Imran Shah Malik was shot. Aban asked, "How do you know he was killed here?"

"He spent the night with me."

"Wasn't he kidnapped in Peshawar?"

"No. He came here from Peshawar. He had once promised to come to Nemogram."

"Tell me all that happened?"

"At the crack of dawn, just after he took his bath and was changing his clothes, they came and took him."

"Who?"

"Men of al Qaeda."

"Was *Abba* associated with them?"

"Absolutely not. But he had good connections with the moderate faction of the Taliban."

"Why did they kill him?"

"They had an argument."

"Over what?"

"Your *Abba* was perhaps not willing to accept what they proposed."

"And what did they propose?"

"I don't know. They asked me to wait outside when the deal

was being struck. But I could clearly make out that they were arguing. When I came in, I saw two al Qaeda men pointing their guns at him. They then took him away."

"Didn't you follow them?"

"No one dare to follow the al Qaeda. But I did."

"What happened?"

"There were four of them. They refused to listen to what Imran said. They tied up Imran's hands, covered his face and stood in a straight line like a firing squad facing your *Abba*. I killed all of them. Unfortunately, a stray bullet hit your *Abba* and he fell down into the river. The current was fast and Imran was swept into a gorge. I jumped into the river to save him, but could not as the current threw me out onto the other side. My head hit a rock and I was unconscious for many hours. When I woke up, I returned to the place and buried the four assailants. Then I contacted Hafiz Saeed and told him everything."

"Didn't Hafiz Saeed know about al Qaeda's plan?"

"I don't know. But he sounded surprised."

Aban was flabbergasted. "If you killed the al Qaeda men, how did the video recording of my father's killing reach different news agencies and TV stations?"

"They had placed the video camera on an automatic MT tripod. I took out the cassette and threw the camera and tripod into the river. When I contacted Hafiz Saeed, he asked me to send the cassette to him."

"So it was Hafiz Saeed who released the footage."

"Maybe."

After thinking for a long time, Aban asked, "Why did *Abba* stay with you?"

"He was on some mission. He was here to bring truce between the tribal leaders and the military."

"Did the Taliban oppose that?"

"They didn't. It must have been something else. Yes, al Qaeda opposed the alliance."

Aban tried to get a larger picture, "Anything extraordinary that happened that day?"

"Yes. Before bedtime, he contacted Hafiz Saeed. I don't know the context of the discussion, but your father said that one day al Qaeda will finish Pakistan too."

"What did Hafiz Saeed say?"

"I don't know. But Imran said that he would never allow anyone to raise their eyes on Pakistan; be it al Qaeda or *Hindustān.*"

"India?"

"Yes. He said that there was not much of a difference between al Qaeda and the *Hindustāni* military."

"Is there anything else that I should know?"

"Come with me." The man took Aban to a secluded place. He stopped at a point and removed twigs and leaves from underneath his feet. A wooden hatchback was exposed. He opened it. A rope was tied to one end of the trapdoor while the other end dangled freely, dropping down to an underground facility."

Aban was surprised. "What place is this?"

"This was my radio signal station."

"Radio signal station? But our government had banned all private radio transmission many years back."

"I used the 138.225 MHz frequency."

"Isn't it the disaster relief operations channel used by the Emergency Management Agency?"

"Yes. That's why I used it. Unless some disaster takes place, no one in Pakistan tunes into this frequency."

"Does the al Qaeda use the same frequency?"

"They used to, but not now. Barring some communication via emails, they have stopped all forms of electronic and radio communication. They only trust the ancient postal system."

"But where is the tower of your radio station?"

The man pointed to a mountain.

The man held the rope tightly and descended into the hole. He resurfaced after a while and handed over a briefcase and a watch to Aban. "Your father stayed with me. During the night, he told me something interesting about this watch. He said that this watch would one day become famous. When I asked him how, he said that the watch had codes, which could move mountains, make waves in lakes and change the course of rivers. Of course, I didn't believe him. But I know your *Abba* never says anything in jest. It seems he hid the watch deliberately before the al Qaeda men started to argue with him. Perhaps, he didn't want it to fall into the wrong hands. I found the watch under the mattress and never opened his briefcase. You know what happened after that."

"Why did you hide them here?"

"I knew that the al Qaeda would come back."

"Did they?"

"Yes."

"How come they did not find you?"

"From that day on, I became a wanderer. I went to carry out relief work for earthquake victims in Quetta. There were more than a hundred thousand homeless and the local government were handicapped because of limited resources." After a pause, the escort said, "I forgot to tell you something; your father said that the watch is unique and if someone tries to open it forcibly, the contents inside will be destroyed."

"How?"

The man laughed, "You are as inquisitive as I was. I asked Imran the same thing. He said that a miniature acid vial is placed inside the watch in such a way that if someone tries to open it without inserting the proper nib in the crown, the acid will spread over the tiny circuit board and dissolve everything."

"Where is the nib?"

"I don't know, but your *Abba* had a beautiful Mont Blanc pen."

"I know about the pen. It was a gift from *Ammi*."

"Oh!"

"But what is the tiny circuit board supposed to do?"

"It can transmit satellite signals."

"Why didn't you give that watch to Hafiz Saeed?"

"I never mentioned the watch and briefcase to him."

"Why?"

"I was waiting for you."

"Why?"

"I could trust only you."

Aban held his breath.

As soon as the stranger removed his shades, a childhood memory came flooding back to Aban. Aban understood why this man had visited the High Commission of Pakistan in India to identify him. Why he had taken so much pain to explain everything that happened to Aban's father?

Aban continued to look at the man.

"It has been long years since I visited you, played with you and held you close. I've missed you as though my soul had parted from me."

Aban waited.

"Aban, I'm your *Chacha Jaan*."

Juhi and Nausheen

JUHI WANTED TO talk to Aban on his birthday, but he was not accessible. The phone rang many times, but Aban did not respond. Worried, Juhi rang up Nausheen and asked about Aban. Nausheen told Juhi that Aban was out and would be back the following day and promised Juhi that she would convey her message.

"Is everything all right with Aban?"

"He is fine. He has just become very quiet. Sometimes, it worries me a lot."

The two women talked for a long time before Juhi hung up. Juhi closed her eyes, remembering her mother. She could barely hold back her tears when she was reminded of the day she passed away.

She remembered the precious moments when both of them walked together to the Washington Memorial; her mother selecting and buying the finest clothes and perfumes for Juhi from Macy's, Nordstrom and Barney's. Juhi never parted with a glittering diamond necklace her mother had presented on her sixteenth birthday and she could never forget how she had coaxed Juhi to attend cookery lessons to prepare the birthday meal for the invited guests. How her mother had reminded her, time and again, why a clean home is home to God and reveals the persona of a family. And also how the garbage in the backyard needed to be cleared or else it would attract bad spirits.

Juhi remembered every word her mother said, her silky voice, her kind advice and her words of caution with a compassionate disapproval. Sometimes she chose to keep silent, but even that spoke volumes. The way her mother smiled, the way she looked intently at Juhi and the way Juhi shared funny as well as sad moments with her were all still fresh in Juhi's memory.

Her mother had loved opera and the Boston Ballet. She would cry while watching a tragic scene and burst out into crackling and uninhibited laughter when light moments were played out on stage.

Even when she was ill, fighting the deadly disease, knowing that it had no medical cure, she would always smile and encourage Juhi to see the brighter side of life. She wanted Juhi to see the world with an open mind without judging people's actions and words. She trusted Juhi more than herself in many ways. She always reminded Juhi to take care of her father after she had left, as he would be a lonely man. How fondly she remembered their love and marriage and how she dreamt about the future of her family and the future grandchildren, whom she hoped to cuddle and to tell numerous stories.

It all seemed just like yesterday.

And then Juhi was all alone, staring glassy-eyed at the roof, in a hollow home; humming with no sound at all. With an ache in her heart, Juhi could not share her grief with anyone. Merely listen to the slow thudding of her own heart.

Penetrate

Aban's uncle recounted his nephew's childhood stories as they walked towards the Hummer. He had fond memories of how little Aban used to throw tantrums to be taken to the nearby market. Aban had taken his *Chacha Jaan* to the same circus fair to board the Ferris wheel no less than twenty times. Even the carousel ducks must have gotten tired due to little Aban's constant hopping on and off on their backs. The candy floss vendor began to wait eagerly everyday for his prized-customer's arrival and sell at least five cotton candies to Aban as long as the circus remained pitched in Rawalpindi.

Nostalgic memories came flooding back. He remembered how he would bring chocolates and candies and watch with satisfaction while Aban would jump and hop around him, trying to grab the gaudy packets from his hands. If his *Ammi* ever suggested that Aban learn the alphabets A, B, C and D from his *Chacha Jaan,* Aban would promptly answer that his *Chacha*

Jaan ought to read. Instead, little Aban would run and get his brightly coloured storybook 'Bobby and the little Birdie', and make his Chacha Jaan read it over and over again.

Each day, the little kid wanted a new toy, some more toys, and still some more. If *Ammi* would refuse, *Chacha Jaan* was ever willing to oblige. In a game of hide and seek or a small wrestling fight on the bed, *Chacha Jaan* had to be the loser and his nephew, a triumphant and satisfied soul.

A very sketchy memory of his own childhood at that time was still imprinted somewhere inside Aban's brain too.

"*Chacha Jaan*, let's go to the airport. I'll take the late evening flight to Lahore."

"You cannot go back to Lahore, Aban."

"Why?"

"Do you think Hafiz Saeed is so naïve that he won't call you and ask you about the watch?"

"But you said you never mentioned the watch to him."

"He is much cleverer than we can imagine. He must have seen the video footage when the Al Qaeda's men were tying your father's hands. There was no watch on his wrist."

"Then why did he want me to find out about *Abba* here?"

"To understand this, let me draw a complete picture for you. When I contacted Hafiz after Imran's mishap, he seemed to be least interested in getting your father out of the Swat River. I became even more suspicious when he began to ask probing questions and repeatedly asked me if Imran had told me something extraordinary. Of course, I answered in the negative. Suddenly, I realized that he wanted my cell phone line open to ascertain my exact location. In panic, I hid everything underground and left the place. As soon as I drove for a few miles and reached the bend of the mountain, I turned back to see my homestead. Several armed people had surrounded my hut and were firing indiscriminately. When they did not find anyone inside, they spread out in the area to hunt me down. From that day, I knew I could not visit this place. But I had to come back when your mother called me, asking me to help you. She was also worried about your relationship with the LeT people."

"I have never told her anything about it!"

"I told her about your visit to Hafiz Saeed."

"How did you know?"

"I've obliged many of Hafiz's men. It was their turn to return the favour."

"I understand, *Chacha Jaan*. But I'll still have to go back to Lahore to take care of *Ammi*."

"She has left Lahore."

"Why?"

"Hafiz Saeed is too dangerous. He can go to any extent if he finds out that you have conned him. And he knows very well how much you love your *Ammi*."

"Where did *Ammi* go?"

"Quetta."

"Is she safe there?"

"I told you that I'd carried out relief work for earthquake victims in Quetta. The Mayor of Quetta was impressed with my work. Surely, he can grant a small request of hosting my guests for a few months till we work out some solution as to how you can return to Lahore."

"But Quetta is not a safe place. It's not far off from the stronghold of the Jihadists."

"Don't worry. If you want to hide, take cover right under the enemy's nose, under the constant vigil of their eyes. They will search everywhere except their own backyard. Own a name that rhymes with the name of their *qaum*, their kith and kin, and they will think you are one of them."

"Still I'm not going anywhere, *Chacha Jaan*."

"You are going to India, Aban."

"Why should I go to India and get caught once again by Indian authorities? You know they tortured me while I was in their custody."

Aban's uncle was silent till both reached the vehicle. He revved the engine and steered it to a dusty road. "I know everything, Aban. It was all a ploy of Siddhartha Rana to fool the Jihadists."

"How could you? How did you?" Aban could not believe his ears. When he did not get reply, he asked, "Can I ask you a last question?"

"You are my beloved nephew. I'll answer thousands for you."

"What do you do, *Chacha Jaan*?"

"I have not told anybody what I do; not even Imran, for many years. Everyone thinks that I work for the LeT. Only when your *Abba* visited Nemogram, did I tell him everything about myself. I trust him. And today I'll tell the truth to another person I trust. I work against all forms of Jihad. I've given my life to preach that the principle of universal acceptance underlies Islam. I have not forgotten the true meaning, which says the meaning of life is reparation of the heart and turning it away from all else but God. Most people seem to have forgotten that.

I'm follower of Sufism. I have learnt the true meaning of it and so, whenever necessary I also pick up the gun, especially to fight injustice meted out to anybody. I don't know whether your *Abba* was close to any Jihadist group or not. But I know that he was a true patriot, a man, who loved his country and could die for his motherland. So, I picked my gun to kill those people, who tried to kill such a patriot. You may say that there is a dichotomy in my character, but that's the way it is. I supported Hafiz Saeed when his organization LeT or JuD worked for the charitable purpose of the earthquake victims, but I hated him when he talked about Jihad, where human beings kill one another."

Aban nodded.

"I've still not told you what I do. Let me tell you everything since I don't know what will happen to us hereafter. Pay attention to the present. Listen to the whispers doing the rounds after the Mumbai attack. It's almost six months now. A few Jihadist groups are making a cause of Jihad, but al Qaeda is silent. If they are silent, it simply means something ominous is brewing and it will catch the world unawares. The Americans are worried about this dead silence, and have doubled their efforts to safeguard the Pakistani nuclear bomb. We all know that the al-Qaeda has tried its level best to lure our nuclear scientists to make a bomb for them. But their efforts have failed. So, the best bet for them is to steal these nukes from the Pakistani inventory. They helped the Taliban to capture the Swat valley with only one purpose. That was to take control of the Pakistani nuclear facility in Kahuta, which is less than five-hours from Swat. Had it not been for the timely information of the CIA to the government of Pakistan, al Qaeda would have succeeded in carrying out its grand design. The Americans also advised the Pakistan Army to take control of Swat to hedge against the danger of the Talibani attack on Pakistan's nuclear facilities. To ensure their safety even further, the government of Pakistan relocated the entire inventory of their nukes to different locations in Pakistan. But al Qaeda was a step ahead. They tracked the movement of the specialized SST vehicles, picking up the whereabouts of not only the nuclear material from Kahuta, but also from other hidden tunnels and secret mines at military bases. The CIA believes that al Qaeda must have infiltrated the personnel handling the nuclear assets."

"But what's your role in this grand game?"

"When the CIA briefed the Prime Minister of Pakistan, he asked me to penetrate the al Qaeda and find out what they know."

"So, you work for the Prime Minister of our country."

Chacha Jaan stopped the Hummer near a spring that poured into the Swat River.

The Swat River has flowed right from Rig Vedic time and was then called the *Suvastu,* a tributary of the mighty *Sindhu.* Of the Vedic rivers, the mystical *Saraswati,* Holy *Gauri* and sacred *Sushoma* flowed alongside the *Suvastu* or Swat. Several gurgling streams, glacier-fed stunning lakes, gorgeous waterfalls, thick pine forests, lush green meadows surrounded by lofty alpine mountains with eternal snow on their crests, make this area appear close to paradise. Such is its pristine state. It also holds some of the oldest evidence in the form of human remains and art and artifacts of an ancient culture when man walked the earth here, thousands and thousands of years ago. Sanskrit was the language of the Swati people of yore. Rama spent three years of his exile in a terraced field, Ram Takht, in the valley. Historian tells us that Alexander the Great crossed this river to enter *Bhāratavarsham.* Ashoka the Great built the Butkara Stupa right here. The Scythians, Kushans, the Swati Pakhtuns and Mughals have all had something to do with this valley. Buddhists and Gandharas inhabited the serene lands years ago. Islam in its purest form flourished here. Numerous forms of art, architecture and culture prospered alongside each other. The fruit-laden orchards of these flower-filled mountain slopes have not only charmed human beings, but also enticed beautiful animals. It is home to the musk deer, the grey wolf, the Himalayan ibex and the snow leopard. This otherworldly bounty of nature has been a home to great civilizations, carrying the vibrations of numerous religion and cultures-- a '*heaven on earth*'.

Chacha Jaan spread a bed sheet on the lush green grass, opened a tiffin box and offered his *Mughlaiparatha* to Aban. Aban continued to watch the white waters of the downstream of Swat. His heart ached to think that the same beautiful, impersonal current had swept his father off into some distant realm.

Aban was brought back to time present, when *Chacha Jaan* said, "You may say that. But I only work for my motherland and my people."

Juhi and the Ambassador

Juhi was now very involved with her 'Billion Tree Campaign' and interactions between father and daughter were few and far between. When Juhi came home, she found her father still away and at dawn when she left for work, the Ambassador would be asleep.

One day, she decided to talk to her father and waited for him to come home. She heard the Ambassador's footsteps approaching his bedroom. She waited for a while and then knocked at the door.

The Ambassador was surprised, "Are you still awake?"

"Yes, dad."

"Is something bothering you?"

Juhi nodded and the Ambassador waited. He loosened his tie and smiled, "Well my sweet little pie, tell me where are you planting trees these days?"

"Near Commonwealth Games Village. But I want to go to the Himalayan region."

"Is your NGO doing something there?"

"No. They are not interested in the Himalayas. So, I need your help."

The Ambassador pondered for a long time. "I'll talk to the Director General of the Indian Council of Forest Research and Education in Dehradun. Let me see if he can be of any help." The Ambassador stood up and came close to Juhi, "What else is troubling you, my sweet little girl?"

"Bless me for..."

"For what?" The Ambassador was slightly uncomfortable. He could see what was coming.

"Will you please contact the Indian High Commissioner in Pakistan?"

"So, it's that Aban fellow. Just wait for a few days. This gentleman will come up with something new on Jihad ideology."

"The heart knows nothing of ideology."

"I can't help you, Juhi. I've shown you the articles he has published in Pakistani newspapers. Watch his TV interviews. I have the tapes. You know as well as I do that he has become a Jihadist. He is writing against our government. My latest information says that he met Hafiz Saeed, the mastermind of the Mumbai attacks. So, forget him. I can't send my daughter to Pakistan to become the life partner of someone working against my own country. It will be as good as becoming a traitor myself and throwing you to a pack of hungry hyenas. "

"I know him, dad. Try to understand. He is not what everybody else or you think he is." Juhi turned back, intending to leave. *"The heart has reason that reason does not understand."*

"Wait, Juhi." The Ambassador reached his cupboard and pulled out a folder. He handed it over to his daughter. "Then read this dossier of R&AW. It is a two-hundred page account of this gentleman."

Juhi took the paper and went to her room. She opened the dossier. Her hands started to shake when she saw the chapter titled—'Interpol Blue Alert on Aban Malik'

Rawalkot-Poonch Road

The Hummer reached the Saidu Sharif Airport. The passengers were boarding the last flight to Islamabad. In fifteen minutes, the aircraft took off. Aban and his uncle waited at the airport for another half-an-hour. "Now power on your cell phone, Aban and talk to Hafiz Saeed and tell him that you missed the flight."

Aban did so and Hafiz Saeed told him to travel by road and reach Lahore as quickly as possible.

"That's great. It gives us time to plan our things better. Now listen, we'll have to reach the Pakistan-India border before sunrise."

"Are you coming with me, *Chacha Jaan*?" Aban was surprised.

"I'll see you off at the border. I have a few friends among the Pakistani Rangers. I've already talked to them. Now you tell Siddhartha Rana to make some arrangements on the Indian side."

"Which place should I say?"

"The Poonch border. Tell him that we'll take the Rawalkot-Poonch road."

"That is a long distance. Isn't it? Why can't we take the Muzaffarabad-Srinagar highway? We can reach the border in less than seven hours."

"Try to understand. This is a busy road with many check posts on both sides of the border. The Rangers will always be suspicious of a young boy in western clothes."

Aban laughed, "Oh! *Chacha Jaan*, look at our young boys. They all are lookalikes of me. Hardly anybody wears a beard and *Shalwar Qameez* in our metropolis."

"But very few look like Brits with an American accent. Moreover, tourists are not allowed in the buffer zone between *Azad Kashmir* and the Indian part of Kashmir. I have lived like a wanderer. I know every nook and cranny of these places. Rawalkot-Poonch road is a safer bet. Before 1947, a nine-seater bus travelled on this road. Each passenger was allowed to carry fifty kg. of goods. Due to partition, this road was closed to traffic. Many generations, who lived together for ages, suddenly could not bear to look at each other. This sector was heavily affected in the 1971 War. Not only were roads and bridges damaged, but also anti-tank mines and landmines were planted everywhere on both the sides. Since the last thirty-nine years, no civilian has ever traveled on that LOC road."

"How will we travel then?"

"My dear Aban, the area in Poonch has many rivers, thick forests and small dirt roads. We'll walk in the darkness."

"What about the landmines?"

"Just pray to Allah."

David Coleman Headley

SIDDHARTHA GOT A call from Robert McLean, "Hi Sid, the FBI has arrested a man called David Coleman Headley aka Daood Sayed Gilani at the Chicago O'Hare International Airport when he was to board a Pakistan bound flight. He seems to be a double agent. Although, he was working as an informant of the Drug Enforcement Administration, it seems he was more interested in passing all vital information to the Pakistani LeT and the ISI. He was even trained by LeT a few years back."

"Great news, Bob. The mysterious cell phone number 0321-5023113 is now somewhat resolved."

"Do you have a lead on this number?"

"Oh! Yes. It seems Imran Shah Malik and the LeT had planned something big. They and a few others including Indians were at some place in the Hindukush Mountain, near Chitral on 14th March 2007. I'm trying to get to the bottom of it. Anyway, you have been of great help, Bob."

"My pleasure, Sid. By the way, where is your boy?"

"Who?"

"Aban Malik?"

To Poonch

THE DRIVE ALONG the Peshawar-Islamabad motorway was smooth. Aban and his uncle stopped at a roadside motel at a small place in Dhowk Manat for dinner. Aban's uncle spoke to a few truck drivers and found out that one of them was driving to Lahore.

"Give me your cell phone." He demanded of Aban.

"Why, *Chacha Jaan*?"

"You are too precious for Hafiz Saeed. He must be definitely tracking your cell phone. Let him find it tomorrow morning in some truck depot of Lahore."

Aban smiled. "Let's enjoy the delicious Peshawari food. Peshawari mutton and biryani are the best in the world."

Instead of driving southwards to Lahore, their journey began towards the east when the Hummer sped on Grand Trunk Road after crossing the rotary bridge at Burhan interchange. After a few kilometres, once again it turned left to accelerate onto N35, the Karakoram Highway Pass. Aban dozed off and woke up with a start when the vehicle came to a sudden halt at a small rapid. "There is no road ahead, *Chacha Jaan*."

"We left the main road long back and have travelled on dusty tracks. We are near Salotri. The Pakistan-India border at Chakan-da-Bagh is less than two miles from here."

"Thank God. We didn't step on a landmine."

"It starts from here, Aban. Any wrong step that you take from here will blow you up and your plans. And I'm not talking about the landmine beneath your feet. You will face unforeseen challenges in the unknown land into which you are about to step in."

"What's that fire?" Aban pointed his hand towards a bush fire, quickly spreading towards the mountain forest.

"The Pakistani Rangers. They have lit up a small bonfire to engage their Indian counterpart, the BSF, who will be busy controlling it for hours. You swim across the Poonch River. It is safe as no one can plant a landmine in the river. Even if a fool does so, the river erodes everything under her bed and deposits it at some faraway place. Climb over that hill. That's safe too. No one plants landmines there because the army will always choose to march through the valley, when it is there, instead of the rugged mountain route. Once you reach the other side of the foothill, you will be in India. *Khuda Hafiz*, Aban. May *Allah* be with you and protect you from harm."

"*Shukriya* for all that you have done for me, *Chacha Jaan*. Do convey my love and regards to *Ammi*. *Khuda Hafiz*."

To Dehradun

JUHI WENT TO the Old Delhi Railway Station to board the Mussoorie Express for Dehradun to see the Director General. Lost in her thoughts, she waited for the train to pull up at the platform. Suddenly, a throng of beggars materialized in front of her. Scrawny little girls, who looked like they had not bathed for ages, crowded around her with extended palms, beseeching her for alms in their nasal tones. At first Juhi tried to sidetrack them, but the crowd of urchins was big and persistent. They ran on nimble feet and crowded around her once again with renewed, higher pitched voices begging her to give them 'something'.

Juhi fumbled in the purse for coins, trying hard to keep away from one girl, who had a little brother astride her hip, and was alternately scratching her head behind her ears and extending the same palm to receive. When Juhi could not find any change, she tried to cut corners by slipping into one of the phone booths, as the gathering of the humming street kids chided her, saying she had enough money to travel in the comfort of an air-conditioned first class, but had no money to spare for the poor.

A red-faced Juhi quickly hurried behind the doors of the comforting phone booth. She rang up Aban's number. Someone else answered the phone, "Who are you?"

"Juhi."

"Aha! Juhi Shergill, the daughter of the Ambassador."

"Yeah."

"Where is Aban?"

"I don't know." Juhi was surprised, "This is Aban's number. Isn't it? Please ask him to call me."

"That son of a bitch has not only abandoned you, but also ditched us."

"Who are you?" Juhi was getting nervous.

"Forget about us. But if you happen to contact him, tell him that we found his cell phone from the truck. He'll know who we are and very soon we will know where he is. Tell the traitor that he may choose to hide anywhere in this world, we'll surely find him. That's our promise. *Khuda Hafiz, Mohtarma.*"

Delhi

"I HOPE YOUR journey from Uri to Delhi was comfortable," Siddhartha Rana smiled.

"Thank you. That's very welcoming. The Indian Army officers were very courteous."

"My pleasure, Aban, and I've wonderful news for you."

"What's up?"

"Juhi was to leave New Delhi for Dehradun. Would you like to meet her?"

"Great. But how do you know about her whereabouts? Are you tracking her?"

"Absolutely not. Why should we? It was just a chance happening. In fact, we were tracking your call for your safety. Juhi called you up on your cell phone and had an interesting conversation with Hafiz Saeed's men," Siddhartha said, and pressed the button of the recorder.

"*That son of a bitch has not only abandoned you, but also ditched us.*"

"The damn terrorist dares to call me a son of a bitch," whispered Aban angrily. "I'll find out whatever you all have planned, Mr. Hafiz Saeed." Aban then turned to Siddhartha, "Where do I need to go to see Juhi?"

Siddhartha smiled, "You don't need to go anywhere. She is waiting for you in the adjacent room."

Hindu Mythology

TEN HARDCORE JIHADISTS, ever willing to sacrifice themselves for the cause of ideology, assembled daily at Jamia al-Qadsia mosque to observe certain rituals. This had been happening for the last fortnight. Each evening, they offered *Namaz* and then whipped themselves in repentance till blood oozed out from their bodies. They repeated before the Qazi the same lines every day, "I, in the name of Muhammad, who will show us the way to carry out Jihad and in that of Allah, who will open the doors of heaven, will carry out the duty assigned to me. Forgive me for the crimes that I have committed, Oh Allah! by learning the Kafir's mythology and by learning to praise the gods of the infidels, the Hindus."

After this catharsis, they assembled in a room full of pictures of Hindu mythological gods and goddesses. Tales of Rama, Vishnu, Brahma, Shiva and Ganesha and every other god or goddess that they could think of was narrated to them.

The teacher was strict since he knew that he could not take

any chances. He had to prove his worth to Hafiz Saeed. So, his disciples had not only to pass the test, but also show that they had a much better understanding of Hindu culture than the average *Hindustāni*. Time was short as he had to produce results within three months.

His students needed to learn by heart: many Sanskrit verses, the methods of offering prayers to Hindu gods and goddess, *bhajans, kirtans*, other rituals, and most importantly, the Hindu way of life.

How to tie the *dhoti* and wear the *angavastram* were clearly the easiest and each one of them learnt it on the first day of training. Learning Hindi was not tough either since these Punjabi youths could all speak good Urdu and had grown up watching Bollywood movies.

The tougher parts were yet to come. Pronouncing Hindi words with the same nuance as that of the Hindu radicals was not easy. The toughest bit was, however, to speak the language of hatred that the Hindu radicals speak.

Dam Security

ABAN WENT TO Siddhartha's office the following day. Siddhartha took possession of Aban's credit and debit cards, his club membership card, the identity card of Cornell, and everything that could prove Aban's identity. He placed them in an envelope, sealed it and then locked it inside the vault.

He asked Aban to sign a few documents that gave Aban a new identity. Protecting Aban was of primary importance to Siddhartha. He signed on an identity protection document, which would enable Aban to get out of legal hassles, in case he got exposed. Two witnesses signed on the paper and it was placed alongside the sealed envelope. Later in the day, it was submitted to the office of the Additional Solicitor General.

Aban told Siddhartha everything that had happened in his meeting with Hafiz Saeed and his *Chacha Jaan*.

Siddhartha tried to solve the riddle. "So, Hafiz Saeed knows you are a civil engineer and have submitted a paper on the environmental impact of big dams and he wanted you to make some calculations."

Aban nodded.

"Hafiz Saeed is the last person to be interested in environmental protection. His interest is clearly big dams and something to do with that. Your *Chacha Jaan* said something about a watch, which your father claimed had codes that could move mountains, make waves in lakes and change the course of a river." Siddhartha was immersed in deep thought, "We know that Hafiz Saeed and Imran Shah Malik worked closely. If we combine what Hafiz Saeed asked you to do and what your *Abba*'s watch can do, it only points to one thing—some big dam is under threat. If so, then we are headed for a catastrophe!"

Siddhartha booted his laptop and searched for big dams in India. He found a listing of more than two hundred and fifty medium to big dams. The Central Water Power Commission monitored more than eighty-two dams. He turned to Aban, "After 9/11, dams are the most vulnerable targets for terrorist attacks. Classified intelligence information is being exchanged between countries, which point out that terrorists are planning to blow up dams. Unfortunately, most information is not specific. However, in the month of March, we intercepted calls amongst LeT operatives, discussing the possibility of breaching the Bhakra-Nangal Dam. It seems that they are training their Jihadists to swim in fast current, climb hills, handle underwater explosives and other expertise that would help to blow up the dam. We passed on the information to the State Government of Punjab to tighten security around the lake and dam. In fact, after the Mumbai attacks, not only Bhakra-Nangal, but the security of all important installations: nuclear power plants, dams, missile sites, offshore oil platforms have been elevated to a much higher level than normal and adequate measures for their safety are being taken up on priority.

Unfortunately our security at the dam is not up to the mark. We have old equipment, which is incapable of detecting any underwater terror attack. What we needed were automatic sensors, modern sonars, sophisticated underwater cameras and monitoring software to be installed to thwart these threats. Since we were concerned with these inputs, we brought this issue to the notice of highest level of government. The government acted fast and ordered the concerned department to procure and import the equipment as well as deploy more security personnel at the dams. However, we still have a long way to go. "

Aban introspected for some time. He turned to Siddhartha, "I shudder to think that I could be one of the reasons for an unprecedented catastrophe."

Semtex

THE GAZA STRIP where Israel and Palestine are engaged in constant battle for a small chunk of land is one of the most volatile regions of the world. The southern part of this hot zone borders the Sinai Peninsula of Egypt. Though the area was previously controlled by Israel, it decided to demilitarize it and handover the important Rafah border to Egypt and the Palestinian Authority.

When the terrorist group, Hamas of Palestine, assumed power in the Gaza strip, they destroyed several parts of the wall bordering the town of Rafah. They took control of a vital route of the Philadelphi corridor and dug many underground tunnels to ship arms from the Egyptian side to their fiefdom.

Poverty forced thousands of Gazans to cross over to the Egyptian side in search of livelihood. A large number of them were porters, who carried weapons and drugs for a living. Some were such pitiable victims of abject poverty that they were willing to do anything to earn a few shekels, the Israeli currency, and risked their lives for a few dimes.

Many of these Gazans, who have lived for centuries on the shore of the Mediterranean Sea, are the world's finest sailors, capable of maneuvering even a small dinghy in the most turbulent waters for thousands of miles without being detected.

Shalim Amīr Khan approached some of these boatmen to transship two thousand kilogrammes of brown color plastic brick of semtex to a small apartment opposite Helnan Hotel of Port Said in Egypt.

When the poor sailors delivered the product at the pre-determined destination, two artists separated the malleable plastic into three parts. Two parts were moulded into the cast model of Pyramids of Giza, figurines and small statues of Tutankhamen, Nefertiti and Cleopatra. They were placed inside glass showcases and packed properly. The rest of it was left as received.

Two days later, Shalim Amīr Khan completed the export related paperwork. He dispatched the first part to a gift shop located in Millennium Mall in Karachi, the second to a handicraft shop located in Sunder Nagar in New Delhi. The third packet was meant for a shop in the small town of Garudeshwar, Gujarat, barely seven miles from the Sardar Sarovar Dam.

The third largest in the world with its spillway discharging capacity, the Sardar Sarovar Dam is also the second largest in the world in terms of volume of concrete used in its construction. The largest is the Grand Coulee Dam in USA.

The first two packets containing semtex were cleared by the customs of Karachi and New Delhi after charging a flat rate duty for the gift items.

The last packet arrived at Mumbai CST International Airport and x-rayed. The Custom Appraiser was bewildered. He did not know how to ascertain customs duty on a brick coloured product, described as 'Plastic material for manufacturing undergarments'. Such an item was not listed in his custom-duty booklets.

Catastrophe?

SIDDHARTHA WONDERED HOW Aban could be the reason for a catastrophe and gave him a quizzical look.

"During my undergraduate program in Cornell, our professor assigned us a special project to analyze the impact of a dam-break and prepare a computer based simulation model of it. We were four students in the group. We visited the Grand Canyon and studied all fifty dams constructed on the Colorado River. The two biggest dams caught our attention. The first was Glenn Canyon in the upstream and the second was Hoover Dam. These two dams are the biggest reservoirs in the United States. Lake Powell behind the Glenn Canyon is the second largest, while Lake Mead on Hoover, holding a colossal amount of water, is Numero Uno.

We prepared a case scenario wherein the upstream Glenn Canyon Dam collapsed. All small dams in the downstream gave way there and then. Huge walls of water reached the Hoover

Dam in four hours, downstream of Colorado River. Even this iconic dam was not able to resist the force of the water, rising to the towering height of one hundred and fifty metres when it hammered against the dam walls for ten consecutive days. An unimaginable cataclysm hit the area after the Hoover failed and the wrath of both the lakes combined. It was a hundred times more devastating than Hurricane Katrina, which inundated New Orleans and the Mississippi Area. Katrina was termed the costliest natural disaster, resulting in property damage worth eighty billion dollars and still counting.

As the two dams and other smaller ones collapsed, the major cities of Las Vegas, Phoenix and Los Angeles were immediately wiped out from the face of the earth. Many other stunning places like Flagstaff, Williams and Grand Canyon National Park became bogs of mud and broken steel. Several picturesque places in the downstream like Tusayan, Cameron, Navajo, Hopi, Laughlin, Yuma, Needles and Blythe became ghost towns, swimming in the murky waters.

Electricity supply to these places was cutoff since the hydro power station and transmission lines were all gone. Roadways, rail lines and airports from where the emergency service could be provided went underwater. Even hospitals and food warehouses got submerged.

The agony created in the aftermath continued not only for years, but many decades. The Imperial Valley of Southern California remained under floodwater as if forever. Massive boulders and gravel were carried to faraway farmlands and totally covered the fertile land, rendering it barren. The surging water stripped off the arable land, making it unfit for farming for many generations to come. The cost of rebuilding these dams came out to be more than fifty billion dollars and the overall cost of destruction was worked out to several trillion dollars. America could never be the same again.

In fact, we also studied a report of an organization called Living Rivers, which wanted to drain the Lake Powell to save America from this 'to be catastrophe'. However, the US District Court of Utah did not permit the organization to pursue further studies."

Aban fell silent. His account knocked the wind out of Siddhartha's lungs. He asked Aban, "But how can your project have a connection with Tupac-II?"

"When we completed the mathematical modeling and computer simulation of the project, it was considered the best project ever presented by undergraduate students in any engineering school of the United States. Our professor sent it to the United States Geological Survey and the Lower Colorado Valley Authority for their comments and feedback. In the meantime, I went to Lahore for my Christmas vacation. I told *Abba* about our project on Christmas Day. He asked me to show the simulation and when I did, he patted me on my back, and asked me to save the file in his computer hard disk. I did just that." After a pregnant pause, Aban said under his breath, "I think he used our project to simulate Tupac-II."

"How can you say that?"

"Today is Christmas day again and it just came to me. I hope it's only a wild hunch, but if *Abba* has shown the simulation to the LeT or JeM, those ideas would definitely have bred other ideas."

Siddhartha held his head in his hands. "What happened to the comments and feedback of USGC and LCVA?"

"When I went back to my engineering school after vacation, I got to know that the U.S. government had classified our project as top-secret on the recommendation of both authorities."

"Why?"

"The government could not risk that people believe a plausible, scientifically proven doomsday."

Customs Officer

A DAY AFTER CHRISTMAS, the Custom Appraiser officer of Mumbai CST Airport Cargo section was still in a festive mood. He planned to clear the backlog only in the coming New Year. He ordered his inspectors to clear the current consignments and leave the pending ones for the following week.

With a bored look, he turned to the late evening edition of the newspaper. His eyes widened when he saw an article— *'Al Qaeda attempt to blow up an American plane averted.'*

By our Bureau
25ᵗʰ December 2009

On Christmas Day 2009, a Nigerian born American citizen, Mr. Umar Farouk Abdulmutallab, boarded a Northwest Airlines Flight 253 from Amsterdam to Detroit. He had purchased his ticket in cash in Ghana on December 16. Two eyewitnesses testified live on CNN that they had witnessed a smartly dressed Indian male' with Abdulmutallab near the plane.

Aboard the flight, Abdulmutallab spent twenty long minutes in the bathroom as it approached Detroit. When he returned to his seat, he covered himself with a blanket. A few passengers clearly heard popping noises and smelt a foul odour. His co-passenger watched in horror as Abdulmutallab's trousers caught fire. The fire threatened to spread to the walls of the plane. A Dutch film director leaped on Abdulmutallab and subdued him. In the meantime, flight attendants used fire extinguishers to douse the flames. The steward took Abdulmutallab to the front of the airplane cabin. When the steward asked him what he had in his pocket, he replied, "Explosive device." The device consisted of a six-inch packet that was sewn into his underwear containing the explosive plastic powder PETN.

The Customs officer racked his brains, "This seems to be similar to something that I encountered a few days back." The words "underwear" and "plastics" suddenly coalesced in his mind. He called the duty inspector. "Do we have something in our terminal that has to do with plastics and underwear?" he wanted to confirm.

"Yes sir. A consignment is still with me for determining customs duty valuation. The product description is 'Plastic material for manufacturing undergarments'."

Horror stricken, the Customs officer yelled, "For god's sake, bring it here quickly."

Stones and Waves

THERE WAS NOTHING that Aban or Siddhartha Rana could do except look for some more leads. Tupac-II and the Dam certainly seemed like a very plausible connection, but it was still not enough for Siddhartha to reach a definite conclusion. Even the conversation between Hafiz Saeed and Aban and Imran Shah Malik's claim about his watch was not conclusive proof.

Siddhartha had already sent the image file of Túpac Amaru II to the National Security Agency in the USA for cryptanalysis. The NSA tried its best with its programs: Enigma, Brute Force Key-space Search, but without success. Siddhartha then sent it to a few other centres: the Government Communications Headquarters of Great Britain, the Canada Communications Security Establishment, the Defense Signals Directorate of Australia and Department of Information Technology of India. All of them failed and a few even said that it contained some hexadecimal or binary garbage, which was not worth trying.

Siddhartha got Imran Shah Malik's watch x-rayed from different angles. He did not open it as Aban's uncle had mentioned that forcibly cracking it open would cause the acid vial to destroy the chip inside the watch. He showed the watch and its x-ray films to watchmakers, distributors, retail sellers, collectors, and even persons claiming to be connoisseurs and experts. Some said that they could not say anything without opening the watch. However, they all agreed that the x-ray film did not show any unusual component in the automatic watch.

Frustrated, Siddhartha asked Aban to take a short holiday instead of hanging around the IB office. He also asked Aban to stay close by, so that he could come to the office if required.

On New Year's Day, Juhi and Aban left for Ajmer by the early morning Shatabadi Express. After offering prayers at the Dargāh, Aban expressed his desire to go to Pushkar Lake. Juhi was surprised. Aban recounted the story that his *Ammi* had told him about the magical charm of Lord Brahma, the Creator.

Both came out of the temple and descended the fifty-two steps of the *Kund* to touch the holy water. A *Panda,* the priest, who stood waist-deep in the water, rotating with hands folded, seemingly rapt in prayer, suddenly sprang into a different kind of action. He ambushed Juhi and Aban, quickly threw his own *angocha,* the cotton towel that hung around his neck, on the grounds of the *ghat.* He instructed Juhi and Aban to sit on it and rapidly began to chant mantras, applied *tilak* and tied a thread around Juhi and Aban's wrists all in such rapid succession that neither of the two friends could utter a word. Before they knew it, the *Panda* blessed them predicting a future together, a brood of four children and a long and happy married life. Even before his 'prediction' was complete, he demanded five hundred and one rupees for the ceremony. An open-mouthed Aban handed him the money as though in a trance.

Shaken and comforted at the same time by the strange episode at the *ghat,* Juhi and Aban settled down on a bench beside the lake.

"To love is to receive a glimpse of heaven," Juhi muttered as if in trance. *"Love is portion of the soul itself, like the celestial breathing of the atmosphere of paradise."*

A couple of kids were throwing pebbles into the water and playing. "Look at the ripples I have created." One of the kids hopped and jumped with joy.

His younger brother lifted a bigger stone and threw it into the lake. "Look, I have destroyed yours."

Juhi smiled while Aban kept thinking, "Can a huge wave or ripple be destroyed?" He continued staring at the ripples till they disappeared.

Submarine Parts

AN AGENT WENT to the Russian submarine maker and took delivery of two of the machines and the manual for reassembly. The first submarine was transported by Rossiya Airlines cargo flight from Pullover Airport, St. Petersburg to Dushanbe in Tajikistan. It was further transported by truck till it reached Wakhan Corridor at the Durand line, touching the northern border of Pakistan. The Pakhtun Tribal Chief of Pakistan had contacts with all the tribal chiefs of Tajikistan and Afghanistan. He made sure that the submarine was transferred safely to its destination in Pakistan.

A few days later, Shalim Amīr Khan visited the same person. He got the second submarine knocked-down into four different parts: Hull, Propulsion, remote navigation system and Robotic module. Two parts were booked from St. Petersburg to Kolkata and Goa in India. The other two parts were destined for Kochi and Chennai from Moscow.

All the consignments reached the respective destinations safely. The different bits and pieces were transported from all four places to a small warehouse near Mazagaon dock in Mumbai. A retired marine engineer read the manual and assured Shalim Amīr Khan that he could assemble the product within a week's notice.

"What if we want you to assemble it at our location?"

"I'll charge more. However, I need a small workshop in case some component needs refurbishing."

"Done. We'll book your train ticket."

Headley again

DAVID COLEMAN HEADLEY was charged with conspiracy to bomb different targets in Mumbai, and of providing support to the LeT. After three months in FBI custody, Headley pleaded guilty and promised to cooperate with the U.S. authorities. He signed a few documents, wherein he accused the LeT and HuJI, Pakistan-based terrorist organizations with links to the al Qaeda of perpetrating the Mumbai attacks. These papers were later submitted in the Chicago court.

The American government shared the information with their Indian counterpart.

A Jihadist, Headley admitted that he had reported to Major Iqbal and Sameer Ali, both serving Pakistani ISI officers. The officers, in turn, were closely associated with Abul al Qama, a dreaded LeT operative. Abu Qahafa and a Lashkar member 'D', who was perhaps Saifullah Muzzamil, were Headley's other links to the underground world of the terrorist-ISI nexus.

Major Iqbal introduced Headley to higher-ups in ISI. One of them was an enigmatic Major Hamza, a major operator. No one could trace Major Hamza, since he had been promoted from the Army to the ISI and the Army promptly listed him as having retired from its cadre role, and removed all his antecedents.

His junior, Major Iqbal provided twenty-five thousand dollars and counterfeit Indian rupees to Headley to start an office, namely 'First World', in Mumbai and also to meet the expenses of his scouting trips to different parts of India. On the streets of Lahore, Major Iqbal imparted training to him about the art of effective and scientific intelligence: how to create sources and when to discard a rogue agent; how to take cover or come out in the open to mix with the crowd; when to work alone and when to involve others. They also trained him in martial arts and unarmed close quarter combat.

Headley accepted that he had started off as a LeT recruit, but drifted towards the al Qaeda. He told the interrogators that he had continued to stay in touch with LeT members after the Mumbai attack. He was told by the ISI that he should never speak about the involvement of any ISI officer. After the attack, he removed all incriminating material from his home in Pakistan at the behest of the ISI.

He also claimed to have made contact with the members of al Qaeda in his two trips to North Pakistan. His most damning account was about an Army officer, who worked with Headley and was very close to Ilyas Kashmiri, number three in the al Qaeda hierarchy. The Mumbai attacks were financed and supported by ISI. ISI officials handled every important LeT member. ISI was also close to al Qaeda.

The ISI-LeT-al Qaeda nexus now lay exposed before the world.

Headley further stated that he had undertaken multiple trips to India before and after the Mumbai attack. He had also visited a hill station in the Himalayas, the National Defence College in Delhi, and Chabad Houses in many cities of India for carrying out surveillance needed for future attacks.

He claimed that a top LeT commander recruited Ishrat Jahan as a *fidayeen* to assassinate the Chief Minister of Gujarat. However, the Gujarat police gunned her down.

A few months later, a bomb was detonated in a popular German Bakery, near a Chabad House in Pune, a city close to Mumbai. The explosion in one of the most cosmopolitan and upmarket areas of Pune left many dead and several severely injured.

Siddhartha analyzed each fact minutely. A few patterns seemed to emerge. The LeT was trying to attack high profile targets. They were choosing places, which drew maximum media attention. They wanted to kill the Chief Minister of an important state. Mumbai and Gujarat seemed to be interconnected. al Qaeda seemed to be the new link, but without much substantial evidence, Siddhartha could not go further. He tried to find an answer to the Tupac-II puzzle, using information from these new revelations.

Crest Telefilms

SHALIM AMĪR KHAN visited the owner of CTEL, Crest Telefilms Entertainment Ltd in Mumbai a few times to oversee the progress of the television documentary script. Each time he watched the film, he rejected it, pointing out some defect in the frames or sound. He wanted everything to be perfect.

After a long ordeal of more than a year, Shalim Amīr Khan finally approved it. The assured payment was made to the owner of CTEL and the film changed hands.

Back in Dubai, one evening Shalim Amīr Khan sat on his Mac Pro and checked the uncompressed wave files of a presenter describing a Megaflood. He noted intently every detail: the reporters giving their accounts of the flood from different locations, the sound of gurgling water, the cries of people and the aftermath of the destruction. He spent ten days mixing the files on the blank soundtrack, to finally create the finished product.

The first two minutes consisted of a video of Shalim Amīr

Khan's voice and a motion picture in which he emerged in the backdrop of a beautiful lake. When the camera panned and zoomed in, the background image dissolved and viewers could only see the probing eyes and the steady head of Shalim Amīr Khan, and hear the resonant voice in which he spoke. Then with a slight tilt of head, he spoke in a very polite voice, "*Aadab,* Mr. Prime Minister and the honourable members ..."

However, this documentary had to wait, till the final moment arrived. Some more tweaking and cleaning was required. He improved the final product several times and smothered out every single rise and fall in the amplitude of the sound, trimmed all unwanted video frames and synchronized the video with the audio many times over.

When he finally ran the video file, he was sure that no one in this world could say that it was not a prerelease of a live commentary.

Garudeshwar

SIDDHARTHA GOT A call from the Mumbai Intelligence Bureau, "Sir, a month back, we got information from the Department of Customs in Mumbai about an unclaimed consignment from Port Said, Egypt. The product description was 'Plastic material for manufacturing undergarments'. The Customs Appraiser officer became suspicious and he called the Mumbai police to examine it. After verification, the explosives experts were also called in. They found that it was a plastic explosive."

"What kind of plastic explosive?"

"Semtex."

"Any detection signature?"

"None. It has no taggant agent."

"What variant is it?"

"1A."

"Oh! This variant has a wide temperature range, is malleable and can be used in any condition: from land to water," After a pause, Siddhartha asked," Where was the consignment bound for?"

"A shop in Garudeshwar in Gujarat."

"Where is Garudeshwar?"

"A few miles west of the Sardar Sarovar Dam."

"Did you make an enquiry at the shop?"

"There is no such shop at the intended place."

"Any enquiry in Egypt?"

"We contacted Mukhabarat, the Egyptian counter terrorism intelligence service. They tried their best, but could not find anything."

"How much is the semtex?"

"Five hundred kilograms."

"Oh God! It's sufficient to bring down an entire neighbourhood."

"Yes, sir."

"However, what is interesting is where the product was bound for."

"But Garudeshwar is a very small and peaceful village. As per our local intelligence, there is nothing in the town that can suggest any link to terror."

"Not Garudeshwar. The target is Sardar Sarovar Dam!"

Tirich Mir

AN AL QAEDA agent reached the film studio in the timber market, Ravi Road, Lahore. The master-mixer was waiting for him. He powered on his old projector and ran the film. The agent nodded, as it was absolutely flawless. The master-mixer had also made a DVD of the film. The agent grabbed both and presented a basket of mangoes to the master-mixer.

The agent came out of the timber market and turned his Toyota right. As soon as he reached the iconic Minar-e-Pakistan, a big blast from behind attracted the attention of many people sitting in the park. The agent ignored the sound, took a U-turn, crossed the Ravi Bridge and sped on to the Grand Trunk Road.

It took him eighteen-hours to reach his destination. He stopped his SUV in the backdrop of Tirich Mir, the highest peak of the mighty Hindukush Range.

Another vehicle was waiting for him. Two men from al Qaeda approached the agent. They took the packet from him and quickly turned around. They casually tossed the packets onto the backseat, and the driver rolled forward the engine. Their white vehicle melted and merged into the distant snow.

Kerala Connection

THE INDIAN CELL PHONE number tagged with the mysterious number 0321-5023113 had been kept in the powered 'off' mode ever since the IB sleuth had started hunting down details from other intelligence agencies like R&AW, CBI, Military Intelligence and the State government CID.

Like hunting hounds, Siddhartha's men were after the identity of the cell phone owner. One of the officers visited Siddhartha's office. "Sir, we have finally found the owner of this cell phone."

"Who is it?" Siddhartha seemed to be relieved as a vital link to Tupac-II and the Indian connection was about to unveil itself.

"It was provided to the Home Department of Kerala. They in turn handed it over to the Assistant Director of the Kerala Crime Branch. But he was killed in a Maoist attack a few years back."

"But how come the phone was still in use until very recently?"

"That is the mystery. I enquired from his family. They say that when his body was brought home, there was nothing missing except for the cell phone."

"Was it taken by the Maoists?"

"Highly doubtful. The policemen, who accompanied the officer on the day of the encounter, say that the Maoists never came close to the officer. As soon as a bullet hit him, the policemen rescued him, immediately picked up his body and rushed to the nearest hospital. Unfortunately, the officer died on his way to the hospital."

"Did you check the records with the Kerala Police?"

"Yes, sir. They say that all records were transferred to the CBI by the order of Kerala High Court."

"How did the High Court come into the picture?"

"His family approached the court since they doubted the circumstances under which he was killed."

"Did you confirm with the CBI?"

"Yes. The CBI closed the matter after making a thorough inquiry. They filed their report before the High Court, which approved the closure of the case."

"What about the cell phone?"

"The CBI says they are not aware of its existence."

"Who says so?"

"Sundaram Iyer."

"Oh! The Joint Director of the CBI. But he is presently posted in Delhi."

"True, sir. But he is a Kerala Cadre IPS officer and is on deputation to the CBI. He held the post of the DIG in the Anti-Corruption Bureau at Kochi at the time when the Maoists gunned down the officer. On promotion as Joint Director, he joined the Delhi office."

"Thanks."

When the officer had left, Siddhartha picked up his phone and connected to the special unit of the IB, "I want all the previous call records of Sundaram Iyer. Put all his phones under tap. "

"But sir, he is the Joint Director of CBI."

"I'm aware of that. I'll seek the mandatory permission from the department. And I want you to be very cautious, since the CBI has an advanced system, which enables them to override their call monitoring."

"Not better than ours, sir. We can break every firewall and all voice-data. I know Mr. Iyer uses Gold Lock encryption. Certified by the Israeli Ministry of Defense by licence # 15252, this technology is presently used by top-class Military Special Forces. However, I will do the job."

"Good. Let me know immediately if you find anything suspicious." Siddhartha hung up.

He called his two agents, "I want both of you to shadow a person, day and night."

"We need to complete our previous work, sir. It will take another two days to complete the report. Should we start shadowing this fellow after two days?"

"Forget everything. I want you on this job immediately."

Plymouth to Mumbai

THE DIVER WHO was working for Her Majesty's Naval Base completed his underwater explosive training. He returned to his regular duties and waited to hear from the agent. He had already procured a multiple-entry visa to India for one year.

After an eight-month long wait, he received an invitation from the Mumbai Scuba and Diving Club to be their guest instructor for a full week. The envelope contained a first class railway ticket of First Great Western from Plymouth to London, a two-day stay voucher at the Marriott Hotel in London, and a first-class flight ticket of British Airways from Heathrow to Mumbai.

The flight, BA 199 from London to Mumbai was most pleasurable. The diver indulged in the best of champagne and wine along with delectable seafood. When he expressed his desire to sleep, the flight steward prepared a fully flat bed and provided a single-piece quilted mattress, a duvet and a soft pillow. After a while the diver drifted off to sleep, dreaming of the wonderful life of sunny blue skies, inviting white surf and cool balmy breeze.

When the flight steward announced at noon that they were going to land and instructed everyone to fasten the sea-belt, the diver woke up, rubbing his bloodshot eyes and grunting that the ten hours had flown by so quickly. Striding across the terminal, like a 'British Lord', the diver reached the concourse and picked up his bags.

An old, dull brown Premier Padmini taxi was waiting for him. Displeased and rudely shocked, the diver had no choice but to get inside.

Instead of going to the diving club towards south Mumbai, it turned right from the Terminal 2 Airport and crossed the suburb. After crossing the tollbooth, it sped on to National Highway No-8. It stopped only once when the diver expressed his desire to attend to nature's call. The driver pointed out a small bush on the roadside for the diver to relieve himself. The taxi stopped again at a smelly *dhaba* where both the driver and the diver ate stale samosa and tea, frothing fumes with goat milk.

The diver looked outside, when the car stopped one more time at a police barricade. He asked the driver, "Where are we?"

The driver turned around, flashing his nicotine-stained teeth in a smile. "Welcome to Gujarat, sir."

Assemble Together

SUNDARAM IYER RANG up Somashekhar Rao, "Be all ears. I'm being followed and it seems that my phones are being tapped."

"Come on man, who can tail a CBI man and dare to tap his phones?" Somashekhar laughed.

"Try to understand, every intelligence agency is in the business of playing with other agencies." Sundaram Iyer sounded livid.

"I think you are just being overcautious. Take it easy."

"Tell Parag to see me at the hotel."

"The same hotel?"

"Yes."

The line went dead. The special unit of IB hooked the line to tap the phone of Somashekhar Rao. The light in front of the panel turned green.

"Hi Parag! What's up?"

"I'm good. Everything has arrived in India except the man of the moment."

"Is he still in Dubai?"

"Yes. He seems to love Arabian Nights."

"When is he coming?"

"I don't know, buddy. Sundaram may be aware of it."

"Well, Sundaram has asked both of us to be at the hotel in a New York minute."

"At this hour? Isn't it a little late? You know I'm already facing a media-trial after that bloody road rage accident. I don't want to expose myself any further."

"You know you cannot deny Sundar's request. After all, he is helping you in the court matters."

"He can't help when the matter is before the Supreme Court. And there is no free lunch, my dear."

"But he has assured you ten million."

"Do you think Parag Nanda is worth only ten million?" Parag Nanda laughed. "I'm helping to complete his grand design for only one reason."

"To get you out off the hook of further investigation when the Supreme Court remands the matter back to the lower judiciary for reconsideration."

"Atta boy, you're getting intelligent!"

"No one can be cleverer than you. But I always trust Sundaram."

"Why trust him at all?"

"You remember he promised to get the refund of my bank guarantee encashed. Well, my company got the money back."

"Don't fool me. I don't see you happy merely because your company is getting some dough. Sundaram has obviously fattened you up."

"I have only got half."

"Why?"

"He is waiting for the water to boil."

Breakthrough?

On the request of the Indian Government, the NSA of the USA dug out the email exchanged between the terrorists groups of Pakistan during the Mumbai attack. The FBI had already achieved a major breakthrough when it located an email sent to a person asking him to carry out some new operation. "A new attack in India on Pakistani Radar" caught the attention of Siddhartha. He dug in for more. There was a reply mail, mentioning the subject, "Their Mad Life."

"What could be the meaning of 'Their Mad Life'? Whose life is mad?" Siddhartha clicked on a pdf file attachment. What opened up was something unintelligible.

Siddhartha called his Systems Expert, "The file attachment seems to be highly enciphered. However, look at these symbols. They represent the *rashis of Jyotish*, the zodiac signs of Indian mystical astrology."

"Intriguing, sir."

Lahore to Nepal

ONLY SEVEN OF the Jihadists could pass the training programme in Lahore. Three of them failed not because they could not learn everything taught to them: the Sanskrit verse, Hindu mythological stories, about Hindu gods and goddesses, the methods of offering, *bhajan, kirtan*, and other rituals. They had answered perfectly well during the interview, but because of some very minute imperfections they were rejected.

The first one failed, when the teacher asked him, "Will you kill them?"

And he replied, "*Insha* Allah."

The second was shown the door, when the teacher asked him, "Who constructed Babri Masjid?"

"The Emperor Babar."

The third replied perfectly to everything. The teacher asked, "Will you kill them?"

"The Hindu never kills his brother and father."

"Who constructed Babri Masjid?"

"The place is not *Babri Masjid*. We, the disciples of God razed the unholy structure of the Muslims many years back. It's *Ram Janmabhoomi.*"

"Good." The teacher was impressed, till he asked the final question, "Will you visit Ajmer Sharif?"

"I won't."

"Why?"

"Sufism is a mystical expression of Islam. Hindus don't go to Muslim Dargāhs."

The teacher was furious, "Go to Ajmer Sharif and see how many Hindus visit the Dargāh. You will forget the count. And now clear from your memory whatever we taught you about the Hindu religion. You're out!"

The other seven were perfect.

The snow had melted and come down in cascades in the month of April. The Indo-Pak Kashmir border that had brought Aban into India became unfit for the seven infiltrators to enter unnoticed.

Each of them was a first time flier and their only experience with planes was that of watching those iron birds, streaking across the sky with open-mouthed wonder. They were handed their boarding passes and the agent motioned them to move on to the security check. One of them discovered that once they had stepped into security, they were on their own. The agent had abandoned them. As word spread across the group, each glanced nervously at the other. When asked to board the bus outside the boarding gate, most of them looked confusedly at their boarding passes. What kind of cheats were these bigwigs, who gave them tickets for a plane and were forcing them to make their journey on a bus! Cursing the thugs and feeling thoroughly cheated, the youths sat crestfallen in their seats. To their utter surprise, the bus stopped in front of the plane. "Allah be praised," they were finally on the plane, the Gulf Air flight number GF 765 from Lahore to Nepal via Bahrain.

They slipped into their respective seats of the economy class, deliberately choosing seats in different rows away from each other. While a few dozed off after some time, the others gazed at the landscape and sea from the windows. Yet others ogled at the beautiful airhostesses, whenever they found the opportunity. These perfect pictures of servitude were dedicated to them, completely at their beck and call. One starry eyed youth stared smilingly at one of the pert girls. He felt like a Sheikh in a harem, surrounded by doe-eyed, half covered, half unclad belles, who served wine as their hips swayed to the lilting background of Persian music. He drank deep from the divine beauty. "*Jannat* cannot be far away at this altitude." he thought to himself. Those whose eyes were blinded by these dazzling beauties, complained and grumbled, since the female flight crews were not in burqa.

But they all had one thing in common. Whenever a turbulent air pocket hit the aircraft, all of them screamed, without exception, in a chorus. Each one would clutch the seat handle tight and those who could, would start muttering prayers. "*Ya Allah! Yeh dua kubul kar. Hamari salamati barkarar rakh. Hamari hifazat tere hath mein. Humein mehfooz rakh. Humein dozakh ka bhagirdar na bana.*" (Oh God! Please accept our humble prayer. Keep us safe and protected. Our existence is in your hands. O Kind One! Send us not to Purgatory, that burning hell)

Those giddy with fear could only think that they were being punished for learning the rituals and the ways of the *kafirs*: the infidel Hindus, the pagans, the *butparasts,* the damned idol worshippers. Alas, they had been defiled and could not even hope for repentance!! Oh! Why did not the *khauf* of Allah, the wrath of God, deter them!

When the aircraft steadied, each one would send a thousand thanks to the Lord Almighty, to Allah the Great. "*La ilaha illallah Muhammadur Rasulullah. Allah-u-Akbar.*" (*In the name of Allah, We praise Him, seek His help and ask for His forgiveness. Whoever Allah guides, none can misguide…*)

Sumptuous food was yet another surprise for these first-time air-travelers. A few blinked at the male stewards and whispered in their ears, "If it is possible, *Janab* to slip in some wine?" "Absolutely, sir. No problem sir." The pat acquiescence was music to their ears. To these strapping Punjabi youth, the small servings of *biryani* simply served to whet their appetites in such a way that 'the giving famished the craving'. Some of them, therefore, quietly offered to pay a little extra for some more of the aromatic grains of rice.

The monotony of the vast Arabian Sea did not deter a few of them from continuously looking outside. These young men had no hunger because the persistent queasiness in their stomachs prevented them from thinking of anything, but the fact that they were thousands of feet in the air. They would have given anything to feel *terra firma* under their feet.

At the close of the day, the aircraft landed at Tribhuvan International Airport in Kathmandu. A bus was waiting for this medley mix of both happy and sad youth.

They mingled with the Hindu devotees, who were on a pilgrimage on the occasion of the Kumbh Mela.

An eight-hour drive took them to Birganj at the Indo-Nepal

border. The immigration officer checked their identity cards that made them residents of remote villages in Nepal. He chanted, "*Jai Sri Ram.*"

In a chorus, all seven responded, "*Sita Ram.*"

The Immigration officer smiled and casually allowed the bus to pass through the porous border. The Indian officers smiled at them when they started to sing *Bhajans* and *Kirtan* together. The bus dropped them off at the Raxaul railway station.

With the sure earth under their feet, they all felt reassured, and ate heartily at the local restaurant.

The Sadbhawana Express whistled and stopped at platform number one. All of them boarded the train, which slowly pulled up, chugging pleasantly towards the west.

Bengali Market

THE OFFICER OF the special unit saved the voice file of the conversations between Sundaram Iyer, Somashekhar Rao and Parag Nanda in a pen drive and hurried to Siddhartha's room. "Sir, I've stumbled upon something important."

After hearing the recorded voice, Siddhartha rang up the Lalit Intercontinental Hotel and contacted the butler. "Go to the reception and see if the same men arrive."

"What if they enter from other gate? There are many."

"Then go to the lift and see what happens."

"I can't be present at ten locations, sir."

"Let's hope for the best. Stay near the reception desk where I think they will pick up the keys to the room. Somehow you have to record the video images through your cell phone. I'll be there in half an hour."

"Got it, sir."

Siddhartha hung up. However, he was not aware that even

though the LeT could not track the Gold Lock protected call of Sundaram Iyer, they had been monitoring Somashekhar and Parag Nanda.

One of the LeT members contacted Hafiz Saeed and informed him about the meeting. LeT contacted a Maulana, who had just returned home after offering Namaz at Jama Masjid, and explained to him what was to be done.

Siddhartha reached the hotel entrance, but the hotel security stopped him. "What's the matter?" Siddhartha asked.

"Sir, something unfortunate has happened. A few gunmen entered the porch of the hotel and shot at two persons as soon as they got down from their car."

"Let me in."

"We can't, sir. The Delhi Police has cordoned off the area and they have asked us to ensure that no one enters or leaves."

Slightly away from the entry gate of the hotel, a car neared the exit, stopped for a few seconds, and sped towards the Bengali Market. Siddhartha reversed, made a turn, and accelerated. He turned right and reached the Copernicus roundabout. Seven roads radiated from that point.

Dubai to India

SHALIM AMĪR KHAN contacted his travel agent. His travel agent booked a first class ticket of Air Emirates on the Dubai-Delhi sector, scheduled for the late evening flight on 2nd April 2010.

Shalim Amīr Khan checked in at terminal-3 of Dubai International Airport, exclusively built for the use of Emirates Airline. The flight was on time and landed at New Delhi after three hours. Sundaram Iyer was waiting for him at the exit.

Sundaram went to Easycab, a taxi service and rented a car.

"I was trying to call you after I landed. Why isn't your phone working?"

"I have dumped all phones since they are under surveillance."

"But you said your phone was safe."

"That's true, but I'm not sure after the killing of Somashekhar and Parag."

"Oh! Perhaps they could not control their tongues. I think we can't take risks with the people talking a lot."

Sundaram nodded. "I suggest you switch off your cell phone too."

"No one in *Hindustān* knows about my number."

"But you made a mistake. You tried to call my number. We can't take any more risks." Sundaram Iyer took the cell phone and removed the battery. He opened the glove box of his car, "Take this phone. These are switched off and I've removed the batteries. Get it activated only after I have seen you off. I'll contact you from the public booth. I'll dial on this new number and hang up after three rings. Exactly after ten seconds, I'll call you and say that Citibank is offering car loans at a very low interest rate. And you'll reply, 'Don't disturb me' and then you will disconnect." Sundaram pulled out another phone and handed it over, "Now you will have the number of the public booth on the first phone, give me a call at the booth number using this second phone."

"Good. We have to tread very cautiously. We can't leave anything to chance." Shalim Amīr Khan kept quiet for some time. "Has the semtex reached its destination safely?"

"My artist from the Sunder Nagar handicraft shop has reworked the cast model of the Pyramids of Giza, the figurines and statues of Tutankhamen, Nefertiti and Cleopatra."

"Why?"

"You can sell Egyptian art to rich men of Delhi and Mumbai, but not to poor people of remote villages. So, I asked him to mould them into Hindu Gods and Goddesses. Then, I got it transported to our site. I have also asked a talented, but poor local artist to re-mold semtex once again into the shapes of the Indian Hill trout and mahseer fish."

"Oh Great! Where is our man Khalil Deek? Only he knows how to make these 'fish' swim."

"He is waiting for you at Maurya Sheraton Hotel."

"I have booked my stay at the Lalit Intercontinental. They offer corporate discounts to Hussein Pharma."

"There are too many enquiries going on ever since the killings. We can't take risks just to save a few thousand dollars."

The car reached Dhaula Kuan, took a loop flyover road to Sardar Patel Road and turned right to the hotel.

"Take back these two cell phones. I don't need them," said Shalim Amīr Khan.

"Why?"

"Were we not safer some seventeen years back, when our part of the world was without cell phones? We used to do our work more efficiently, without bothering to worry about who was listening to us all the time and who wasn't."

"Still, just in case I need to contact you."

"Mr. Sundaram, no questions. I've lived in the jungle all alone for forty days and climbed beyond the Hindukush Mountains without any radio communication. Whenever I wanted to talk to someone, I always found a way out."

"I don't trust my phones anymore. How will you contact me?"

"From this moment onward, I'm taking command of the *Hindustāni* operation. Keep in mind that we won't be contacting each other anymore. I also direct you not to contact anyone, even remotely associated with Tupac-II. Talking too much is dangerous and you know it."

Sundaram shivered. After a long silence, he asked, "What do I do then?"

"Nothing, but relax. Go to the hotel room and ask Khalil Deek to check out immediately. Tell him to see me at the New

Delhi railway station. Our train leaves before the day peeps through."

"Why are you leaving today? I have booked your air ticket for tomorrow's flight."

"*Hindustān* is a large country and the trains are crowded. I love the crowds when I move and a deserted place when I work."

"Should I cancel your booking in the hotel?"

"Why at all? You have paid for a two-day booking. Today is Saturday. You can relax for a few days in the hotel itself."

"Why don't you stay the night too and enjoy the company of the girl, waiting for you in the suite? She is very pretty. You will have a rather gala time."

"I'm completely loyal to my wife. No other woman exists for me."

"Tell me when will we be meeting then?"

"See me at the dam on D-day. We will watch the giant waves together."

Tracking

SIDDHARTHA RECEIVED A call from his special unit informing him that an unidentified international number had tried to call Sundaram Iyer's number from the Indira Gandhi International Airport. Siddhartha instructed the special unit to track the man with the help of the Air Intelligence Unit.

He had time since immigration would take at least an hour, even if someone had cleared the green channel. In the wee hours of the morning, when there was very light traffic on the road, Siddhartha drove to the airport and parked his car near the exit.

He saw Sundaram Iyer along with a man walking towards the rented cars. Who was the man so important that Sundaram Iyer himself was accompanying him? The tall man was wearing a hat, a dark glass and an overcoat even in the heat of April. The man continued walking with his tilted head and did not raise it even once.

Siddhartha was surprised to see the man's posture and gait.

He knew that photographing him would be of no value because recognition systems fail if a person drops his head at more than a thirteen-degree angle. These were techniques in which the people of intelligence and army were trained in. The man seemed to know all of this.

Siddhartha stood staring helplessly. He could not arrest anyone on the basis of suspicion. He could not even confront them, because if he did, it would put them on their guard. He was not even sure if Tupac-II was just a figment of imagination, never to materialize or something actually so big that would turn the course of history.

Siddhartha started to follow the car. He switched on the portable cell phone tracker machine and obtained the number of the man. The machine cloned the SIM card and started to catch the conversation between Sundaram Iyer and the mystery man. It continued to record till the signal went off. Siddhartha understood that someone had removed the battery and that the phone was as good as dead.

With no option left, he followed them into the Maurya Sheraton Hotel. Siddhartha waited for a few minutes and entered the hotel lobby. He saw both men walk up to the lift. When, they were out of sight, Siddhartha went to the reception desk and placed his identity card on the desk, "Which room did the two gentlemen go into? I need the keys of the room."

"To the Presidential suite on the top floor, sir. I'll get the keys from the manager."

Siddhartha nodded.

After a while, the receptionist walked back with the manager. "Sir, we cannot allow anyone to enter a guest's room without a warrant of authorization."

"Getting a warrant will take time and we are running really short of it. Try to understand that this is a matter of national security. "

"My apologies sir, but I'm bound by government directive. I have a copy of the circular from the Ministry of Home Affairs. One of the guidelines clearly mentions that under no circumstances can a stranger be allowed to enter restricted areas."

"I'm sorry, gentlemen. I'm here to breach government orders in the greater interest of the nation." Siddhartha turned and ran towards the lift before the hotel staff could react. The lift doors closed and Siddhartha made a swift ascent.

He ignored the footsteps on the top floors. He tried turning the door handle to open it. To his utter surprise, it gave way without resistance.

Sundaram Iyer smiled, pouring out scotch into his glass. "Welcome Siddhartha. I was expecting you."

"Where is the man who accompanied you?"

"I can't see anyone. But for your satisfaction, I suggest you check the adjoining rooms, and please don't forget the bathrooms."

The hotel staff, the security guards and the manager entered the suite. Sundaram Iyer spoke, "Well manager, nothing to worry about. Both of us are government servants and are on a mission, rather on the same mission. He is my guest."

When everyone left, Siddhartha asked, "How did you know I would be here?"

"Siddhartha, why do you forget that both of us are trained Class-One police officers? We know each other's way of working. Aren't we in the habit of sniffing out everything? It was not a big deal to realise that my phones were being tapped, that two guys were shadowing me, that a car had followed me all the way from the airport to this hotel? It was all too simple, my friend. I expected the cleverest officer of the Intelligence Bureau to come up with something more innovative."

Playing his cards close to his chest, Siddhartha responded, "Don't forget that I have proof."

"Oh Yes! Those stories of my visit to Chitral in Pakistan, my pleasure trip in a yacht in Dubai, and call transcriptions—they will surely stand scrutiny." His sarcasm was cutting. "How could you be so naïve, Rana? You will get ensnared in the warp and weft of the net of espionage, if you are not careful."

"I can still charge you for acting against national interest."

"Well, well, Siddhartha. Sounds quite convincing. Why don't you check the reports from Dubai and Pakistan that your friends in the FBI sent to R&AW? It's a pity that neither the FBI nor R&AW send the report to the IB, even though you asked for it. Isn't it ironic that our own intelligence agencies don't trust each other? The question is what will you do now? If you want the report from R&AW, it will take you a lot of time to overcome the bureaucratic hurdles and obtain a copy. I don't want you to suffer the agony of suspense. My dear friend, my Director sanctioned all of my foreign trips as official tours. I never went to Chitral. I was in Jordan at that time. I went to Dubai, but never left my hotel room."

"You cannot deny the call records," Siddhartha retorted.

"Oh! You're still stuck with the Kerala officer's phone. The poor guy died while fighting the Maoists. Brave, wasn't he? The CBI traced the shopkeeper of Kochi, who sold the phone to a Muslim immigrant in Dubai. Isn't it true that many Keralites go to Dubai in search of jobs? We traced the man, but unfortunately he had thrown away the phone and the old SIM card. He says that he got a brand new iPhone and a new 3G connection. We got his statement recorded. If you want, I'll certainly provide it to you."

"Then how has the phone continued to be active till a few days back?"

"Oh dear! Didn't I tell you that the missing phone of the Kerala officer was with an NRI Keralite? You know cloning of sim-cards is so easy nowadays. Many wives get their husband's sim-cards cloned to listen to what they talk with their girlfriends." Sundaram Iyer laughed, "I cloned my wife's phone only once. She is very boring. All that she can talk of is her children or gossip with her female friends. So, I threw the SIM card away after a few days. It isn't exciting if one can't flirt on the phone."

"But you do flirt with the country's enemies. Don't you?"

"Come on, Siddhartha. In our diplomatic world, there are no enemies. And friendship is a matter of convenience." Sundaram Iyer continued, "Let me complete what happened to the cloned sim-card. For your information, the CBI had registered a criminal case against the shopkeeper and an unknown person who had misused the cloned sim-card. I'll definitely let you know, when we find the unknown guy. The IB can then flirt with that guy." "Care for some drinks?"

"Thanks," Siddhartha stood up and reached for the door. He turned back swiftly, "Remember our training in the police academy, Mr. Iyer? Remember the famous paradigm, 'The enemy's enemy is a friend'? I relearned that 'The enemy's enemy may not necessarily be a friend, but the enemy's friend is almost always an enemy in this world." Siddhartha smiled. "I love a challenging enemy, but I will never have anything to do with an enemy's friend."

Constitutional Avenue

ABAN'S UNCLE REACHED Islamabad and sought an urgent appointment with the Prime Minister of Pakistan. Although the PM was to attend the Monday morning cabinet meeting at his Secretariat, he granted time to Aban's *Chacha Jaan*.

Chacha Jaan rented a cab and reached the grand residence of the PM at Constitutional Avenue. The staff at the reception escorted him to the living room. The PM came and shook hands with *Chacha Jaan*, "I think you have something very important to tell me."

"Mr. Prime Minister, I want a secluded place."

"You can speak here. We sweep for bugs every day."

"I'm afraid, Mr. Prime Minister. The bug sweepers are from the Army."

The PM looked at him for some time and asked him to come to the study. When *Chacha Jaan* explained what he knew, the Prime Minister was deeply disturbed. "Are you sure al Qaeda can pull off something as big as that?"

"I'm certain, Mr. Prime Minister. These are some of the photographs, which prove their recent activities."

"When did the semtex reach Karachi?"

"Two months back."

The Prime Minister watched some more photographs. "According to you, the diver and the submarine have already placed the explosives. But who is behind all this?"

"Saeed al-Masri, the financial chief of al Qaeda."

"Any news on Indian dam sites?"

"I cannot substantiate, but I have come to know that the semtex was sent from Port Said to Garudeshwar in Gujarat."

"Garudeshwar?"

"It's a very small town, near the Sardar Sarovar Dam. If we combine this information with the recent event of the assassination bid on the Chief Minister of Gujarat, there is a high probability that the dam might be sabotaged."

"What will anyone gain by doing this?"

"The hatred of the Muslim community for the Chief Minister of Gujarat is well known. Not only do Indian Muslims target him, but he is also under the radar of JeM, LeT and to some extent of the al Qaeda too. What is more perturbing is the LeT's stance. They think that the Hindus of Gujarat should also be taught a lesson for their blind support to the ruling party of Gujarat.

Chacha Jaan described the scenario of the dam break, in no uncertain terms.

"The Sardar Sarovar Dam broke. It inundated the fertile plain of south Gujarat while the wall of water moved at ferocious velocity; smashing, crushing and devouring everything in its path. The megaflood flowed half a mile above the tallest building and surged ahead to meet the Arabian Sea. All the cities of Southern Gujarat came under the deluge. The industrial belt of Vapi-Surat-Bharuch was ruined. The fertile land and green belt from Valsad to Vadodara became a wetland for many years. All major road and rail lines connecting Mumbai to Delhi got swamped, crippling the movement of goods from major ports of western India to north India. The canal supplying drinking and irrigation water to Ahmedabad and the Saurashtra region dried up forever."

"But there is a sizeable Muslim population too in Gujarat." The Prime Minister was perplexed.

"That's true, Mr. Prime Minister. But who cares for a handful of Muslims when it is a question of Jihad?"

The Prime Minister began to pace up and down the room. He lit a cigarette, brought it to his lips, but snuffed it out in the ashtray without even taking a drag.

Chacha Jaan handed over a few more photographs to the Prime Minister, "I've been tracking the al Qaeda movement to our nuclear sites. These photographs, which were picked up from an Air Force Base, are scary."

"So you think our nukes may be compromised too?"

"Absolutely, Mr. Prime Minister."

"Which Air Force Base is this one?"

"I don't know, Mr. Prime Minister. We need to find out."

The Prime Minister stopped to consider, "Pakistan is already under pressure from the USA to secure all nuclear weapons. They have offered to put PAL, the permissive action link in the nuclear warheads to eliminate chances of any unauthorized use. However, the Pakistani Army declined the offer, fearing that America may sabotage the nukes by remotely changing the electronic lock and thus turning them into nothing more than dummy warheads. We have been able to secure the warheads to some extent through the coded switch devices that we procured from America."

The Prime Minister sipped a glass of water. He continued to weigh the pros and cons, still pacing the floor. "The situation today is very complex. In case the Americans come to know about the possibility of our nukes falling into the hands of al Qaeda, the US might even launch a preemptive attack on Pakistani nuclear sites?" The Prime Minister was trying to find a solution to the conundrum. "It will be a bad strategy to involve America in this matter right now. Even though our efforts are fraught with tremendous risks, Pakistan will have to solve the dilemma on its own."

After mulling over it for a long time, the Prime Minister stood up and shook hands with *Chacha Jaan* once again, "I'll do whatever is best for our country."

Chacha Jaan left. The Prime Minister picked up his hot line and made a call.

Samadhi

SIDDHARTHA WORKED WITH his team for almost a week. On many occasions, he slept for only a few hours in his office. He compiled and scanned each and every clue and lead to Tupac-II.

Siddhartha became increasingly convinced that if the riddle of Tupac-II had to be solved, it only had to be through Aban's laptop and his father's watch.

The details he got from the FBI office in Dubai were not sufficient. The photograph and the video file of the four people in the yacht were grainy, even after enhancing them digitally. Siddhartha could not obtain much information except the height of the two unknown people. One silhouette seemed to match Sundaram Iyer's; another shadowy outline seemed to belong to the mystery man, who had come to India.

The discussions in the conference room of the yacht, which was bugged by the woman agent of the FBI, threw very little light on the actual course of events.

To analyze the technical aspects of the discussion in the yacht, Siddhartha invited a team of engineers. They could only decipher that a resonance in a pool can cause the successive rising of tidal waves with some destructive potential. That the effect of the biggest Tsunami could not break a strong dam in Italy was a fact confirmed by the best engineers. The effect was also termed harmless for a big dam. According to them, the biggest known damage caused by a seiche was the one, which created a ten feet wave in the Lake Michigan. It hit the Chicago waterfront, swept away eight fishermen and drowned them.

Two disturbing facts emerged. The first was the unnoticed oscillation of the reservoir of Koyna dam, which had created a highly destructive earthquake in the past. The second was the possibility of a water-pancake effect, which can be caused when a dam structure begins to resonate with the frequency of hammering tidal waves. Because of oscillation, the center of buoyancy of a huge water-mass can progressively shift both upward and downward. Resonance and shifting buoyancy could be a dangerous combination. The latter could cause the buoyant force of the water body to bob up and down. Every time the force hits the top portion of the dam, it will push it away towards the downstream and each time it will move down and affect the lower part of the dam, it will try to topple the dam towards the upstream side. A moving torque will be created. This will weaken different parts of the dam. The capacity of the dam to resist overturning, sliding and crushing at the toe will diminish with each passing minute. Finally, the dam will give way once the overturning force becomes more than the weight of the dam. In a worst-case scenario, an upheaval similar to Koyna dam might occur. No dam can withstand a high seismic surface acceleration and the dam will buckle under the pressure and give way.

But which dam? The question remained unanswered. The simulation of the actual dam under threat was not available to Siddhartha, since Somashekhar Rao had run that simulation on his laptop in the conference room of the yacht. Saeed Masri had prevented its transfer to even a remote server for complete confidentiality.

Another fact that caught Siddhartha's attention was the date assigned to the catastrophe. As discussed in the yacht, it had to be the the date of the death anniversary of the philosopher and sage Ramana Maharishi.

Siddhartha checked the date. It was 14th April. He picked up his pencil and encircled the date on his table calendar—14th April 2010 and scribbled "Place—???" in bold right next to the date.

There was another hint regarding the place—it was the place where a great saint had taken 'Water *Samadhi*', which is supposed to bring ultimate Nirvana.

Siddhartha searched through the lists of saints, who took *samadhi*. There were hundreds. A few important ones were: Saint Dnyaneshwar at Alandi, Nivrutti at Tryambakeshwar and others. But most of the places were not near any lake or river. Some were. The great saint and music composer Thyagaraja had attained *samadhi* on the banks of river Cauvery, Saint Eknath in the holy Ganges River and a few more.

One of the places that kept coming back to Siddhartha's attention—the temple of Vasudevanand Saraswati, was situated on the right bank of Narmada River at Garudeshwar, Gujarat. The Saint propagated the philosophy of respecting all religions.

He would instruct the Muslims to chant *Ayats*, the verses from Qur'an. Parsis visited him to receive grace. Before taking *samadhi*, he sat up, facing the Lord in the west, performed *tratak* (steady gaze), controlled his breath and quit the body with a loud chant of Om.

Siddhartha thought aloud, "Garudeshwar is hardly seven and half miles from the Sardar Sarovar Dam. All leads, including the consignment of semtex to Garudeshwar and the assassination bid on the Chief Minister of Gujarat points to this dam. He lifted the eraser and rubbed the question mark, put against the heading; 'Place' in the calendar and put 'Garudeshwar' against the blank.

He now scribbled 'SS', the abbreviation for Sardar Sarovar inside the date encircled—14th April 2010.

The game was on........

Part-III

U.S. President

THE PRIME MINISTER of Pakistan disconnected his hotline. He asked his secretary to contact the Chief of Staff of the White House and inform him that the Prime Minister needed to talk to the President of the United States.

Within half an hour, he received confirmation. The Prime Minister explained the gravity of the situation to the President.

"So, you think the al Qaeda may be involved."

"Indeed, Mr. President."

"What do you want us to do?"

"We would need the satellite images of the movement of the al Qaeda men in the area. Deployment of the US Special Operation commandos in select locations of Islamabad will also be required. The Marines, who are experts in underwater explosives, should be repositioned from the Gulf region. Drone attacks on the intruders is imperative."

"But your parliament has recently passed a resolution, condemning our drone attacks."

"You are aware of our government's limitations, Mr. President. We support the Allies War against al Qaeda, but we also need to address our constituencies, since public opinion is against the presence of Americans on Pakistani soil."

"Do you have a specific target in mind?"

"Yes, Mr. President. My source has provided me with accurate photographs."

"Anything else?"

"I want U.S. experts to bug my residence, office and the PM Secretariat."

"What?" The President could not believe his ears. It was perhaps the first time in the history of any sovereign country that the Head of Government of one country had asked another country to bug its most important office and residence.

Home Minister

THE HOME MINISTER of India called an emergency meeting of the different departments of intelligence: R&AW, IB, CBI, the Director General of Police of Gujarat, CISF and CRPF in the conference room of North Block. The Chief of the Armed Forces was a special invitee.

Siddhartha Rana accompanied the Director of IB. When he entered the conference room, he saw to his dismay, Sundaram Iyer shaking hands with the Home Secretary. Their eyes met. Sundaram smiled while Siddhartha squirmed in his seat.

The Home Minister started the discussion, "Gentleman, we have a grave situation. The Prime Minister has received information that terrorists from Pakistan and possibly al Qaeda have infiltrated India. They are all set on a mission to blow up a big dam in order to bring massive destruction to our country. We have concluded that Sardar Sarovar Dam may come under attack. We still don't know exactly when, but it may be sooner than we think." The Minister went on to explain about the leads and shared everything he knew.

The DGP of Gujarat could not stop himself any longer. He blurted out, "Sir, we've been pointing out this fact for a long time that Gujarat is not only on the Pakistani terrorist's radar, but also on that of the al Qaeda. And the problem is magnified because even Indian Muslims support al Qaeda and LeT. These flesh mongers have their guns trained not only for the destruction of Gujarat, but also plan to assassinate top politicians including the Chief Minister of Gujarat. Unfortunately, the Central Government has turned a blind eye to all our concerns." The DGP was really exasperated.

"Well, now we have Gujarat as our sole point of focus." The Home Secretary said drily.

"I need to convey the wishes of the Gujarat Chief Minister. He makes it very clear that if the Central Government continues to support the fundamentalists at the cost of the majority population, Gujarat is not going to cooperate." The DGP said with stubborn finality.

The Home Minister joined in, "We are not here to score points against each other. The nation stands above any state. As a top IPS officer, you are expected to keep your brief limited to security concerns and not dabble in politics." Sundaram Iyer almost rubbed his hands with glee.

"The Gujarat police forces have their own limitations. We may not be in a position to deploy sufficient police force at Sardar Sarovar."

"Why?"

"We have more than a dozen major dams to guard, and many other vital industrial installations. We face a perpetual threat from Muslim fundamentalists. How can we forget the attack on Akshardham Temple that led to major casualties?"

"Please get this clear in your head that we are a nation first." The Home Minister said firmly, "The CISF takes care of Sardar Sarovar. And the Central Government will deploy central forces at other sensitive locations."

The DG thought it fit to keep his mouth shut for the time being. The Home Minister continued, "Any more suggestions?"

Siddhartha raised his hand. The Minister nodded and Siddhartha spoke out, "Sir, my Director has already briefed you about everything we have come to know about the Tupac-II plot. However, I could decipher the date only an hour before this meeting."

"What date is it?"

"14th April." When Siddhartha said this, Sundaram Iyer shifted uneasily.

"14th April is just two days away." The Home Minister was obviously alarmed. He turned to the Director of CISF, "Has your unit noticed anything unusual at Sardar Sarovar in the last few days?"

"Sir, I've verified with the Deputy Commandant at Sardar Sarovar. There is nothing unusual except that some fishermen tried to reach near the dam. The patrolling party intercepted them and questioned them thoroughly. The DC said that the fishermen seemed to be innocent people from Garudeshwar, a small village near the dam."

"How long did they stay near the dam?"

"About two hours before our people sighted them."

"That's a pretty long time for anyone to dump explosives." Sundaram Iyer chipped in, "I suggest that the CISF carry out extensive sweeping for explosives around the lake, but more intensively at the toe of the dam."

The Director of R&AW was worried. He turned to the Home Minister, "Sir, you need to discuss the matter in the cabinet. We have already taken a stand after the Mumbai attack that if Pakistan is involved in any further attack on India, we will retaliate with all weapons at our disposal. Even the President of the United States supports our view. America is willing to attack inside Pakistan territory, if something like the Mumbai attacks originates from Pakistani soil."

"I can understand your point. Before coming to this meeting, we had a long discussion in the National Security Council meeting. The Foreign Minister doesn't subscribe to this philosophy. Moreover, we should not blame Pakistan if some non-state actor tries to do mischief."

"If the dam bursts, it won't be an innocuous mischief. The impending cost will be unimaginable. Our option in view of public opinion will be limited," Sundaram Iyer rejoined.

"Well Mr. Iyer, the government will decide the course of action. We have mechanisms to deal with such situation." The Home Minister turned to the Chief of the Armed Forces, "What is your assessment of the situation?"

"We have information about troop movement of Pakistani Armed Forces at our LOC and also at the Punjab and Rajasthan border. We tried to ascertain this with the Pakistan Chief, but he was evasive in his reply. Our Defence Minister has given us the go-ahead to match their strength. We have moved our army from the hinterland and put the Air Force and the Navy on maximum alert."

The Home Minister wondered how Siddhartha could

pinpoint the date of the impending attack and asked for an explanation.

"Sir, we tracked a yacht which sailed from Dubai. The agents of the FBI bugged the yacht and recorded the conversation that took place in the conference room. The participants talked about the date and the place of attack also. The date is confirmed and the place is the best possible guess according to the information available to the IB." Siddhartha said, and then turned to see the reaction of Sundaram Iyer. Sundaram was leaning on one side of his chair, staring at the floor blankly.

"See me in my chamber after the meeting." The Home Minister told Siddhartha and moved the motion that the meeting be adjourned.

Chaklala

THE WING COMMANDER at Chaklala, Rawalpindi, received an order from his superior to open three vaults at underground locations.

The officer followed the instructions and asked his men to follow him into a deep tunnel, leading to different underground facilities. Two fissile cores, two trigger devices and two implosion modules were loaded on to a mobile van and taken to the surface for assembly. Within two hours, the expert assembled two nuclear weapons of a hundred kilotons each. Another technician fitted the GPS enabled parachute and calibrated the destination, where the nuclear bombs would be dropped. These nuclear bombs were put in a capsule, fitted with two small rockets on its underside to ensure precise delivery of the bombs at the intended destination.

Ground staff placed everything into a waiting Dassault Falcon aircraft. Another technician removed the transponder of the aircraft so that it would fly undetected for many nautical miles.

From Moradabad

THE SEVEN JIHADISTS pretending to be Hindu devotees deboarded Sadbhawana Express at Moradabad, a small town in Uttar Pradesh. They had to wait in a dilapidated, dingy *dharamshala* till instructed to move further.

When the Jihadists got the signal to go ahead, they got into the general compartment of 2369, the Kumbh Express. They joined the group of men and women, singing and chanting devotional songs. A few of the onboard toddlers and children watched these strange worshippers curiously, while some of them would occasionally wail because of suffocation, caused by the throngs of people and the extreme summer heat. The slightly grown up and young kids were more interested in peanuts and the snacks which vendors sold at railway platforms. Every time the train stopped, they pleaded with their parents to buy something or the other.

The Indian Railways was operating many special trains from

different parts of the country to carry the devotees to the Kumbh Mela. All trains were running jam-packed and many people were left stranded on the platform, waiting to get lucky with the next train. Thousands of private bus operators and cab drivers were doing brisk business. More than a hundred thousand private cars were stuck in a several miles long traffic jam.

Three hours later, when the train was about to reach the destination, the devotees started to sing till their voices got hoarse and their lungs threatened to burst. The Jihadists too would stop for a few seconds, inhale and rejoin the chorus one more time, one more, and then again for one more time.

From the railway station, the Jihadists went to Har-ki-pauri. They ate heartily at a local food stall. Later, they decided to take a bath and what could be more refreshing than the fast flowing cool water of the Holy Jahnavi River. After a lot of bargaining and coaxing, they engaged a photographer, at a dirt-cheap price, to capture their photographs on the pavement. They all looked very pleased with themselves. Only one of them missed all the action, because ever since he had reached the *ghat*, he had been hit by a bout of dysentery. He could only stand in the long queue in front of the public lavatory, holding his stomach, looking at his friends from afar. The group moved on to the tiny shops in the narrow by-lanes to buy trinkets and little curios. One boy found the cheap steel bracelets and aluminum chains too costly as they were priced at five rupees each. He settled for a two rupee six inch, orange plastic trumpet with a green snout. He blew it loudly and waved the wand high in the air, signaling to the others to join him. They all seemed to have forgotten the purpose of their visit and got lost in the elevating air that enveloped the place. It was as if they were on vacation. The blue sky overhead and the swift current of the holy river seemed to infuse them with the same life energy as she did to devout Hindus and to everything else.

The photographer delivered their photos within an hour. Each one peered closely into them, excitingly pointing their own images. "I am here." "Hey, my eyes are closed." "I am looking so many shades fairer." "Look at the way this fool is crouching." They were full of comments.

It was time to buy bus tickets to the final destination that lay nestled in the mountain. In the overcrowded bus, five of these youths had to find a place on the bus rooftop, ducking and braving the slaps of the branches of the tall trees all along the four-hour journey. Two of them had to make do by holding tightly onto the narrow bars of the back ladder leading to the rooftop.

The bus stopped at the security post. The policemen casually checked the baggage of devotees and asked the driver of the bus to proceed.

With nothing much to do, the youths had dinner, spread out newspaper sheets on the bus station floor and fell asleep.

Before the crack of dawn, a man's voice commanded them to rise and shine. The next stop was to be the CISF office.

NIST

WHILE THE HOME MINISTER held a closed door meeting with the Director of the CBI, Siddhartha waited in the PA's room. When they were through, he went to see the Minister in his office. He further briefed the Minister about Tupac-II.

"Where is the boy, Aban?" The Minister enquired.

"He is at the guest house of the Army Cantonment."

"What about the daughter of the ambassador? Is she with Aban?"

"No, sir. She went to the Indian Council of Forest Research and Education in Dehradun for the billion-tree campaign. But we have information that she has come back to Delhi to spend some time with her father."

"Isn't Pakistan aware of Aban's whereabouts?"

"They are, sir. Hafiz Saeed came to know about Aban's trip to Ajmer and Pushkar with Juhi. Gunshots were fired at him when he was coming back to his hotel. Since we were guarding him, our men somehow took control of the situation. After the incident, we thought it fit to hide him till we got to the bottom of Tupac-II. And Aban is doing his best to solve the riddle."

"Still the contents of his laptop are as elusive as ever."

"Yes, sir."

"I talked to the Secretary of Commerce at your behest during my last visit to the USA. I requested NIST to help us to break the image password. Even though they could not decipher the Amaru Tupac-II file as they could not find the images to fit the 2X2 grid, they did come up with a definite conclusion. Three image password files are in uncompressed format and should be the size of 480 X 360, each of about thirty-three kilobytes, with the same hue, saturation, colour temperatures etc, which will reveal the mystery. Surprisingly, the fourth image is panoramic."

Siddhartha Rana listened in rapt attention.

"Well, I have some good news for you. Our R&AW Agents penetrated the office of the new ISI Chief and got hold of three image files of similar descriptions. I have them with me. Perhaps, these three are the first three images, which will help to crack the password." The Home Minister handed Siddhartha a pen drive. "The fourth, however, is still missing."

"Sir." Siddhartha said, and then stood up, intending to leave.

"Sit down, Siddhartha. I want to tell you something else."

"Sir."

"Certain facts have come up about this gentleman Sundaram Iyer. A few days back, we got information that he was up to some mischief. He seems to have gone on a wire-tapping spree without prior sanction of my Ministry. Not only has he bugged phones of the cases he was handling, but also yours and mine. He has even dared to wiretap the phone of a few Cabinet

Ministers and senior bureaucrats. Worst of all, he even intruded upon the National Security Advisor last week. R&AW has found his overseas connection and the Enforcement Directorate has unearthed details of his foreign banks accounts in tax-havens. "

"I'm also aware of his dubious role, sir, but my hands are tied for lack of concrete evidence." Siddartha went on to explain everything he knew about Sundaram Iyer.

The Minister was incensed. He said, "Now we have conclusive proof against him. So I've asked the Director of the CBI to suspend this man pending a departmental enquiry."

"Sir, I've another suggestion. Let's not do anything for the time being."

"Why?"

"If he is working for the Jihadists, he is an important link for us. Any knee jerk reaction could be disastrous as they will smell a rat and get alert. We still have two days' time, but hasty action may leave us with no time at all."

"What should we do then?"

"Let the Director CBI pretend before Sundaram Iyer that he is not aware of anything and watch closely how Sundaram plays his cards."

The Minister agreed. He asked his PA to connect his telephone line to the Director of the CBI. After a brief conversation, the Minister turned to Siddhartha, "We've bad news. The Director says that Sundaram has faxed a two-day casual leave application to his office."

"Where is he?"

"The Director says that he tried to contact Mr. Iyer, but his phones are switched off. He left his official car at North Block after our meeting."

"Let me try his home number," Siddhartha dialed and talked to Sundaram's wife. She told Siddhartha that she was not aware of her husband's whereabouts and that her daughter and she were going to Kerala by the evening flight to spend their summer vacation."

That set Siddhartha thinking. He turned to the Minister, "It's quite surprising, sir. Sundaram's daughter studies in the Delhi Public School and she is in the same class as my son. Their exams commenced today, yet they are leaving."

Deputy Commandant

IN THE MIDDLE of the night, the office of the Central Industrial Security Force received a message from the Ministry of Home Affairs. The officer on duty rang up the Deputy Commandant's residence and informed him about the fax message.

The DC drove his official car from his residence and reached his office in five minutes. He looked at the fax message, which had instructions to elevate security to maximum level around the dam site and the reservoir.

The security guard entered the room of the DC, saluted and snapped in attention. When the DC nodded, he said that an officer of 108 Rapid Action Force Alpha platoon wanted to see him.

"Send him in."

A man entered, "Sir, my command office has asked for the deployment of additional force for the security of the dam." The man handed a letter to the DC. "Our Commandant is at

Cham, at the upstream of the river. He has asked you to convene a meeting of your officers at seven in the morning. He wants to take stock of your preparedness. But before that he wants to see the security arrangement around the reservoir. If you could depute your officer to accompany him, it would be easier for us."

"At this time of the morning," the DC said, " I've my doubts that I can spare any officer. Anyway, I will give him a quick tour."

The Deputy Commandant rode his vehicle with the man on NH94 and sped towards Cham. A SUV coming from the other side crossed the bridge and steered slightly left blocking the DC's vehicle. Before the DC could react, four people surrounded his vehicle. They pointed their gun at him and asked the DC to come out of the vehicle.

Another man walked towards the DC with powerful strides. When the man came closer, the officer was taken aback. He was his exact clone! The clone addressed the DC in measured tones, "Officer, from now on, I'm the Deputy Commandant of your CISF unit. Give me your vehicle key and the keys to the vault of your office. I'll take proper care of your installation."

"How can he speak in my voice and style?" The DC looked bewildered.

"Well, well, you must be astonished at my appearance, officer. I not only speak as you speak, but also think as you think. I even know each of your family members, about your grand-grandfather as well as grandchildren and of course, the name of your dog. Sorry to say my men injected a heavy dose of sedatives in his veins because he would have recognized me and I needed to guard myself. But you need not worry; he will wake up by tomorrow afternoon. He will live long."

"What do you want?"

"Revenge, officer, revenge!"

"I don't know you. I have never seen you before."

"I would never avenge a personal grudge, officer. But when a country slaughters another country, I take it personally, very personally."

"What are you talking about?"

"The pain inflicted on my country when your country split my country into two will always keep our wounds green."

"Are you from Pakistan?"

"I belong to none except Allah, brother."

"What's the point in talking about the painful stories of history? Indians too never overcame the pain of partition."

"Partition was destiny, my dear, but the 1971 War was never our destiny. The war was imposed upon us. I can still feel the pain when your men divided my country. That pain never leaves me. Tell me what should I do?"

"I still don't know who you are."

"I too am searching for the answer to the existential question, 'Who am I?' But I certainly know why Allah sends his men to bear suffering in this world. He sent me to fulfill a cause, and that was to take revenge."

"But..."

"No questions." Shalim Amīr Khan turned to his men, "Take everything from him. "

The men disarmed the DC. Two of them started to drag the officer towards the river, but Shalim Amīr Khan stopped them. "When I reached this place, I had no place to hide. I went there and stayed the night," Shalim Amīr Khan said, pointing to the Shiva Temple, about a mile north of the reservoir at Killu Khaal. "There is no one there except the God guarding both mountain and gorge. Even the priest has left the *mandir* and gone for the *Shahi Snaan* on this auspicious day. There is a small antechamber with heavy iron doors at the back of the temple. The rusted handles of the door do not seem to have been opened for eons. When I touched it, the doors opened with a long squeaking sound as the rings on it made a loud clang. Worried that someone had heard the strange sound, I waited. When all remained quiet for a long time, I entered the dark room. The place was full of an almost palpable, though invisible energy. And even though I was thirsty and exhausted, I felt rejuvenated within minutes.

"Take the officer there. He who looks after all of us, will take care of everything. Put him in handcuffs, but don't seal his mouth. Leave dry fruits and water beside him. The priest will come back by evening. Oh! Yes, don't forget to take one more precaution. Administer a soothing tranquilizer to him. He needs to sleep for twenty-four hours. He will not endure the pain of isolation."

Turning to the DC, Shalim Amīr Khan continued, "My sincere apologies to you, sir. You are an honest officer and I honour the trait. Unfortunately, today, my choices are limited. But I promise you that if I live to see tomorrow's dawn, I will come back. You may then choose to punish me for my deed."

Shalim Amīr Khan turned and reached the official vehicle. His men proudly occupied the back seat. He entered the car and adjusted the rearview mirror. Nearby, on a dusty road, the SUV climbed over a mountain in the opposite direction quickly moving towards the north.

Shalim Amīr Khan pressed the pedal, crossed the bridge, steered at the bend and accelerated.

Their Mad Life

A CONTROL ROOM was setup in the North Block. The Home Minister authorized Siddhartha Rana to take every possible measure to save Sardar Sarovar Dam and report the progress to the Home Secretary.

The Joint Secretary of the Department of Internal Security with other officials boarded a special aircraft to Vadodara, Gujarat. They travelled further, about sixty miles from the airport, to the dam.

Siddhartha called Aban from the North Block and told him about the three image files that the Home Minister had given him. He uploaded those files to a newly created email account. Aban downloaded the file.

"We still need to search the fourth image," said Siddhartha.

"When will you be back in your IB Office? I need to know everything that you can tell me about Tupac-II because I have a hunch that there might be a clue in those details."

"The work in the control room of the North Block keeps me from my office until tomorrow afternoon."

"Will see you then."

For the entire day and night, Siddhartha stayed in the control room, arranging logistics for the security of the Sardar Sarovar Dam: the explosives experts, divers from the Navy, intelligence officers, engineers and the officials of the hydro power project. He also coordinated with the anti terrorist squad and the CISF office.

It was late evening the next day, but he still could not get time to go to his own office. The systems expert rang him up, "Sir, I need you to be present here in the IB Office. We have decoded the *rashis of Jyotish*, sent by the FBI."

Siddhartha rushed to his office and entered his room. Aban and the system expert were waiting for him. Siddhartha turned to Aban, "I think you could use some sleep."

"I have been trying to work out the solution ever since you provided me with the three images."

"Any progress?"

"I'm sorry. I've used thousands of combinations to arrive at the fourth image, but still nothing."

Siddhartha moved his gaze to the systems expert, "Tell me how did you decrypt the elusive attachment file?"

"The pdf file attachment shows many symbols. I tried to decode through normal decoding, but nothing came out of that. These Jihadists always come up with some innovative idea or the other. They are always a step ahead of us. Therefore, I tried to think the way they think. The answer was to look at the problem in the simplest way. I took a printout, scanned it and saved it as a document. I ran the optical character recognition program with pre-selected fonts. Nothing came out when I chose the English and Roman fonts. Then, I tried Indian fonts like Mangla. Still, without success. Then, I searched for the fonts relating to astrology as the symbols represented rashis. Finally, I got the answer. When I set the OCR to read the Astrology font, the symbol turned into Arabic language with phonetic and thematic structure. I used my computer translator and got a clear message."

"Absolutely wonderful." Siddhartha was delighted. "Show it to me."

"Sir, first look at the symbols once again." The expert unfolded the sheet paper.

"The Arabic version seems to have carefully maintained the rhymed form, as if an Oracle was delivering the sounds with profound effect." The system expert clicked on the version:

.حققنامراقبةبحيرةبهم
.وسوفتكونالبياناتجاهزةللمحاكاة
.نحنبحاجةللعملعلىعددقليلمنالأشياء
.الفترة،والتردد،المرحلة،اتساعالحركةالتوافقيةالبسيطة

He then ran the translator. "Now see the converted message in English, derived from the combination of mystical *rashis*, numinous *Jyotish and* magical Arabic."

We have made a surveillance of their Lake.
The data will be ready for the simulation.
We need to work out a few things.
Period, frequency, phase, amplitude of simple harmonic motion.

He continued, "Sir, each of the four lines contains eight words. Unfortunately, it does not represent the image password."

"That's true. However, this is a very important file. The last line is interesting. They are talking about period, frequency, phase and amplitude of simple harmonic motion. During my last discussion with the engineers and technical experts when we were analyzing the data sent by the FBI from Dubai, the most worrisome fact was the lake moving in a simple harmonic motion."

Aban was worried. "We still don't know which lake they are talking about."

Siddhartha tried to assuage his fears, "Most probably, it is the Sardar Sarovar."

"Are we doing something to prevent the sabotage?"

"Yes, we are. Our team of underwater explosives experts,

divers, engineers and the anti-terrorist squad have already started the operation."

"Have they found anything?"

"They are trying. But the lake is huge. They could not do much during the night. They say that it'll take another day to declare the lake completely sanitized. We may come to know about it by tomorrow evening."

"How much time do we have?"

"There is the possibility that the dam on target is not Sardar Sarovar. In that case, if we get to know the exact status of Sardar Sarovar only by tomorrow, then perhaps we will be left with no time." Siddhartha's words hung over in the office like an ominous cloud.

Siddhartha continued to look at the last line. The word 'Simple Harmonic Motion' mocked at him in the same way as the subject line of the email—'Their Mad Life'.

"I hope I'm not going mad," Siddhartha drank a glass of water and turned to Aban, "I know the date, but still don't know the place."

Mother's Ashes

A CAR WAS STRUCK in the traffic snarl near Roorkee. Long queues of buses, private vehicles, trucks were all lined up, waiting for the traffic police to clear the logjam.

Juhi asked her father, "Why did you choose today, the 14th of April, for the immersion of Mom's ashes?"

"I could not come to India when your mother died three years ago since the Prime Minister of India was on an official visit to the US. Even after we came back to India after my retirement, I waited for this day since 14th April is the most pious day of *Kumbh*. Today is the *Mesha Sankranti*. On this date, the sun rests at the equator for the whole day. The *Vishu*, our Vedic calendar says that on this date, the sun starts its *Uttarayana*, the northward journey. The saints celebrate the day as the beginning of the New Year. So, I chose this date."

"But why did you choose the occasion of Kumbh?

"To understand this, you need to know the origin of Kumbh.

At the time of the mythological *Samudramanthan,* when the gods and the demons churned the primordial sea, a golden pot emerged along with many other treasures from the belly of the *samudra.* This pot called *Kalash,* contained divine nectar, which could make anyone immortal. A fierce battle took place between the gods and the demons as they quarreled over who should have the pot of nectar. The demons being stronger than the gods took possession of the golden pot or *Kumbha.* So, Vishnu disguised as *Mohini,* or the beautiful enchantress, lured the demons into giving her the pot of the elixir of immortality. Vishnu started distributing the nectar to the gods, but one of the demons realized that they had been tricked and alerted the other *Asuras.* Immediately, the demons rose up in battle against the gods and one of the gods, *Indra's* son, ran away with the golden pot. This skirmish lasted twelve days, corresponding to twelve human years after which the *Kumbh Mela* is held. During the fierce battle, four drops of the nectar fell in four different places—Haridwar, Prayag, Ujjain and Nasik, and took the form of four holy rivers: the Ganga, the Yamuna, the Shipra and the Godavari. Ever since then, it is believed that whoever takes a dip in these rivers during *Kumbh* or the special celestial configuration, is absolved of all sins and blessed by the Almighty.

"What ritual will we perform there?"

"We will take a dip in the sacred Ganges and then scatter her ashes in the holy water."

The traffic ahead had not moved much. The Ambassador turned to Juhi, "I think we should have some light refreshment."

"It would be better we check-in into the hotel and then have some tea. I'd packed pastries and patties for you. You can have them in the car."

"You must be tired after driving all the way from Delhi."

"I'm fine."

"Still Juhi, a half hour break will do us no harm. Steer left. There is a very nice multi cuisine restaurant Fuzion. I love the vegetarian *tandoori* fare they serve at this place."

"How do you know about it?"

"Your mother and I used to stop by whenever we planned a trip to these parts."

Juhi slowly turned the Mahindra Xylo to the porch of the hotel. The restaurant was full, and the manager asked them to take the garden seats. Snacks were served after a while. Juhi had gone silent and the Ambassador did not know how to start a conversation.

"Do you still miss your mother?"

Juhi nodded.

The Ambassador continued, "She was a wonderful woman. I miss her every day, each moment. She wanted you to be a doctor. But I never interfered with your dream when you chose to pursue environmental studies. I want you to be happy. I love you and cannot bear tears in your eyes. Ever since you have come back from America, you have not been your cheerful self."

Juhi kept nodding.

"Your grandfather was an army officer, who fought both World Wars for the British Empire. When I qualified for the Indian Foreign Service, he was on cloud nine. I joined the LBS Academy at Mussoorie as probationer and every time, I came home, my mother would pester me to marry this beautiful girl, who was studying medicine. When I finally told her that I was in love with another girl, she was still happy. When I told my parents that the girl I had fallen for was a Christian, my mother, though not very happy, was still willing to compromise for the sake of my happiness. But my father was dead against the relationship. I tried to convince him, but finally succumbed to his emotional blackmail and married the girl of his choice. For a long time, I could not accept your mother as my wife. I even refused to take her to Buenos Aires, when I was posted in the Indian Embassy in Argentina. She was too evolved a person and too strong to do anything about my audacity, even though she disliked it. When I realized what she truly was, I began to feel small." The Ambassador fell silent.

"Will the story of two love birds come to an end?" Juhi stared blankly to a dimly lit lamppost for long time. A while later, she turned to her father, "Do you still love your first love?"

"Yes. I do."

"Do you want me to forget my first love?"

"No, my sweetheart. Not at all. I don't want to repeat the same mistake your grandfather did because it just results in wasting years in the lives of two people."

Both father and daughter kept quiet for a very long time.

"Where is Aban?"

Roosevelt Dam

SIDDHARTHA RANG ROBERT McLEAN, "We have decoded the file 'Their Mad Life'. It talks about the surveillance of a lake and some simulation details -- *Period, frequency, phase, amplitude of simple harmonic motion.*"

"I'm afraid, Siddhartha, this is a very dangerous situation. In fact, our counterterrorist experts have known for many years that al Qaeda has been preparing to attack big dams. They possess photographs and notes of the target locations in the USA. Even more chilling are the disturbing facts that have come up with our military findings in Kabul. They have seized a computer from an al Qaeda office, which has models of a dam that has been created using structural architecture and engineering software. The simulation, attached to the file, is about the catastrophic failure of a big dam. However, we cannot identify any specific dam, which might be their target. The simulation is the proof of their complete preparedness and not a mere feasibility study.

They have engineers, who use Microstran and AutoCAD with complete mastery. So, obviously they have advanced software for analyzing steel and concrete structures and classifying rocks and soils. They can conjure up architectural designs in three dimensions like a magician with a flourish of a wand. In fact, the simulation shows precise calculations of how a wall of tidal water, surging downstream, can bring an unimaginable catastrophe.

"Have you run the simulation, transposing it on a real-life dam?"

"Yes we have. We took help of Aban's project and chose the Roosevelt Dam to see the results of simulation. The hydrological engineers told us that this dam backs the largest man made reservoir, holding gallons of water. What I saw was beyond imagination."

Robert McLean described the details like a movie was playing in front of his very eyes.

The Roosevelt Dam broke. It swept off the city of Phoenix from the map of America. Scottsdale, Mesa, Chandler, Glendale and many other nearby cities got inundated, killing millions. The entire area, being saucer like with no water outlet was a disaster waiting to happen. Once the area got submerged, the water did not drain out for years. Nothing could be done for decades except for people to pray that the water would evaporate quickly.

"Still, the breaching of a dam requires massive explosives, and in all likelihood, a big dam will withstand most shockwaves."

"That's true, but technology today can enable a person to breach anything from cyberspace, even if he has never seen the place. A twelve-year-old boy, sitting thousands of miles away, hacked into the SCADA system, which runs Roosevelt Dam and opened the massive floodgates. If this could happen a decade back, think of the possibilities that the technology of today can unleash."

CISF Office

THE SEVEN JIHADISTS burned all their clothes: *angavastram, dhoti,* turban and any attire resembling Hindu dress. They offered *Namaz* and proudly got into their new olive green uniforms of the 108 Rapid Action Force Alpha platoon, the Indian Commandos. The shining badge, the embossed insignia, the black shining boot, -- all of them were a perfect replica of the uniform of the Alpha Platoon. They drove an SUV mounted with a red beacon light and siren straight to the CISF office.

Shalim Amīr Khan entered the Deputy Commandant's chamber with the air of a man who owned the place. He retrieved the CISF security deployment map of the dam and the reservoir. He called the radio operator and asked him to change the frequency 138.225 MHz of the VSAT antenna, atop the temporary shed on the far side of the hill. Shalim Amīr Khan smiled to himself, because he knew that even if the *Hindustāni* Intelligence jammed all other frequencies in the event of an emergency caused by an attack on the dam, they could not block this particular frequency, since it was the disaster relief operation channel.

Little did the Indians know that the same lifesaving frequency channel could turn into a life-threatening medium at the hands of Shalim Amīr Khan!

As soon as the frequency changed, the timer device of the massive explosives underneath the three big hills started their pre-determined countdown.

Shalim Amīr Khan called the Assistant Commandant and discussed the fax received from the Ministry of Home Affairs. "The reinforcements from the Alpha Platoon have arrived and are waiting in the adjacent room. Since they are experts at anti-sabotage operations, they will guard the sensitive locations around the reservoir and dam."

"But sir, the protocol of redeployment needs approval from the office of the Director General in Delhi."

"I've already briefed him over the phone regarding this fax message. He will send the formal approval as soon as he reaches office."

"But sir…"

"No questions."

The officer nodded and left the room. The redeployment was done within an hour. The majority of the CISF Security personnel were deployed at the most unimportant places: Machine Hall, Bus-Duct Gallery, Diversion Tunnels and the Computerized Control Room. All strategic positions were reserved for Jihadist control.

While four Jihadists took control of the diversion tunnels T1 to T4, another went to the surveillance room, adjacent to the Computerized Control Room. The room monitored the entire dam and reservoir site by video camera, fitted at different locations. Real-time video data was captured and sent to a centralized computer server. An inbuilt program pinpointed any perceptible change and would trigger off an alarm if any suspicious activity were captured.

The Jihadist took charge of the equipment. He pulled out a DVD from his pocket and loaded a new program into the server. As soon he had done so, the monitor began to screen data captured a year back, instead of giving real time output.

The technicians sitting in front of the monitor could not detect the change. They stared at the monitor showing the shoals of fish swimming and algae clinging tightly to the wall of the dam wearing a thoroughly bored look.

Khalil Deek, the explosive expert reached the office of the CISF and straightway went to the room of the Deputy Commandant.

"Good you are not late." Shalim Amīr Khan smiled.

"I had to survey all four diversion tunnels. They were dug so many years back that they are now overgrown with grass leaves and covered by foliage. These tunnels run into miles, and are sealed by concrete lining with steel reinforcements at the reservoir side. Stone, earth and concrete linings cap the dry side of the downstream. So, it is a prerequisite to calculate the precise timing and the placement of semtex for the plan to work perfectly."

"We don't have much time. You'll need to place them quickly."

"My device is ready. I only have to enter the diversion tunnel one by one. Within eight hours, my work will be done. The system that I've designed will work simultaneously in all four diversion tunnels. When the first semtex explodes, it will blast off the seals on the reservoir side. Water will gush inside, filling up all four tunnels. Precisely at that moment, the second firing of the powerful semtex will push the water outwards into the lake with a tremendous unidirectional force. It will create an underwater wave of three metres, albeit imperceptible on the surface. This will travel rapidly to the opposite side. Then your roles come into play. As soon as the water strikes the hill, which is five miles from the dam, you will explode the first hill using your remote. A massive amount of soil, earth, trees and stones will suddenly fall into the reservoir. This will amplify the underwater waves and simultaneously create a surface wave of thirty metres. The wave will return, rushing towards the dam. Since the reservoir rests on the canyon, which narrows down as it progresses towards the dam side, the water will go higher and higher in height, creating a huge wave front."

He continued, "When the wave will return to the dam, my explosives inside the diversion tunnel will explode, again amplifying the underwater wave. This combination of underwater wave by the semtex explosion in the diversion tunnel and surface water wave caused by the landslide will continue to grow."

The description continued:

"In this stage, we will allow billions of gallons of heaving water to move to and fro in simple harmonic motion for thirty minutes. You will not blast any of the hills during this time. The world has seen the greatest elemental display of fireworks in the thunderous eruption of fire-spewing volcanoes; it has witnessed the biggest craters created by thudding meteor impacts, it has watched tidal wave fronts and devastating tsunamis; the world has also beheld swirling tornadoes that have whipped up cattle and human dwellings like twigs in the air. Now imagine the scene when the gargantuan body of the water of this lake will begin to sway like a mammoth in a state of *masth*. Such a water show has never happened in history and it will be the greatest that man will ever see."

Almost at the point of exhaustion, he continued giving details:

"After half an hour, when the wave reaches the far side of the dam, you will explode the hill on the left side of the tributary. The surface water will grow to one hundred metres while the strong underwater currents of the wave underneath the surface will gain immense power. Phase three will be a repeat of the preceding phase. The only difference will be that the height of the water, rushing towards the dam, will grow beyond imagination."

After listening with rapt attention, Shalim said, "Not even God or the Biblical times have created such a phenomenon on earth. The forty days of incessant rain, which caused Noah's Arc to float in the bubbling Mediterranean, was probably nothing compared to what the last forty minutes of this show will be." However, a little doubt crept into his mind, "What if the wave still does not break the dam?"

Khalil Deek laughed. "I'm going to open the hatch covers of the diversion tunnels. But where is your diver and submarine? It's time they placed the explosives at the toes of the dam."

"I want you to do one more thing."

"At your service."

Shalim Amīr Khan handed a jacket to Khalil Deek. "Spare a small amount of semtex for making a transparent lining on the inner side of this jacket and put a timer so that it explodes only when it touches water."

"Oh! That's very simple. A very thin metallic tube, almost invisible to the naked eyes, with the wire connector at its two ends will act as a trigger. We all know how well water conducts electricity. As soon as the water enters the tube, the circuit will be complete and the button cell will charge the miniature capacitor inside the jacket. A tiny pulse will ignite a miniscule fire that will be sufficient to blow up the semtex."

"Wonderful!"

"Do you want to wear it, sir?" Khalil Deek smiled sheepishly.

"I have an honourable guest to do the honours."

Drone

A FEW YEARS AGO, a sleepy village Kotgala, in the North West Frontier province of Pakistan, on the left bank of the Indus River was severely affected during an earthquake. Death and destruction had turned this village into a ghost town. The few of them, who survived went to Lahore and Karachi to eke out a livelihood. Government officials took no interest in reviving a dying village and so the victims and saviours alike forgot about it.

However, an old man and his daughter continued to live in a small hut.

They hosted a small group of people who offered the old man a few thousand rupees and a promise of more. He never suspected that the burly men, who came to the village in an ambulance, painted with the Red Cross sign, were from the al Qaeda. He happily did everything the guests asked of him. The daughter prepared delicious meals and served steaming, aromatic *Kahwa* whenever the men demanded.

After offering evening *namaz*, all of them got into the ambulance and sped off on the Karakoram Highway. The cleverly hidden boxes of RDX and mortar went undetected with them.

Instead of crossing the Youi Bridge on the Indus River, the ambulance climbed a rugged mountain and then descended on to the banks of the river. A speedboat was waiting for them.

In the sky, invisible to eyes on the ground, an American Drone picked up the location of the ambulance, painted the target and fired its missile.

A blinding flash lit up the entire area. Within seconds the ambulance was torn into smithereens. Charred bones and flesh scattered all over the place. The mortar and RDX, kept in the vehicle, turned to dust. A small portion of it fell into the Indus River with a small splash.

The high-resolution video camera of the Drone captured everything and relayed it to the Command Centre.

The speedboat laden with explosives and mortars sped away towards the dam. The Marine commando fixed the crosswire on the boat captain and triggered the sniper rifle. The boat lost control and exploded after a while.

Another Marine commando recorded everything and activated his 3G systems on camera. He uploaded it to the Command Centre before the sky darkened once again.

Landing at Rawalpindi

THE **USAF C-17** Globemaster declared full emergency over the Pakistani AFB (Air Force Base) at Rawalpindi, Islamabad, asking for immediate priority landing. Permission was granted and the ATC cleared the runway.

The Globemaster taxied to a remote area of the tarmac. Two shipment trucks, labelled 'United Nations Organization' neared the aircraft. Weapons and gears were unloaded on to the trucks that headed for Constitutional Avenue. They drove into the National Library of Pakistan, opposite the Prime Minister's Secretariat. Once again, the unloading of weapons and gears started.

Two hours later, a United Airlines Plane from New York landed at Benazir Bhutto International Airport. The passengers, who were US Special Army Personnel in plainclothes, deplaned and boarded the waiting bus, which took them to a building, opposite the Indian High Commission Office in Islamabad.

They formed small groups and crept into the National Library in the dead of night. They got into uniform, picked up the weapon and entered the Prime Minister's Secretariat, positioning themselves at vital exit points and other strategic locations.

The Central Control Room, set up earlier on the first floor of the residence of the Prime Minister of Pakistan captured the movement of the US Special Army Personnel and informed the Prime Minister.

Another team, which had already bugged the entire perimeter, was left with the last job of installing small concealed video cameras, a big-sized LCD monitors and state-of-the-art audio-video device for the next show.

Fitting

THE STEALTH SUBMARINE had been working silently in the reservoir for the entire week without surfacing even once. It had profiled the contours of the entire bottom surface of the lake. This data was fed in the computer of Khalil Deek to determine the exact timing of the successive blasts of the explosives.

A night before, the submarine had dived near the dam, reaching maximum depth. Semtex, molded in the shape of Indian Hill trout and *mahseer* fish, were tied to the submarine's tail end with wafer thin transparent glass strings.

When the winding rotor of the submarine activated, it slowly pulled at the strings. The semtex floating and swimming on the surface of the water as a shoal of fish dived and followed the predetermined path. When the 'shoal' reached close to the submarine, the autopilot activated the robotic arm, isolating the 'semtex fish' from one another and patched them at pre-calculated gaps on the entire one-kilometre stretch of the toes of the dam.

Although the semtex would not blow the dam on its own, Khalil Deek was to time the precise moment at which the semtex would explode. This would happen when the massive underwater wave and the surface wave would strike together with full force.

While the humongous wave force would cause the dam to overturn, slide and get crushed, the semtex would cause the liquefaction of the soil. Even a slight liquefaction can cause dam failure because the gooey soil beneath the dam begins to act like a greasy lubricant, dislodging the dam from its very foundations. This had been proved by the case of the Lower San Fernando Dam in California.

The rest of the job lay on the shoulders of the diver, who came from Her Majesty's Naval Base in the United Kingdom. He would connect the semtex with electrical wiring, fit the capacitors, set up the blast caps, adjust the actuator and trim the timer like a master musician preparing his instrument in order to play.

Sardar Sarovar

THE JOINT SECRETARY, overseeing the operation at Sardar Sarovar, rang up Siddhartha, "We have checked the entire dam but have not found anything that indicates sabotage or a terror operation. I think we should wind up the operation."

"Please ask the team to check all the dams on the upstream of the Narmada River and also the dams in the adjoining area. We absolutely have to be on guard."

"It's going to be the small hours. We can start it only after daybreak. In fact, I'm not even sure if we have any time left, if you say that the date is today, the 14th of April, because that day is already here."

"I'm dead sure about the date. But, the place can be any dam of Gujarat, if it is not the Sardar Sarovar."

When the talk ended, Aban, who was listening, asked Siddhartha, "How did you deduce the date and place?"

Siddhartha told him about the conversation among the four

men in the yacht that had sailed from Dubai. One of the men, still unidentified, had said that the date of ultimate destruction would be the one when the great philosopher-saint Ramana Maharishi died. He also alluded to another great saint, who took *samadhi* in water to attain the ultimate nirvana."

"How did you zero in on Sardar Sarovar on the basis of this information?"

"Well, we had some more information. We learnt about the plans to assassinate the Chief Minister of Gujarat. Then, a consignment of semtex was dispatched from Egypt to the small village of Garudeshwar, which is only a few miles away from Sardar Sarovar. At this place, the famous Saint Vasudevanand Saraswati took *samadhi*."

"Did Saint Vasudevanand Saraswati undertake *samadhi* in the Narmada River?"

"Why do you ask?"

"Because the unknown man in the yacht talked about *samadhi* in water."

"Now that you mention it, Vasudevanand Saraswati didn't take *samadhi* in the Narmada River. Oh my god! How could I have overlooked such a vital point?" The horror of the sudden realization struck Siddhartha like a lightening bolt.

"I know about a Saint, who took *samadhi* in the Bhagirathi River." Aban said.

"Who is that?"

"Swami Ram Tirtha."

"How do you know about him?"

"My father studied in Foreman Christian College in Lahore. Swamiji was a mathematics scholar and a professor in his college. He was a member of the Undergraduate Mathematics society.

The society and all its members still revere Swamiji."

"So?"

"Even my father, who was a devout Muslim respected Swamiji for his mathematical genius. There is still a photograph of Swamiji in his study. He told me that Swamiji once met Swami Vivekananda in Lahore and was so impressed with the latter's philosophy that he decided to become a *sannyasi*. Swami Ram Tirtha went to a small town, where he attained enlightenment on the banks of the Bhagirathi. Swamiji also wrote a book on practical Vedanta, which won great acclaim. The people of the Himalayas loved to listen to his discourses and would throng around him every day until one day Swamiji withdrew completely from public life. He moved to the foothills and began to spend all his time in solitary meditation. A few years later, on the day of *Deepawali*, he gave up his body in the Ganges. In other words, he undertook water *samadhi*."

Siddhartha had been listening to the story intently. He continued to gape at Aban even after he had finished. He pondered for a long time. "What images are we using as the password to unlock the file Túpac Amaru II?"

"All three image passwords show catastrophes caused by unbridled water. The first image is that of the Banqiao Reservoir of China, the failure of which had caused more casualties than ever recorded in history due to water. The second is the image of a breaking St. Francis Dam of the USA. The last image is that of the deluge called Johnson Flood, created by the failure of the South Fork dam.

"Interesting! The first image shows a reservoir, the second a dam and the third a deluge, but all three speak of unprecedented devastation and all are caused by the force of water."

Aban waited.

"Dear god, Aban. Both of us have missed something that has been staring us in the face for a long time and is of such utmost importance that it can spell life or death. The fourth image that will crack open the file," Siddhartha leaned forward and said, "…is the image, which adorns the wall of your father's study. It is Swami Ram Tirtha."

"Oh my god!" Aban held his head in his hands and ran his finger through his hair in exasperation, "I have lost count of the number of times I've gone into my father's study in search of a clue to explain the Mumbai attacks and his mysterious death. Every time I've glanced at Swamiji's photo, I have missed its import." A wisp of doubt crossed Aban's mind. Did his father really intend such unprecedented destruction of human life or did he at the bottom of his heart want to save the very same people he was killing, if he got what he really wanted?

Aban pressed the enter button of his laptop, which flickered into life out of its sleep mode. He searched for an image file of Swami Ram Tirtha on the Internet and selected one with 480X 360 dimensions. It had also the required size of thirty-three kilobytes. With a few manipulations in the Aperture software, he matched the colour, contrast, definition, hue, resolution, shadow, sharpness, saturation, tint, temperature and exact RGB numerical value of the new picture with the other three image files. The image with a perfect matching histogram was saved in the hard disk of his laptop.

Aban opened the mysterious Túpac Amaru II file and placed the three pre-identified image passwords on to the grid. With trembling hands, he dragged the last image on to the grid.

Open Sesame!

The flash player started showing an animation of a huge reservoir behind a dam. The dam collapsed and the resulting deluge surged and drowned everything in its path. As soon as the film ended, the mysterious Amaru opened up.

The details of the deadly plan of Tupac-II were now available in front of the two men. Everything starting from its initiation inside the mountain cave of Chitral, the film developed in the film studio of Mumbai, the procurement and dispatch of semtex, the diver from Plymouth and the submarine from Russia -- everything was as clear as day. The black hearts of the AIG, Somashekhar, Parag and Sundaram Iyer lay exposed for everybody to see.

Both Siddhartha and Aban had somewhat guessed the place where Tupac-II would unleash its fury, but they were walking a tightrope, which left no room for error. Their conjecture, although intelligent, was something, which was too little and had come too late.

Time was running out......

PTV

A TRAGIC TRAVESTY comes up every time Western Intelligence reports establish a link between terrorist activities and Pakistan. Pakistan throws up her hands helplessly or sits down in complete denial.

One such incident was that of American born Adam Pearlman, who had inherited both Christianity and Judaism. However, in the late '90s, he converted to Islam at a mosque in California with a lot of fanfare and rechristened himself as Adam Yahiye Gadahn.

He also denounced Christianity. According to him, the apocalyptic ramblings of Evangelical Christianity were paranoid and hollow. Fed up with American liberal society, he moved to Pakistan and married an Afghan refugee girl. However, he maintained contact with his parents for a few years. He lied to them that he was a journalist in the Pakistani media.

Impressed with the ideology of al Qaeda, Adam Yahiye

Gadahn became their propagandist. He wrote profusely in blogs, claiming to be a cultural interpreter, spokesman and media advisor for the al Qaeda.

A few months earlier, he had released a video, entitled 'A Call to Arms', asking Muslims to be prepared to play their due role in responding to and repelling the aggression of the enemies of Islam. *"Choose high-value targets, such as military installments and mass transportation systems, as well as symbols of capitalism whose ruin could cripple their economy. Rise up to the occasion and take action to clinch this once-in-a-lifetime opportunity to reap the rewards of jihad and martyrdom. So, unsheathe your sword and rush to take your rightful place among the defiant champions of Islam."*

The anchor of the Pakistan Television Corporation News channel was also indoctrinated into the ways of Jihad. Adam Yahiye Gadahn had rewarded him handsomely with two hundred thousand U.S. dollars and an assurance from a top Air Force official that the government, including the Federal Minister for Information and Broadcasting, would not touch him. All that the anchor needed to do was to relay a breaking-news at 08:15 am on the appointed date.

In the early morning hours of 14th April, the TV anchor received the expected phone call from Adam Yahiye Gadahn. "I've uploaded two video files to your media-server. The first is my message. Run it half an hour before the final show. The final show has a cipher key, which I'll provide fifteen seconds before it starts."

"I'll do it. Can I see your message before running it?"

"Why not?"

When the phone disconnected, the anchor ran the file.

Adam Yahiye Gadahn, with his cold look, started to speak softly, "My dear fellow Islamic brothers, recall what Mohammed ibn Abdullah preached to us. His call of duty reminds us to do everything possible to slay the non-believer…" His speech continued for ten minutes. The real tone and tenor of his tirade were reserved for the last few minutes, "So, dear friends, we have finally launched our holy plan to slay the *'Kafirs'*—the *Hindustāni*. The satanic *Hindustāni* Government will attack our country of Pakistan in retaliation and our coward government will turn a blind eye to their unpardonable crime. They are scared of *Hindustān*. So, you all have to rise up in arms and wipe out the enemy, using every resource that you have. My last and final call is to our valiant army. Brothers, you alone can save our motherland. So, roar like the lion and devour these goats…"

The message stopped.

Samadhi

"Swami Ram Tirtha took *samadhi* in the Bhagirathi River," Siddhartha thought for a long time. He rang up the office of the Deputy Commandant of Tehri.

Shalim Amīr Khan answered the phone, "Yes sir, as per the instruction of the Ministry of Home Affairs, we have deployed the 108 RAF Alpha platoon at sensitive locations and secured a few more sensitive places by redeploying the security officials of my CISF unit."

"Anything unusual?"

"Nothing, sir. Everything is fine."

"Report to me immediately in case you find anything suspicious."

"Sir." The line went dead.

Aban overheard the entire conversation. He asked Siddhartha, "Does the date 14th April have some special significance?"

"Yes. Today is the *Mesha Sankranti,* a very important date for Hindus."

"What do they do?"

"They bathe in the holy rivers and offer *puja* to deities."

"Would you expect a big congregation of devotees or long queues of people at particular places?"

"Yes. We do. The Haridwar Puja Officer is expecting more than ten million devotees to visit the place during the day."

"Ten million!" Aban was surprised with the number. "Is it that important an occasion?"

"Yes. It's one of the most important days of the 2010 *Kumbh*. It is said that bathing during this particular time will absolve the devotee of all sins and the devotee will then attain salvation." Siddhartha explained everything about the *Kumbh* to Aban. He asked, "Why do you ask?"

"I don't know. But ten million people gathered at the banks of one river and the location of Tehri Dam in the upstream of the same river seem to be somewhat connected."

"I just talked to the Deputy Commandant of Tehri. He is satisfied as there is nothing unusual at the dam site."

"I'm not sure, but let me access the simulation of my father's program again. I would like to compare the dam in the simulation with images of the Tehri Dam, the reservoir and the contours of the hills to find out if the two are the same."

"There is one more thing. We have another file named 'Their Mad Life' from the FBI. But it talks only about some surveillance of a dam and about some Simple Harmonic Motion of the Lake."

"Could you please repeat the name of the file?"

"Their Mad Life."

"Their Mad Life," Aban repeated the name many times in his mind, trying to find some method in the madness. "Oh my god!

Just rearrange every word. Life become File, Mad become Dam and lastly 'Their' is nothing but Tehri. So, 'Their Mad Life' is an anagram of 'Tehri Dam File'."

Siddhartha was shocked as the rearranged 'Tehri Dam File' mocked at him. He turned to Aban, "Dear god! Time has truly run out for us."

"Just wait a second." Aban once again reached the Tupac-II file and closed it. He double clicked the file to reopen it and dragged all four-image passwords on to the grid. The flash player started showing the collapse of a dam, followed by a Megaflood. He compared the flash image of the Tehri reservoir, Tehri Dam and the downstream of the Bhagirathi River with the Google Earth images of the same.

"Their target is Tehri. It is nothing else, but Tehri."

Aban immediately superimposed the simulation data with MBT, the Main Boundary Thrust in the Central Himalayan Seismic Gap and other rupture lines of the mighty Himalayan Range. He did a few quick calculations and shut down his MacBook. He got up in one swift movement, "Let's go."

"Not you, Aban. I can't risk your life anymore."

"I have nothing to lose, Siddhartha and in any case, the issue here is much bigger than either you or me."

"What about Juhi?"

"We haven't been in touch for the last several months."

Aban's cell phone rang. "Aban? Juhi here. I have to come to you. We need to talk."

"I'm in Delhi. But I'm going somewhere," Aban was too dazed by the events that had just unfolded to say anything more than that.

"I'm dying to see you, darling, but it will be sometime before we can reunite. My father and I are on our way to Haridwar to immerse my mother's ashes..."

Before Juhi could utter other word, Aban screamed into the phone, "Where are you right now?"

"About to reach Har-ki-pauri."

"Juhi, Leave the place immediately and go right away to Dehradun. Climb up the Himalayas as fast as you can and reach Mussoorie."

"What's got into you? Why do you sound so paranoid? And why on earth should I climb up the Himalayas?"

When Juhi did not seem to understand, Aban blurted out, "If Tupac-II materializes, nothing will remain in Haridwar."

"Did you have a bad dream? Will you please explain what you are talking about?"

"Go away. Run for your life."

"Aban, you are scaring me now! Are the LeT after your life and mine? I'm here to immerse my mother's ashes and I won't go anywhere unless I have done that."

"It's Tehri, Juhi. Listen to what I'm trying to tell you. It's Tehri Dam. The dam may not withstand the most devious conspiracy ever hatched in human history." Aban explained everything briefly.

"Are you in Tehri?" Juhi sounded worried.

"No. But I'm going there."

"Do you remember you asked me many times about what I wished for at Ajmer Sharif Dargāh? I declined each time since I believe that a *mannat* is never told to the person, who is dearest to one. But the time has come when I should tell you. I prayed to Salim Chisti Ji to bless me that even if I did not get you in this life, I would wait for you in the lives to come. I do not fear death as long as you are with me. I'm coming to Tehri."

"No. You won't. The water wall will wash everyone away, before they can reach even the doorstep of Tehri."

"Who cares when dad has permitted me to chase you till the edge of the world! I'm willing to follow you in the yonder world too."

Dive

THE DIVER SURFACED on the far side of the Tehri Lake and took off his mask. He smiled at Shalim Amīr Khan and flashed a thumbs up sign, "Mission accomplished!"

"Great! Why don't you remove your SCUBA?"

The diver removed the suit and handed over a remote control device to Shalim Amīr Khan, "I've put in the blast cap, and adjusted the actuator."

"There is no abort button on this remote?" Shalim Amīr Khan looked surprised.

"Yes. I had instructions to make it a never-fail system."

"Give me the schematic diagram of the placement of the charge."

"I can't."

"Why?"

"I'm not authorized."

"Do as I say. I'm in control of this operation."

"You do not control me."

Shalim Amīr Khan was furious, "Then who controls you?"

"al Qaeda."

"So it's their plan to blow up everything, even if the Government concedes to our demands."

"I know nothing about that."

"Do you know who in the al Qaeda controls you?"

"Indeed. Saeed al-Masri. He has promised me an incentive. al Qaeda will pay me double."

"You don't seem to understand Saeed al-Masri's language. Try to get this straight. This is the al Qaeda that you are working for. They never leave a trail behind. The 'double payment' is nothing but a honey trap to lure you back to their den, where they will pump two bullets into you and do away with the whole story of the gallant scuba driver who once worked for Her Majesty. Think. I have kept my promise and simply on trust paid you in full even before you started the work. Had your al Qaeda friends trusted you, they would have done something similar."

Quietly, the diver pulled out the schematic diagram from his inner pocket, handed it over to Shalim Amīr Khan and walked away, a wiser man.

Shalim Amīr Khan wore the SCUBA and dived deep into the lake.

NSG

SIDDHARTHA TALKED TO the Home Minister and explained the new situation. The bewildered Minister asked, "But you said that the Deputy Commandant was confident that there was nothing unusual."

"That is what is more worrying. I want commandos to be airlifted right now to Tehri. They will para drop on the mountain side and approach the dam very cautiously, without raising any alarm to avoid panic reaction among the Jihadists."

"We've already deployed hundreds of commandos in Delhi in view of the upcoming Commonwealth Games. I'm not even sure that I can spare any. Moreover, even if I somehow arrange for the commandos, we are too hard pressed for time. The NSG, based at the Indira Gandhi Airport, will need at least two hours to reach, and two hours to climb the mountain to reach the dam."

"Aban and I are on our way to Tehri," Siddhartha informed the Minister.

"What do you hope to achieve by going there?"

"Aban has a watch which will perhaps help us save the dam."

"How will you ever reach there on time?"

"Neither Aban nor I are trained to paradrop. So, we cannot accompany the commandos in their aircraft. We will have to look for something else."

"Take my helicopter. Will you require anything else?"

"We cannot evacuate millions of people from Haridwar. It's impossible. Please talk to the Chief Minister of Uttarakhand to evacuate people from Har-ki-pauri and other bathing places on the Ganges without any delay."

"That's another heck of a problem. There will be chaos and many lives will be lost in the stampede that is sure to occur if such an order is given."

"The police in Haridwar will not be informed of the reason. I'll ask my IB officer at Haridwar to contact the Heads of a few *Akharas* just now. It's common for them to fight amongst each other for the *Shahisnaan*, the royal bath. They will do the same thing, this time too. The police will then cordon off the entire area, disallowing anyone to take a dip until the matter is resolved."

"Is there any loose end that we need to tie up?"

"Yes sir. We will need the Air Force Base in Dehradun to be ready with very powerful explosives. We will also require the radio frequencies of the fighter jets when they reach the destination so that we can communicate to coordinate our action."

"What? Are you talking about explosives?" The Home Minister sounded jaded. "Powerful explosives can blow up the dam. Definitely not save it. Correct me if it's otherwise."

"Aban has something more in his MacBook. I've seen it and

it is beyond anyone's imagination. I'll explain to you later, sir. Please trust me on this one and have this done."

"I'll have to talk to the Defence Minister. Let me correct myself. We need to brief the Prime Minister about this entirely baffling turn of events."

Flying from Chaklala

IN THE DEAD of night when everyone was asleep in Pakistan, the Dassault Falcon aircraft with two nuclear warheads took off from the Chaklala Air Defense Command in Rawalpindi.

After flying east for a hundred miles towards India, it suddenly turned to Lahore. A few miles before the city, the pilot ejected one of the bombs.

The parachute opened; the GPS calculated the position and fired a small booster rocket from the capsule. The parachute slowed down on its descent and the capsule floated into *Anderoon Shehr*, the walled city of Lahore. It dropped with a thud and five persons immediately surrounded the delivery from the sky. They carried it to a shop near Bhati Gate in a hand driven cart. They lifted the shutter and moved the bomb to an underground chamber.

The same aircraft turned northeast towards the tribal area of North Waziristan.

One of the Saabs AWACS aircrafts, flying near South Waziristan, picked up the signature of the Dassault Falcon. It immediately connected to the captain on the radio, directing him to return to the nearest Air Force Base.

When the captain ignored the instruction and bent the throttle instead, an F-16B took off from the Sargodha AFB, locked the target and fired the missile on the Dassault Falcon.

However, before the missile could hit the Dassault, the captain released the hatch opening without bothering to activate the parachute. The capsule carrying the nuclear bomb fell freely and hit the sand bed where the Domal River joined the Zhob River.

Except for a little tribal girl, no one saw anything unusual falling from the sky and none heard the sound of the deep impact.

The impact created a deep vertical depression, which was quickly filled by quick sand, concealing the deadly nuclear weapon in its womb.

Repentance

SHALIM AMĪR KHAN resurfaced from the lake after two hours. Khalil Deek was waiting for him, "We are getting late. We should initiate the pre-defined procedure within half an hour."

"I know, but a few important things need to be worked out first." Shalim Amīr Khan walked towards his vehicle. The man's hands and legs were tied up and tapes sealed his mouth. Shalim Amīr Khan asked one of his men to free him.

Sundaram Iyer fumed at Shalim Amīr Khan, "This is what is expected from a Pakistani bastard."

"This is what I do to every traitor. A traitor has no nationality."

"Shut up. I did everything you told me to do. I even put my high-profile job at stake. Do you know how powerful the Joint Director of the CBI is?"

"That is why you are a traitor. Am I wrong?"

"So you were behind the cold blooded murders of the AIG, Somashekhar Rao and Parag Nanda?"

"Only you can answer this question. Why did you keep in touch with al Qaeda even though I asked you not to share anything with them? Why did you trust Saeed al Masri? I know the answer is money, money and money and nothing else."

"Do you know what will happen to you, if you do this to me?"

"Only He Knows."

"Are you hare-brained?"

"Hold your breath, Mr. Iyer. You'll need all the air in your lungs. It's your type, who has sold the world to the devil. Neither ideology nor faith drives your kind. You are simply a worshipper of Mammon."

"What do you want from me?"

"I want you to repent."

"Repent for what?"

"No questions." Shalim Amīr Khan walked away.

His men forced the semtex-lined jacket on to Sundaram Iyer.

"You can't do this to me. I'll get drowned. Be afraid of Allah."

"It will just be a spark, Mr. Iyer."

The Prime Minister

THE HOME MINISTER visited Panchavati, the official residence of the Prime Minister of India at 7 Race Course Road. The Defence Minister, the Foreign Minister, National Security Advisor and Air Chief Marshal were already present.

The Minister explained the latest situation about the possible terrorist attack at the new location, Tehri. The Prime Minister said, "A few days back, I had a long talk with the PM of Pakistan. He is apprehensive that the al Qaeda is up to something big."

The Home Minister responded, "As per our intelligence source, the LeT and a few rogue elements of the ISI are also involved in this matter."

The Foreign Minister, who was a very seasoned politician, cut in, "It may have been true in the past, but the present democratic government of Pakistan does not approve of any hostile act against India."

The Defence Minister joined in, "What's your perception?" He turned to the Air Chief Marshal.

"I talked to our Army General. As per our military intelligence, the Pakistani army has not de-escalated the situation at the border, in spite of the flag meeting. Our Army General has been trying to contact his Pakistani counterpart but to no avail. Instead of strengthening their forces on the Afghanistan border, as the Americans would want them to, they are moving their forces to the Indo-Pak border."

The Principal Secretary walked inside the room, "Excuse me Mr. Prime Minister. But we seem to be on the brink of some grave danger. We have just received a courier, containing a DVD, entitled 'Save *Hindustān* if you can'. We ran the DVD before bringing the matter to your attention. It also says that a man from Tehri will contact you at 08:15 hours, exactly ten minutes from now. I think everyone should have a look at it."

"Can't we wait till our meeting is over?"

"I'm afraid not."

The Prime Minister nodded and the Principal Secretary switched on both the DVD player and a plasma TV. The video file began to run.

Shalim Amīr Khan stood in the backdrop of a reservoir, surrounded by high mountains, "*Adab,* Mr. Prime Minister and the honourable members, watching this brief documentary. I won't take much of your valuable time and keep you in suspended animation. However, I'll ask you only two questions—What pleasure did you derive by liberating Bangladesh and who gave you the right to take away the pride of Pakistan? Try to find out the answers while you watch the next show. Open your eyes. This is not Sardar Sarovar, where you have been trying to find us. Look closely. I'm presenting Tehri Dam before the august audience."

The scene cut to disclaimer, which mentioned that the show was not real, but a realistic simulation of what would happen.

The text image of the disclaimer dissolved slowly and the beautiful and serene Tehri Reservoir appeared on the screen. A commentary described the catchment area, the reservoir, the two rivers Bhagirathi and Bhilangana, Tehri and Koteshwar Dam, Hydel Power Stations and the holy city of Deoprayag, Rishikesh and Haridwar.

The wave of the water in the reservoir started gaining height. A hill collapsed and the wave rose higher and higher. The bridge on the Bhilangana River collapsed without much ado. It hit the dam which crumbled like a coconut cookie.

A wall of water, several thousand feet in height, surged ahead, uprooting everything that came in its path. It gained more and more height and momentum as it traversed the narrow canyon. When it reached Deoprayag, the gigantic pressure of the wave pushed the water of Alaknanda River ten miles backwards. The small town of Deoprayag vanished from the map.

The water continued to travel in a zigzag canyon and hit Rishikesh. Within no time, all temples and buildings, even at high elevation were flattened out like pancakes. The wall of water carrying dense slurry, mud, trees, logs, gigantic boulders, bridges and entire buildings rumbled, tumbling forth with tremendous momentum before reaching Haridwar. As the water followed the zigzag path of the narrow canyon, the waters behind the wall turned into rapidly moving vortices.

The scene cut sharply to the city of Haridwar.

Millions of people flocked at different *Ghats* to take a holy dip in the waters. The arterial road leading to Haridwar was jammed with incoming traffic for many miles while a sea of devotees covered the narrow by-lanes.

Suddenly, a half a kilometre high water wave, moving at great speed, overwhelmed the entire landscape. Nothing remained of the city, but a flat mud-plain.

The water oozed out devouring Saharanpur, Meerut, Muzzaffarnagar, Ghaziabad, East Delhi, Hapur, Agra, Kanpur and many towns and cities one after the other. The fury of the river continued further to the major cities of Allahabad, Varanasi and Patna, uprooting every barrage, bridge and road in its life-quenching wake. It crushed Farraka Dam in West Bengal and the water diverted into two parts. One went to Bangladesh and the other to Kolkata.

The scene cut once again to show the after effects of the great deluge.

The wild water had carved out wide *gullies* and *nullahs*. It had stripped off the entire fertile topsoil, turning the place into a wasteland. At some places, the water logging in huge pools turned these places into permanent wetlands. Heavy boulders and stones, carried from the Himalayas, were dispersed all across the Gangetic Plain, as if some demon had lifted them off from the mountains and hurled them at the plains below. The gigantic vortices had dug several hundred feet deep wells. The entire place was in complete disarray. Order displaced by complete chaos. Health had given way to pestilence. The once incense-perfumed Ghats of the Ganga reeked of rotting man and matter. What seemed unchanged in this changed world order was the course of the River Ganges, which flowed unperturbed, though quiet.

The movie stopped and static frames popped out:

Death toll—Twenty Million,

Economic cost—3.5 trillion dollars,

Time to recover—Twenty years, or God only knows.

The movie restarted and Shalim Amīr Khan made a reappearance, "Your Excellency, you must be wondering why I sent you a simulation before the real story, which will start exactly at 08:47. You will ask me a question, what do I want? Well I will answer the first one. I want you to get a feel of things to come, since many of you may not live to see it. As for the second question, "What do I want? The phone will ring in your room, Honourable Prime Minister. I'll answer your question then."

The phone rang just then. The Prime Minister picked it up, "What do you want?"

Assistant Commander

THE **NSG** COMMANDOS initiated Operation Cactus-II. Forty miles south east of Tehri Dam, they jumped from the rear cargo door of the Ilyushin II-76 Jet. A few dropped right into the valley, while the strong mountain winds pushed some of them further away. An hour later, all of them assembled at Molnau, about fourteen miles east of the Tehri Dam.

The Assistant Commander asked them to load their SIG weapons, the Laser Designator, the Advance Audio Communication Set, GPS device and other gadgets into the vehicle.

The vehicle crossed many hills and mountains and it took an hour to reach the left bank of the Tehri Reservoir. They got down half a mile before the dam and crawled over the mountain, overlooking the dam. They took their respective positions while the AC inspected the area with his binoculars. There was nothing to be suspicious about. He asked his commandos to descend the mountain and try to reach the dam and report thereafter.

Suddenly, his attention was drawn towards a helicopter, landing on the right side of the reservoir. He trained his binoculars once again.

Two men stepped out of the helicopter and ran towards the Dam. His Commandos locked the crosswire of their IMI Galil sniper on the two men. One of them said, "Sir, target engaged. Waiting for orders."

The AC raised his hand and increased the gain of his binocular, "Hold on. I think I know one of the men." He strained his brain, "Oh! He is Siddhartha Rana, the Joint Director of Intelligence Bureau. I met him during the meeting on the Mumbai attacks. But what the hell is he doing here?"

He got the answer, when his audio communication set caught a signal. "Listen very carefully, commander. I'm Siddhartha Rana on your communication line. I've orders for you from the Home Minister."

"What order, sir?" The AC was perplexed.

"We don't have to act in haste since the Government of India still doesn't know the purpose of the Jihadists."

"They have only one aim, Sir. They want to destroy India."

"Still hold your position. The Prime Minister of India is aware of the situation. He wants to negotiate. So, let's wait."

"But I need to send my men to the opposite side of the dam; the side where you are standing."

"Don't send them." Siddhartha thought for some time. "Is your unit carrying any Mini Remotely Operated Vehicles?"

"Yes, sir. We have very advanced Unmanned Ground Vehicle."

"Well, send one of them to the dam. And give me the frequency of your UGV. I want to listen to everything that goes on there."

The commando activated the UGV and placed it on the mountain slope. The UGV started to map the contours of the terrain. It descended the mountain slope, maneuvered onto the dam wall just above the surface of water, stopped to catch a human voice, rotated in the direction of the sound and finally, climbed the wall two feet below the edge. The actuator became active and an optical fibre cable slid out. The sound receiver at the end of the cable started to catch a conversation.

"What are you listening to?" a soft female voice came from the back.

"How did you find us, Juhi?" Aban whirled around astonished.

"The heart has its ways that reason does not know."

Demand

"I WANT PEACE between Pakistan and *Hindustān*," Shalim Amīr Khan said in a very soft tone.

The Prime Minister of India was surprised. "We also want permanent peace with all our neighbours including Pakistan."

"Aha! Permanent peace!" Shalim Amīr Khan laughed and then quickly changed his tone to a stentorian voice, "Mr. Prime Minister, my apologies. But your country has never done anything to establish permanent peace with Pakistan."

"We have tried a lot and are still doing enough to thaw the ice."

"Don't play a cat and mouse game. Give us permanent peace. Give our people peace."

"What do you propose?"

"Plebiscite!"

"What?"

"Don't shut your eyes and ears, Mr. Prime Minister. You

know as well as I do what plebiscite is. I want the people of Kashmir to decide their destiny. A plebiscite in Kashmir is my demand."

"Try to understand. It's too complicated. We followed the Simla agreement in the right spirit. Unfortunately Pakistan never did."

"I know what your agreement did to us. I know what it did to me."

"Listen…"

"No questions. Call a press conference and declare that in view of international peace and for the cherished brotherhood with Pakistan, *Hindustān* will hold plebiscite in Kashmir within a month from today."

"It's not possible to take such an important decision without talking to my cabinet colleagues, the Leader of the Opposition and other political parties. We have to take Parliament and our people into confidence. As on today, no one will agree to your proposal."

"Forget about the others. Do you agree?"

"I don't."

"Stop me if you can. Stop a small seiche from turning into a giant."

"Listen, please."

"No questions." The line went dead.

Initiation

SIDDHARTHA, ABAN AND Juhi listened to the tense conversation between Shalim Amīr Khan and the Prime Minister.

Aban turned to Juhi thoughtfully and repeated the phrase, "No questions."

"What?"

"I'm disturbed with the repetition of the phrase 'No questions'."

"It's very common in our part of the continent."

"I know. Still…" Aban was thinking aloud, "Can he be? But the voice is so different. How could he?"

Suddenly a thunderous explosion shook the earth. The semtex in the four diversion tunnels removed the sealing cap. The water rushed inside. The second explosion in the tunnel pushed the water outward towards the lake. The harmless seiche of the lake, swaying in tranquility now gained momentum.

"Oh God! He has initiated his operation!," Siddhartha broke into a cold sweat. "Who can stop him now?"

"But where is he?" Aban was frightened and very anxious.

Siddhartha trained his binoculars and pointed his hand. "He is there, standing on the dam, holding something like a remote control device."

Aban looked at the dam. He asked Siddhartha to lend him his binoculars, "I want to see who he is."

The underwater wave surged ahead and reached a small hill on the far side of the dam. Another explosion on the hill shook the earth. The hill crumbled and a huge mass of earth, forest, timber, logs and a small CISF booth fell into the reservoir.

"Look at the wave approaching the dam. It's almost a thirty feet tall wall of water." Juhi shouted.

Aban continued to look at the tall man, "No. It can't be. It's impossible. He looks so different." He blurted out, adding to the general confusion.

The AC of the NSG contacted Siddhartha, "Sir, we've engaged the target. If we don't act now, this dam will not stand the waves."

"Hold on for a second." Siddhartha turned to Aban and told him that the AC wanted orders to shoot the man standing on the dam.

Aban responded, "This wave can do no harm. The dam can sustain much bigger impacts."

"But if he fires more explosives, the wave will go on increasing."

"Try to understand. They are prepared. They made an exact mathematical model and have done a perfect simulation of the destruction. They are not fools. I believe the whole process must be automated now. Killing him may be counterproductive, because if he dies, we will never be able to stop the catastrophe.

He has to live. Only he knows how to abort what he has initiated."

"How can we just wait and let the inevitable happen?"

"I propose that you ask the Air Force to fly down from their airbase, loaded with explosives. Let them encircle the airspace and await your instructions to bombard the reservoir."

"It'll worsen the situation. I don't buy your theory."

"Trust me. That would be the last solution. However, we'll exercise this option only as a last resort."

The wave from the far end approached and struck the dam with full force. Exactly at that moment, four more semtex exploded in the four diversion tunnels. The underwater wave synchronized with the surface wave and once again moved away from the dam to the far side of the river. The water of the Bhagirathi and Bhilangana swelled in the upstream as the strong wave pushed it backward.

"Damn it! We can't do a thing while this man is doing exactly what he wants."

"We have a little more time."

"How?"

"After the hill on the far side collapses, the wave will move uninterrupted twenty-eight miles to the far end of the Bhagirathi River. Even if the wave is travelling at sixty miles an hour, it will take more than fifty-five minutes for it to travel back and hammer the dam."

"What if another hill is exploded just a few miles from here?"

"Then, we won't have any time. But it's not the waves that I'm worried about."

"What worries you, Aban?" Juhi joined in.

"Oscillation."

The UGV started to catch Shalim Amīr Khan's deep-throated laughter. "No questions."

Aban trained his binoculars. The man continued laughing, strode to the downstream end of the dam. Quickly, he turned back to reach the lakeside and watched the dancing waves. "No questions. No questions." Suddenly Shalim Amīr Khan became excited like a soldier in the middle of a war, when cannon shells are booming all around. His hands started to tremble and moved to his thighs, scratching it vigorously.

Aban was stunned. He turned to Juhi, "I know who he is!"

Juhi stared at Aban blankly.

Siddhartha spoke out, "He is a rogue. He is the Deputy Commandant of the CISF, an antinational working for Pakistan."

"You have got it all wrong. He is my *Abba*," Saying this Aban ran towards his father, MacBook in one hand and tears streaming down his face.

Siddhartha tried to stop Aban and ran after him in hot pursuit. Juhi stood still, shell-shocked.

Aban shouted, "Stop it for god's sake, *Abba*," and continued to run towards Imran Shah Malik, aka Shalim Amīr Khan, "Stop it, *Abba*!"

Imran Shah Malik turned.

Threat

FIFTY PAKISTANI ARMY TRUCKS, each crammed with soldiers and modern weapons, waited a few miles away from the residence of the Prime Minister of Pakistan at Muree Road, near Rawal Lake.

The official car of the Army Chief of Pakistan entered the Prime Minister's residence. The General ran inside, pushing aside an American Special Armed Force offcier guarding the entry who did not know that he was the Army Chief and allowed unbridled access to the PM. Other Pakistani security guards gestured the man to allow the General to go.

The Prime Minister was talking on his hotline. The Army Chief turned his attention to the big sized LCD.

PTV, the Pakistan Television News channel stopped its programme midway for an important announcement. The anchor of the program appeared, "We have got an important tape from al Qaeda. Adam Yahiye Gadahn, the media spokesperson of al Qaeda, will start addressing you in a few seconds.

Adam Yahiye Gadahn appeared and spoke in his deep, serene voice, "My dear fellow Islamic brothers, recall what Muhammad preached to us. His call of duty reminds us to do everything possible to slay the non-believer…" The message continued.

The Prime Minister put down the phone on its cradle and turned to the Army General, "Weren't you supposed to be in Rawalpindi? How come you are here?"

"We have a situation, Mr. Prime Minister."

"I know that Tehri Dam in India is under threat. Our people are trying to explode it."

"You know they are non-state actors."

"This time I have confirmed information that few people are actually state-actors."

"Have you shared this with anyone?"

"Yes."

"To whom?"

"The Prime Minister of India."

"Do you know the international ramifications of such an admission?"

"I'm aware of it."

"The Pakistani Army will never tolerate such nonsense."

"I think the Army should know by now that terror in any form is just terror."

The message of Adam Yahiye Gadahn ended and the anchor reappeared. "A few minutes back, the Government of *Hindustān* has informed Pakistan that the Tehri Dam in their Himalayan region is under Pakistani terrorist attack. In fact, our media correspondent heard three explosions. I'll update you with the latest after a short commercial break. I'll be right back; till then don't go anywhere. Stay tuned."

The Army General sounded jittery, "Our AWACS have caught the signature of the Indian Air Force aircrafts, which have taken off from Dehradun and other Indian AFBs that are not far off from our borders."

"They may be on their regular sorties."

The anchor was back on PTV once again, "We have just received information that the *Hindustāni* Air Force has retaliated with a vengeance. Their Sukhoi-30 and Jaguar have invaded Pakistani airspace. Their course indicates that they are flying towards Tarbela Dam in Haripur District. If they attack the biggest dam of Pakistan, this hundred and fifty metre high dam will collapse at once. A colossal amount of water of more than one hundred square cubic miles will empty out in a few hours. All our major cities including the capital will be submerged under water in a matter of another few hours." The anchor continued explaining the disaster in waiting.

The Army General turned to the Prime Minister, "What are you waiting for? Our country is under attack. I want you to give orders for appropriate countermeasures."

"What countermeasures do you want?"

"You know that I don't need your authorization for striking down their plane with our anti-aircraft missiles and engage them in air combat. I've full authority and I'm ordering this."

"Go ahead."

"I want your authorization for nuclear code access."

"Why?"

"You are aware that we cannot match their air superiority. If they have decided to destroy our biggest dam, they will do it. I've no doubt about that. But if we announce right now that Pakistan will exercise the nuclear option right away if their aircrafts do not turn back, it will surely have a deterrent effect."

"I'm sorry, General. As the first in the hierarchy of National Command Authority, I won't allow it. In my view, the nuclear option is the last resort in our doctrine."

"It's not. We have reserved the right to exercise the first-attack, if we are under threat from an enemy country. I don't need to repeat what our book says on nuclear protocol."

"Well, I amended the nuclear doctrine only yesterday with the approval of the Cabinet Committee. You may get a copy of this from the Secretariat of the NCA."

"It's illegal. I am ex-officio member of the NCA. Decisions in the NCA take place through consensus and I have my vote in the decision making process. You cannot do it without taking into confidence all the ex-officio members of the NCA including me. Moreover, the concurrence of the President is also mandated."

"If you remember, our parliament Majlis-e-Shoora has already received the assent of the President, this year, on 11th March. Don't forget that I'm the Chairman of the NCA. Moreover, your role is limited to overseeing the functioning of Strategic Plans Division. In addition, nuclear doctrine is a government political decision and does not require convening a formal meeting of the NCA to vote on this subject or endorse it. I think I'm clear that I don't need your advice."

"I have no time for unnecessary arguments. From now on, the patriotic Army of Pakistan is taking control of the government."

"You can't."

"Who will stop me?" The livid Army General was trembling with fury. He pulled out his phone and pressed its keypads.

However, he could not connect his phone. He tried a few more times, wondering what had gone wrong.

The Prime Minister smiled, "We have blocked your access from the time you entered the premises."

"How dare you do that?"

"Turn around and look at the men behind you. I suggest you hand over your Army revolver to these people without any protest."

The Army General turned around and was taken aback when he saw US Special Army Personnel. One of the officers smiled, "It's the Black Ops, buddy."

The PTV Anchor was live once again, "We have just received sensational video footage. The fighter aircraft of the *Hindustāni* Air Force has blown up Tarbela Dam."

The TV screen filled with the Sukhoi-30 and Jaguar firing missiles on the dam. The dam crumbled and water rushed out, submerging the Tarbela Airport instantly.

The Anchor continued, "Our correspondent will try to get more video footage. Stay tuned for further updates."

The Army General said, "We need to evacuate Islamabad and Rawalpindi without any further delay. Islamabad is hardly thirty miles from the dam. The capital will be submerged in no time. Mr. Prime Minister, I suggest an immediate evacuation of the President, you, your cabinet colleagues and my military personnel. I'm afraid if we do not do it, there will be no government in Pakistan."

"Hold your breath, General. Nothing is going to happen."

"Are you blind? Can't you see what your government TV channel has just broadcast?"

The Prime Minister smiled, "I know you aren't blind. Look

a little below the screen. The DVD player is running this documentary."

"Isn't it a live program?"

"It was to be. Fortunately, it is not so now."

"Thank God! I should inform the army to de-escalate the heightened situation. Perhaps I'll need to talk to the Chief of Air Staff to hold fire."

"I didn't ask you to put your army on alert. But the action of a few ISI officers put me on alert two days back. Let me give you the complete picture. When I came to know about the real intention behind the Tupac-II program, hatched by the al Qaeda, I did everything possible in the supreme national interest. US Special Army secured this place just in case the army tried to usurp power in panic. It is true that the Tarbela Dam was under threat in the same way as Tehri is today. Al Qaeda got hold of a spare submarine and a huge quantity of semtex. They planted the explosives at the bottom of the Tarbela Dam, on its diversion tunnel and at three other places in the hillside, just like our people in the Tehri Reservoir did. It was an exact mirror image of what is happening in India right now."

The Prime Minister continued with an air of knowledge, "Unfortunately, till a few hours ago, we were sure that the Sardar Sarovar Dam in India was under attack. Accordingly, I informed the Prime Minister of India, so that he could secure and sanitize the Sardar Sarovar. However, the Indian Intelligence found out that it was not the Sardar Sarovar, but the Tehri Dam, which was the target. If something happens to Tehri Dam, we all will live to regret it — both India and Pakistan. As of now, I can do nothing, but extend the support of our government to the Indian government."

The Prime Minister sipped water and continued in his calm tone, "Coming back to Tarbela Dam, US Marines explosives experts have removed all explosives from the dam planted by the al Qaeda. But the al Qaeda had a plan-B too, in case something went wrong with their original plan. Saeed al-Masri sent his Jihadists with rocket launchers and explosives to board a speedboat and attack the dam from the Indus River." The Prime Minister stood and went to the DVD and loaded another disk. "Look at this disk and see how the drone missile eliminated each of the Jihadists at a place not very far away from Youi Bridge on the Indus River."

The Army Chief was stunned. "Oh God! Al Qaeda is driving us to disaster."

"Not as long as we are together. Sadly, two very high-ranking officers: one in the Air Force and the other in my own office was involved in this affair. They were in constant touch with Saeed al-Masri."

"Who is the Air Force officer?"

"None other than the one who gave you false information about the AWACS getting the Indian fighters' signature."

"We really need to cleanse the system. But how did you get wind of it?

"We came to know of many things after I asked the President of the United States to bug our complex."

"Is this place bugged?"

"Yes. Perhaps, for the first time in history, the Head of State of a sovereign country has made such a request to another country."

"But what about this documentary on the Tarbela Dam?"

"Truth is stranger than fiction. Strange are the ways of the al Qaeda. One minute, they are a crude tribal clan of mob mentality and the next -- sophisticated, techno savvy masterminds. al Qaeda prepared a fake film at a small film studio at Ravi Road in Lahore. This was the same film that was to be broadcast live on our national channel PTV. Imagine what would have happened had they succeeded in their plan. Your anti-aircraft missile and combat aircraft would have still been searching for some elusive Indian fighter jet as we spoke. With each moment ticking away, I would have slipped into panic too. I might even have considered using the nuclear option."

"How does al Qaeda benefit by this?"

"We all know that al Qaeda is fully aware about the locations of our nuclear arsenal. Still, our nuclear facilities are so well bastioned that nobody, not even the al Qaeda can storm in and steal our nuclear heads. So, they took our topmost Air Force officer and a few middle-level ranking officers into their fold by luring them with money and promises of putting them at the pinnacle of power, when they came to power. Our topmost officer of the Air Force became a pawn in the hands of these terrorists. So, he ordered the nuclear facility at Chaklala to assemble two nuclear warheads, load them into an Air Force Jet and delivered them straight into the hands of al Qaeda. A Dassault Falcon aircraft with these two nuclear bombs took off from the Chaklala Air Defence Command and delivered one of them to the walled city of Lahore. When the Commodore of Sargodha located the mysterious aircraft and shot it down somewhere in the north of Zhob, the other nuclear warhead was hurriedly dropped and presently lies somewhere in the vast land of North Waziristan."

The Army Chief heard in rapt attention as the Prime Minister elaborated on the complexity of the 'game'. "These nuclear devices, however, are still useless for al Qaeda because they do not possess the nuclear code to trigger the nukes. Hence, the devious plan to bring India and Pakistan to the brink of war by showing us this fabricated video footage. If we in Pakistan thought that we were under attack from India, I would have called a meeting with the Defence Minister and you, our Chief of Army. The Defence Minister and I would have signed the documents and handed over the codes to you without so much as batting an eyelid. As defined by our protocol, you would have had no choice, but to pass on the codes to the Air Force and our good friend there would have promptly handed it over to his bosses in the al Qaeda. Armed with the power to detonate the nukes, the al Qaeda would have turned the tables of the balance of power in their own favour. They would have immediately slapped the demand on us to stop all operations against al Qaeda or else they would destroy Lahore. The next line of action would have been to threaten America. They would have ordered the Americans to vacate Afghanistan, remove their dummy government from Kabul and hand over power to them. In case of any dithering on the part of America, the al Qaeda would have detonated the nuke, pulverizing Kabul.

With two nuclear weapons in hand, al Qaeda becomes a stronger force to reckon with. Just imagine, even though India is a regional power, it cannot retaliate against us after Kargil War and the Mumbai attacks, because of the nuclear deterrent that we wield. The same nuclear bombs would have boomeranged on us. They would have become an albatross around our necks and we would have been forced down on our knees in front of the al Qaeda because of the threat they posed to us. We would have been forced to give in to their demands. On the face of it, I would have resigned, perhaps on 'medical grounds' while you would have given way to a more 'efficient', 'younger' colleague of yours. Similarly, men in top positions would have had to bow down, surrendering their positions to different sympathizers of the al Qaeda. Pakistan would then have had a dummy government and our hapless citizens would not have the slightest inkling of the lightning bolt that had struck them. Afghanistan would have been under the direct rule of al Qaeda while the world watched helplessly."

"Oh! Doomsday!" The Army General turned to the Prime Minister. "We need to trace the two nukes immediately."

The Prime Minister nodded.

The Army General contacted the Vice Chief of the Army and ordered him to immediately cordon off the walled city part of Lahore and start a door-to-door search operation. An entire brigade of the army was put in charge to search for the capsule in Waziristan.

After the order, the Army General turned to the Prime Minister, "Can I seek one last clarification?"

"My pleasure."

"How did you know that this fake film was to be broadcast?"

"Pakistan will always be obliged to Imran Shah Malik and his brother. His brother gave us the initial lead and Imran Shah Malik sent us a few details of Tupac-II."

"But Mr. Malik is dead."

"That is what I too thought until a few hours ago. He is a man of mettle and has survived many battles. He is very much alive and ticking under the new name of Shalim Amir Khan, which, if you look closely, is the name Imran Shah Malik, rearranged."

"Where is he?"

"When he gave me the details of Tupac-II, I asked him where he was. To this he replied, 'Tehri' and hung up."

"What is he doing there?"

"Allah knows."

Oscillation

EVERYTHING WAS NOW quiet on the Tehri Dam. There was neither any further explosion from the diversion tunnel nor any massive landslide from the faraway hills. But it was only the lull before the storm.

The massive wave created from the earlier explosion hammered the wall of the dam and turned back to the far end. On its way, it broke the inlet gate of one of the penstocks of the hydroelectric plant. Water rushed inside with tremendous velocity and pressurized the surge tank, which threatened to burst any moment.

The emergency siren went off inside the machine room, resulting in chaos and panic all around. The control room Manager asked his deputy to check the extent of damage at the inlet gate. The Deputy came into the machine room. He ran back to inform the Manager that the machine area had flooded.

In a few minutes, the frequency of the oscillating waves

synchronized with the frequency of the dam. The unique hollow structure in the dam echoed with a groaning, humming sound, magnifying with each passing second. The occasional rumbling beneath the bottom of the dam sounded as if some fearful giant of the netherworld was angry because he had been rudely awakened from his long slumber.

This unusual voice from the deep was caught by the teleseismometers, the modern seismograph instrument and the accelerograph and fed as data to the control room. Ironically, there was no one to take note of this frightening bar on the monitor, which had already entered the red zone since the Manager of Operations had ordered evacuation of the Hydel Station.

"Go back, Aban." Imran Malik shouted, torn between an overwhelming desire to run and hug his son in his arms and push him out of the way of the horrifying danger that he faced.

"I won't, *Abba*."

"Don't come any further. It's too dangerous."

Aban reached his father. Between laboured breaths, he said, "What on earth are you doing, *Abba*? Try to understand the consequences of your actions. The magnitude of the disaster would be beyond anybody's comprehension. Not only millions, but billions of precious lives will be lost."

"Let doomed and damned be their destiny."

"No, Abba, no. Why do we forget that we are one? Our culture has evolved from the same roots. Our way of living has not changed for centuries. It is the pain of partition that has parted our hearts. Just like two brothers fall out over trifling issues and keep drifting further and further apart from each other, so have we. All this because neither is willing to forgive and forget. Yet, we are one and for generations to come are sure to tide over these differences because each of us is now tired of fighting futile wars, which simply create pain and more pain on both sides. Our destinies are intertwined. If they die, we die too."

"It pains, my son. It is always painful. Pain has left a scar on me, which no one can remove, not even I, even if I want to. It is unbearable. I cannot overcome it."

"What scar, *Abba*? What pain are you talking about?" A perplexed Aban asked his father, who seemed to wear a strange glint in his eyes.

"This may be the last time that we meet. So, I will tell you the whole story. The wave will not return for the next forty minutes. I have ample time to tell you. I know your *Ammi* must have told you the story of the 1971 War between Pakistan and *Hindustān* and the trauma I faced when the *Hindustāni* Army captured me and sent me to Alipore Central Jail as a POW. One day, I got into a long discussion with the Jailor to grant us the rights of a POW as per the Geneva Convention. The jailor was a kind man. He listened compassionately and promised to do his best. Unfortunately, he was transferred from the jail. A few months later, with the cessation of the war, the *Hindustāni* Government decided to return the POWs to Pakistan as per the Simla agreement. I was a proud solider, who wanted to go back to my country and serve my Army once again."

The story continued:

"However, someone, who was up to mischief, removed my name from the Jail roll. After that, my name or prisoner-number was never called out during the attendance roll call by the jail authorities. When I became suspicious and asked the administrators for a reason, they would just get away with a promise to rectify the mistake. Days turned into months and I waited and waited. One day, *Hindustāni* Army trucks arrived to take back the POWs to Pakistan. I offered *Namaz*, thanking Allah for giving me a reason to live. I smoothed out the crease on my jail uniform, so that I could look as presentable as possible when I returned to my *watan* after such a long time. The minutes went ticking by as I waited expectantly, but no one called my name or came to open my cell. When I heard the last truck labour its way out, away from the Jail, I knew they were not coming back ever."

Aban's father heaved as he continued:

"That same night, another vehicle came. Before I could understand what was happening, four people bound and gagged me and bundled me off into the van. Sleep overcame me. I woke up when somebody opened the backdoor of the van. I had been handed over to the extremists of Bangladesh. These merciless savages took me into the deep forest of Rangamati, the eastern part of Bangladesh. They tortured me for four long years, asking me to give them sensitive details of Pakistani Army and intelligence. I never uttered a word against my country. My answer to their every question was that *Hindustān* had cut my country into two."

Aban listened intently to his father's words:

"One dark night, six people came and tied my hands and wrists. They threw me on the ground. One of them took out a knife from his pocket while another pulled off my trouser and undergarments. The former laughed and said since you had only one answer that *Hindustān* has cut your country into two parts, today I'll cut you into two parts. I closed my eyes, praying to Allah to forgive my sins. I was not scared of dying. But I could not bear the pain when he cut off one of my testicles and the last thing that I heard before fainting was a cruel laughter."

Aban was shell-shocked. He came closer to his father, hugged him and put his arms around his shoulder. Tears welled up in Imran's eyes while he continued, "People talked with a lot of interest about an almost forgotten historical fact about Adolf Hitler. A Soviet doctor, who performed an autopsy on Hitler, revealed many years later that Hitler suffered from monorchism, the medical condition of having only one testicle. His photographs bear testimony to the fact that whenever he participated in the rallies and his marching army shouted '*Heil*'; Hitler would snap into attention and raise one arm to take the stiff armed salute. But his other hand would unconsciously slip down to his crotch, as though he was trying to hide something. This posture of his became the butt of ridicule, but it is only people like me, who can understand the agony that such a deformity can cause. If a man like Hitler, who considered himself to be powerful enough to conquer the world, was plagued by a sense of inadequacy because of this physical condition, think of what it can do to us."

Aban wiped tears from his father's eyes while father continued, "When I escaped from their captivity, I came back to Pakistan, but never told anyone about what had happened to me. I was still haunted by nightmares and the sinister laugh of the man, who had severed me into two. Before coming home, I went to the Army Hospital where an adept surgeon reconstructed me. However, the scars of those days ran too deep. Even today, when I'm very tense or under extreme pressure, my hands begin to tremble and I start scratching my thighs vigorously. I tried to overcome this habit. I tied my hand and even bit it to cure myself, but failed. This is my pain; I'm destined to bear it forever." When Imran lifted his head, he could hear sounds of Aban's weeping. He gently stroked his son's head and pulled Aban closer to his chest.

The Assistant Commandant from the far side of the mountain saw two Jihadists, holding Siddhartha Rana. He took aim and both men dropped dead on either side of Siddhartha. His commandos ran from the mountainside towards the dam while Siddhartha walked from the other end.

Imran Shah Malik pulled out his pistol and pointed it at Siddhartha. His hands trembled.

"No, *Abba*. Don't do it. Siddhartha saved my life." Aban pleaded.

Siddhartha reached father and son. "Give me your remote. Abort the sequence, Mr. Malik."

"I'm sorry, gentlemen. No one can stop it now. Once it is set in motion, even I can't do anything. I tried to reason with your government, but they were not ready to even consider my demand. I was left with no other option, but to initiate the sequence."

"I know your demand. You'll never have Kashmir the way you want it."

"I never wanted Kashmir. I'll hate my government if they ask Kashmir to merge with Pakistan against the Kashmiris' free will. I do not approve of the historical mistake that my Government made when it occupied a part of Kashmir. Do you want to know what I want?" After a small pause, Imran Shah Malik said under his breath, "I want the Kashmiris to decide their destiny."

"No, *Abba*. You don't want that. You want to cut India into two parts, the same way it happened to Pakistan in 1971," Aban interjected. "You want to split India, the same way those people cut you into two parts."

"No questions!" The father turned to his son.

Siddhartha was looking for the opportunity. He jumped and pushed Imran Shah Malik, who fell down. He snatched the remote from his hand, trying to locate any abort sequence.

"I've lived long, dear boy. Sixty-six years has been a long time to live and fifty years is enough to serve one's country. However, I have only one regret. There wasn't enough time to serve Allah. Take my life. Living anymore will be a waste, since I now seek nearness to Allah. I want to serve Him only. But trust me, you cannot stop the inevitable with this unworthy remote. It's not even a child's toy now."

The wave came back and hammered the wall of the dam once again. The explosives inside the four diversion tunnels exploded simultaneously. The rumbling sound of the bottom of the dam faded due to the booming sound of the surging waves. The massive dam looked small in comparison to the oscillation set in the lake when the resonance of the canyon matched with the resonance of the dam and synchronized with the wave. The tremendous upsurge grew and grew while the earth beneath the lake seemed to split into several parts.

"Now no one can save *Hindustān*, my son," The father's palm opened up.

"Oh my God! Try to understand, *Abba*. You are not going to split India into two parts with your plan. In fact, you are going to rip open the entire sub-continent including Pakistan. The geological forces that have built the deep gorges and high peaks of the Himalayas, will lead to a catastrophe beyond imagination. You don't know what you have set in motion today. None of your engineers programmed a simulation that incorporated a very important aspect."

"Nothing will happen to Pakistan, my son. Everyone knows our country's name is Pakistan. Pak means 'pure'. So, the land of the pure cannot be destroyed by Allah."

"It is you who will make all this happen."

"Sorry, my son. Nature is beyond the comprehension of man. Man cannot bring a catastrophe."

"I agree. But remember even innocuous activities of man like constructing large dams, drilling and injecting liquid chemicals into wells and coal mines and even drilling ocean beds for oil has brought about untold devastation. Dams are known to fluctuate the pressure on fault lines and accelerate the movement of the faults. A massive earthquake and underground eruption spawned from a fault in Newcastle that was activated when miners dislodged million of tons of rocks."

"Today is not a day of minor magic tricks like building a dam or digging up the earth. Today will be a day of the greatest water show man has witnessed till date." Imran Shah Malik said cryptically.

"The earthquakes of Alaska, Chile, Indonesia, China will go down as footnotes in geological history. Vegetation like the Ghost Forest of the Western American Coast will replace our lush greenery. The rupture of Cascadia will shrink to a minor event compared to the catastrophe you are going to cause. Thunderbirds and giant whales will shake up the earth to its very roots. Water and earth will join hands in a dance of destruction"

"I know these geological myths and mythological truths."

"Trust me. Today, this show will be the last show, *Abba* for anyone to watch. Tomorrow, no one will survive to see anything similar." Aban looked worried, "Let me show you." Aban pushed the power button of his MacBook, and continued, "Did anybody bring to your notice that the dam is situated right over the eight-hundred mile long fault knows as the Central Himalayan Seismic Gap? This gap has not released its strain in the form of an earthquake for more than seven hundred years. If I'm not mistaken, this gap released a very miniscule amount of energy in the year 1255 AD in a very limited zone of Nepal. That small energy leak killed more than hundred thousand people in Nepal, including Abahya Malla, the king of Nepal. That was a very local phenomenon, where an insignificant amount of energy brought about a devastating upheaval."

Aban took a deep breath and continued, "The unfathomable energy that has accumulated for millions of years is still intact in the entire stretch of the fault line. Normally, ruptures in the fault generate seismic acceleration and makes the water of a reservoir turn into waves. Today, you have reversed the sequence turning the whole thing upside down. An earthquake that occurs naturally happens when the blocks of the earth's crust rub against each other on the fault line. This releases a great quantum of energy, which travels to the surface of the earth. This creates surface acceleration, and in a sea or in a large mass of water, it creates huge waves. If these waves dash against a dam, the force of it can break a dam. In your case, you have just upturned the process. You are creating an acceleration on the surface of the earth by making the water mass sway. The force generated by this will move downwards towards the fault."

Aban looked deeply in his father's eyes. "You know *Abba*, that the fault is prone to distortion by even minute changes in its geomorphologic structure, which may be caused by minor movements inside the earth. However, the saving grace is that the continuous fault is punctuated at intervals by small joints made of lumps of molten matter that has come up from the mantle and is like clumps of gooey clay that hold it together. These clayey joints, which bind the gap, do not allow it to rupture, thereby maintaining a delicate balance preventing displacements." Aban clutched his father's hand and said, "Let me show everyone what is going to happen now."

Aban's MacBook booted. He clicked on a file and ran the simulation program.

Everyone watched with bated breath.

The swaying motion of the huge water body generated a momentum of such monstrous force that it induced an earthquake on the bed of the lake. The vibration created a downward acceleration, which began to move downward, beneath the earth's crust. Coupled with the shifting line of force of the oscillating mass, it seemed to plunge an invisible sword deep into the heart of earth. It then started moving to and fro, ensuring that the earth's heart was cut through and through into two distinct pieces.

The gooey plugging holding the fault line at intervals failed and were expelled out one after the other with a muffled popping sound. The two blocks of the earth began to slip against each other. The friction generated a gargantuan megaquake from the deepest belly of the earth.

This fault-rupture released energy equivalent to millions of megatons of nuclear explosion. It was much more than the explosion that could be caused by the entire inventory of nuclear bombs of the world.

A mega earthquake of more than nine magnitudes shook

the earth. It did not confine itself to the Tehri area, but went on bombarding one joint after another in the adjacent faults, running parallel to each other and at oblique cross-section to the Central Seismic Gap. The tremor that was produced in each of these parallel faults magnified the preceding seismic activities with rippling effect.

The seismic wave reached and ruptured the MBT, the Main Boundary Thrust of the Kashmiri Himalayas, cut through the Karakoram fault zone, raced to the Indus suture, amplified the most active Kunlun fault, shook the Pamir knots, propagated to the complex fault system of Hindukush Mountain, and beyond to many intertwined megathrusts. The name 'Hindukush' lying in Pakistan was totally erased from the scene.

Each dam collapsed and every city turned into dust. Mountains moved to smother and trample the dale.

The simulation cut to another scene.

The virtual camera zoomed in from space. It showed the Great Himalayas tumbling down into the Gangetic and Indus Plains, crushing them out of existence.

This phenomenon tilted the Indian sub-continental plate raising up the Pakistan side and lowering the Bay of Bengal region in a sickening seesaw motion. Because of this permanent slope, each river, flowing from the Himalayas and Karakoram towards Pakistan vanished from the map, promising to make Pakistan barren for millions of years.

The simulation stopped and a note appeared. Imran Shah Malik and everyone else read it.

"*A simple calculation about the tilting of the plate presents a scenario that actually happened one hundred and twenty million years ago. An uplift of the Western Ghats of India tilted the Indian*

Plate in the eastern direction. Though the tilting created a steep mountain, it also submerged a major eastern portion of the Indian subcontinent under the sea. That phenomenon did not happen suddenly, but took millions of years. However, today the same phenomena will happen just in a few minutes before anyone can even react. Such is the might of manmade calamities."

The simulation started once again.

The eastern boundary submerged in the Bay of Bengal. Bangladesh, entire South India, most of eastern India and the Gangetic Plain became part of the seabed within minutes. The higher hills like the Nilgiris, the Western Ghats and few plateaus like the Deccan remained as islands, cropping out of the Bay of Bengal. Mount Everest was not the tallest peak of the world anymore. The K-2 peak in the Karakoram usurped its position.

Subsequently, the tilting of the sub continental plate displaced the water of the Bay of Bengal and the Arabian Sea, creating a tsunami, several miles in height. People, who were fortunate enough to survive the massive jolts and underground eruption, did not have time to escape from it. The tsunami devoured Eastern Africa, the entire South East Asia and Western Australia in a matter of hours and continued moving towards the Atlantic and the Great Pacific.

The simulation ended. Aban powered off his MacBook.

Siddhartha Rana shook his head in dismay while tears welled up in Imran Shah Malik's eyes. "I'm not Muhammad. I'm not Allah. I haven't been sent by him to bring *al-Qiyāmah*. I'm no one to decide, who is righteous and who is not."

"Stop this catastrophe, *Abba*. Tell us how to abort the sequence."

"I can't. Only Allah can." The father stood, but again fell to his knees, lowered his head and prayed, "I'm willing to sacrifice myself. Take my *Qurbani*, but don't let this happen…"

Haridwar and Dehradun

THE DISTRICT MAGISTRATE of Haridwar requested the Brigadier of Dehradun cantonment to immediately dispatch five hundred army personnel to Dehradun, as the local police were unable to control the millions of devotees, who had refused to accede to the request of not taking a holy dip in the Ganges. The CISF unit of Bharat Heavy Electricals Limited had spared fifty guards and sent them to Haridwar. But it had not proved sufficient.

Five MIG-29 jets carrying twenty thousand tons of high-grade explosives took off from Dehradun AFB and within ten minutes started to encircle around the Tehri Dam, waiting to receive the signal from the ground.

Resonance

IMRAN SHAH MALIK stood up and turned to Aban, "Is it the same watch that your *Chacha Jaan* handed over to you?"

Aban nodded.

"Thank Allah. Now listen, Aban. Take my pen." It was a Montblanc Meisterstück 149, which his wife had gifted him on the diamond jubilee of their marriage. "The pen and the watch go together. Do as I say."

Aban followed the instruction of his *Abba* step-by-step. "Fix the date as 14th, the day Wednesday, and the time to 07:08:06. In the next step, pull out the crown and insert the nib of my pen into the crown-slot of the watch. That will activate a small pin inside."

Aban completed the task and the watch began to tick.

"Good job, my son. You did it." The father smiled.

"I don't see anything happening."

"As soon as you completed the procedure, the pin released

the eccentric weight, the winding rotor of the watch. Then, the spiral mainspring unwound. When the watch started to tick, it ran a tiny dynamo that supplies power to a miniature chip and a hidden antenna inside your watch. It transmitted the destruct code through Ku-band 138.225 MHz emergency frequency. The same frequency was set in the explosives device in the far away hills. So, nothing exploded at the far side. That is why you didn't see anything happening. "

The AC of the NSG and his team shot down the remaining Jihadists and then reached Imran Shah Malik. The AC pointed his SIG pistol at him, "Turn around and put your hands behind your head." The other Commandos overpowered him. "Take him to the base."

"If we have to avert disaster, I'll have to dive into the lake." Imran Shah Malik resisted.

"Shut up." The AC thundered.

"Try to understand, mister. The explosives at the toes of the dam will explode in half an hour exactly. If that happens, then no one can prevent the dam from breaking."

"Free him," Siddhartha interjected.

"I can't trust you anymore, Mr. Siddhartha Rana. I'll do everything to protect the dam. I've seen enough explosions in the dam and waves in the reservoir."

"You have just seen the tip of the iceberg."

"That's enough. If you say a single word now in defence of this terrorist, I'll be constrained to take you in custody."

The oscillation in the reservoir went on increasing. The wave returned from the far side of the river towards the mid reservoir. Aban turned to Siddhartha Rana, "It's time. The coordinate is 30°24'56" North, 78°27'51" East and the elevation is 699 metres."

"What's that?"

"The exact location in the middle of the reservoir. Tell the commander to drop the bomb this minute."

The AC was hopping mad. He shouted at Aban, "So, you are also with this bastard. Whom are you instructing to drop bombs?" He turned to his commandos, "Arrest the boy."

Siddhartha pulled out a small communicator from his pocket, wrote the coordinate and elevation and set the beep code. He pushed the green button and the message transmitted to the IAF Mig-29. Then, he turned to the AC, "Look in the sky. They are our Air Force. They are going to bomb the mid of the lake. That is what Aban meant. Let's move out of here."

"Why should they drop bombs, when we already have had enough explosions?" The AC was befuddled.

"It'll kill the oscillation of the lake, the resonance inside the hollow structure of the dam and in the canyon." Siddhartha explained very calmly, "And now I want you to free both Imran and his son Aban. Forget about this dam. It's only a small accident compared to what can happen in a few minutes. Only they can save our entire sub-continent."

The AC hesitated. Suddenly, a flash of light of a relatively mild explosion snapped their attention. Siddhartha asked, "What was that?"

"You know about a traitor of your country, who was alive till a few seconds ago. He wore a jacket and went to that far hill. Both water and fire conspired against him," Imran Shah Malik responded.

The MiG-29 dropped twenty thousand pounds of bombs in the middle of the reservoir. It created a high wave which moved outward in concentric circles. It collided with the incoming wall of water. It was as if two giants were engaged in a royal battle, waiting to tear each other apart. The combined waves rose to hundreds of metres and then collapsed. Two big trailers moving on the National Highway turned turtle, while a few cars were swept away to the far side of the hill. The water reached the New Tehri Village and smashed the houses and shops with full force. The Principal of the All Saint Convent School was worried after he had watched the oscillation from the window of his room. So he asked all students to climb to the roof of the school building. The water struck the school with a loud slap, but moved on without causing much damage.

Slowly, the oscillation of the water in the lake died. The swaying dam stabilized. However, the new explosion generated a sixty-foot wave, which surged ahead at sixty miles an hour, strong enough to hammer the dam with full impact."

Juhi, who had been watching the entire scene in horror, ran to Aban. Imran Shah Malik saw her. He turned to Aban, "Is she Juhi?"

"Yes, *Abba*."

"Your *Ammi* told me once about her after you left for America. That time I asked your *Ammi* to convey my disapproval. I wanted you to keep away from any *Hindustāni*. I was wrong."

"Oh! My God," the AC shouted, "The dam is going to crumble."

"No, it won't. The wave will simply overflow over the top of the dam, taking all of us with it," Aban said calmly, "unless we remove the explosives at the toe of the dam."

"How much time do we have?"

"Ten minutes."

"Well, I'll dive and try to remove the explosives," The AC volunteered.

Siddhartha interjected, "Hold on, Commander. Do you know the depth of the reservoir at this point? It is more than two hundred and fifty metres. No one can dive beyond thirty metres without SCUBA. Beyond that, the water pressure will crush you. Secondly, you will find the place too dark at that depth. How will you remove the explosives then?"

"I can still try." The AC was persistent.

"I'm a recreational Scuba diver. Only nine people have been known to dive below a depth of more than 240 meters, even with the most advanced SCUBA. So, free Imran."

"Mr. Malik is neither a superman nor a fish. He can't dive to such a depth!"

"I've read his file. When he escaped from Bangladesh, he jumped into the Bay of Bengal at Sitakunda and stayed inside the sixty-metre deep water for five long minutes without any breathing apparatus. Perhaps, that is a new world record, albeit undocumented."

The AC nodded and the commandos loosened their grip on Imran.

"Move away from this place. Climb up the hill as high as you can." Imran Shah Malik said, "It's time for me to go." He turned to Juhi, "Take care of Aban. I love him more than anything else." His eyes met Aban. "Tell your *Ammi*, how much I missed her when I could not return to Lahore after I fell into the Swat River. I love all of you."

"Why are you saying this, *Abba*? You have to come to us."

"You know, Aban. I'm a fighter. I'll try." The father said and ran to the place, where he had kept the SCUBA. He lifted his eyes and saw the NSG commandos and the AC climbing over the hills. He turned his gaze to the dam. Juhi and Aban were still looking at him from the top of the dam.

Someone tapped Imran Shah Malik from behind, "Hey man! You're a true nationalist and brave."

Imran Shah Malik smiled, "Time to say goodbye to another patriot."

"Good luck."

While Siddhartha slowly walked towards the road, leading to New Tehri Town, Imran Shah Malik activated the submarine. He fed the schematic data and commanded it to remove the semtex from the toe of the dam. He wore the SCUBA suit and dived deep to remove the capacitors and other electrical devices, which were fitted earlier by Khalil Deek.

"We will be swept away by this huge wave." Juhi hugged Aban.

"It's not the water, but the air that bothers me."

"Air?"

"Yes. Bend down and hold that chain tightly. I'll join you." Aban pointed out to the loop of chains fixed with the spillway motors, just beneath Juhi's feet.

"Come, Aban. Be quick."

"I can't, Juhi. My *Abba* is still under the water."

Imran cut the wire of the serial connection of the semtex explosives, affixed at different positions of the dam. Sixty of them went dead. Only the last one, connected with a battery and a capacitor remained to be neutralized. He reached, but before he could snap the connection, the strong eddies generated by the waves threw him upward and pushed him towards the surface of the lake.

The submarine completed its computed task and turned its direction to nose up. It quickly emptied its ballast tank and moved upwards with high velocity to resurface. When it whisked passed Imran, a semtex carried by its robotic arm got entangled in Imran's leg. The propeller of the leaving submarine created a vortex that pulled Imran inside the funnel. Imran allowed his body to be sucked in for a while, then turned his head downward, headed straight into the funnel, reached to the upside down tip of the funnel and then swam parallel to the vortex. Finally, he pushed hard to propel himself out of the water.

The submarine emerged from the water, sailed towards the northern part of the river and then activated its self-destruct code.

When Imran Shah Malik resurfaced, he felt a sensation in his leg. Someone touched it and tried to remove the explosive, "How did you come here? I assumed you had left much earlier."

Khalil Deek responded, "Did you feel proud of what you did today? However, I have to fulfill my duty. I told Saeed al-Masri everything. He asked me to bring you to him. He will deliver justice to you."

"Go to hell. I'll pluck out the eyes of anyone, who dares to raise his eyes at our *watan.*"

The huge explosion broke the eddy. Aban saw a small portion of the water turn red.

Juhi pulled Aban to her and wrapped the chain to his body. The tidal wave, moving with tremendous velocity struck the edge of the dam. It flung away and dropped with a thunderous splash into the downstream canyon, almost a kilometre away. The canopy of the water compressed the trapped air. As soon as the wave passed, the compressed air rushed to meet the vacuum created by the moving jet. The immensely powerful forward draft pulled Juhi and Aban, who dangled between sky and the concrete of the dam, clinging tightly to the chain, waiting for the worst to pass.

Epilogue

CHHOTA BADRINATH WAS an ancient temple in Old Tehri Town. Those who could not reach the high altitudes of *Badrinath,* would offer their prayers here and go back home, carrying the same blessings as those obtained at the main *Badrinath* Temple. When the Tehri Dam was built, the temple was submerged alongwith Old Tehri Town in the backwaters of the lake. Wise men of the village used to say that it was located on a Ley line, and so, extremely powerful. They said that these Ley Lines were like puppet strings, in the hands of Brahma, Vishnu and Mahesh.

In the same area, a fisherman had ventured out with the return of normalcy. He saw an old man's well-built body, drifting steadily ashore. He quickly pulled out the body onto his boat, rowed to the bank and shouted to his fellow fisherman for help. He removed the unconscious man's hand that rested on his thigh and pumped out the water from his lungs.